"I contribute my truth", John Coltrane

Needleham

Terry Simpson

Stairwell Books //

Published by Stairwell Books
161 Lowther Street
York, YO31 7LZ

www.stairwellbooks.co.uk
@stairwellbooks

Layout and cover design: Alan Gillott
Cover image: Bob Pegg

ISBN: 978-1-913432-33-1
P6

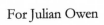
For Julian Owen

January 2001

The town of Needleham sits just inside Yorkshire's border with Lancashire, high in the Pennines. Successive invading waves of Romans, Danes, Angles, Saxons and Normans looked up at that inhospitable land from more habitable plains below and decided it wasn't worth the bother of conquering – they would wait for the hill people to come down to them. Some never did, and the region has maintained its insular quality to this day. Rain that crosses the Atlantic and disdains Manchester finally gives up the struggle in these hills, and the sky above Needleham is often heavy with low, brooding clouds. The small villages and towns nearby are mainly concerned with managing the hardy sheep that dot the hills like mobile limestone boulders, but Needleham itself owes its existence to the discovery of coal a few hundred feet under the surface of the moor in the early nineteenth century. A cluster of stone terraces grew around the winding wheels of three pits named Faith, Hope and Charity after the daughters of the pit owner. Faith collapsed during the long lay-off following the General Strike of 1926. Hope struggled with geological problems and closed exhausted in 1979. The long strike of 1984/5 saw the end of Charity, waterlogged as she was by the yearlong absence of pumping. After that the only major employer in the town was Needleham Hospital, (formerly The West Riding Pennine Pauper Lunatic Asylum), built when the asylums of Leeds, Bradford, Halifax and Huddersfield were full to overflowing, between 1895 and 1901. The British Empire was at its peak, but in the industrial heartlands of its engine room, insanity was booming too. The casualties of global success were accommodated far from the centres of population.

Now, almost a hundred years later, the hospital itself was one of few such asylums still open. A great humanitarian wave had censured the cruelty of those old establishments, and politicians of all parties had joined in a chorus of condemnation. Their concern had absolutely nothing to do with the rising costs of such big old institutions, and the huge surge in the value of the land they were built on, or at least they never mentioned this. Within a short time, the asylums were an anachronism, and Needleham was saved only by being so unfashionably placed.

Time had not been kind to the old buildings. There had been a steady deterioration in the fabric of the hospital in the northern wind and dampness, and much of it was now sealed off and slowly decaying. The clock in the tall square tower at the centre of the main administrative block stopped working in 1966, at the exact moment (some said) of Germany's late equaliser in the World Cup Final of that year. The high room behind the clock had been locked since that time. There was a persistent rumour that the hospital was haunted by a spectral figure, but sightings had become fewer since 1974, and the policy of the then Medical Director, Professor Bolt, to prescribe courses of electro-shock treatment to people who were so deluded. But if there had been a ghost, and should it have chosen that room as its spiritual home, and had it been looking towards the main road from Myllroyd on the first Monday of January 2001, it would have seen a bus arrive at the hospital gate and drop off a solitary man, a newcomer, who proceeded to make his slow way up the drive towards the main building.

*

The large blue sign said:

NEEDLEHAM MENTAL HEALTH NHS TRUST

Your mental health is our business!

Through the trees, the structure rose before him like a lost city among the fields, an ancient, impossible place; a prophecy in the sudden burst of sunlight through grey cloud cover, its acres of stone bathed in supernatural brightness. The towers and sheer extended bulk of the place reminded him of a poem he had learned in school, a grim narrative about a hopeless journey through a dark, forbidding landscape.

A hospital.

A hospital for the mentally ill no doubt, but at the end of the day, a simple hospital, the original Pauper Lunatic Asylum on the very edge of the town, at the boundary between civilisation on this side and wilderness beyond. For on the other side of Needleham Hospital were the moors and hills of the Pennines, where there were only sheep farms and the occasional dark satanic mill, or carpet warehouse as it now was.

It took ten minutes to walk along the curving tarmac path past grazing sleet coloured sheep, which sometimes raised their heads to pronounce a word that sounded suspiciously like 'Maaad'. A long fence behind which earth moving machinery could be heard, grinding forward and retreating, proclaimed ABETTOR GAS & OIL. Finally, behind the long sweep of a wooded corner, the main building appeared again, with the high clock tower and its discoloured battlements surveying the whole scene. It was his first day of work as the Patient's Advocate, and he felt a sense of unease that bordered on terror. This was almost certainly a bad idea.

What was that poem? There was a child and a tower and a long, bleak journey. It was endlessly dreary, like school itself.

The hospital's main door had a carving of a ship at sea. The wind was strong enough to be visible as lines, like wires scored against the sky. Below it a wooden sailing ship was crossing a turbulent sea, sails bulging. Waves towered over its deck, where a row of grotesque faces grimaced with terror and confusion or laughed with exhilaration. One dancing skeleton seemed beside himself with glee. The ship's sails were ragged, about to be torn away by the storm. Its figurehead was a plump, troubled woman with long dishevelled hair, facing out the tempest with great determination and bare breasts.

The carving was done with fine detail as well as boldness, each finger of hands raised up to ward off the destroying storm picked out in loving detail. For the newcomer, the panel stood out among the four carved scenes on the door of ancient oak. It spoke to him, but as if in an unknown language. The other panels showed more traditional symbols of Yorkshire – the sheep that prospered on the stony slopes where agriculture had failed; mining tools that helped to launch the Industrial Revolution; a luxuriant plant that may have been rhubarb. But it was this symbol of peril and mental disturbance that caught his eye.

This ship of fools he had come to.

He stepped forward, twisted the brass knob, and forced the carved door with an effort. It opened onto a broad, short corridor. A ceiling of vaulted wood, carved and varnished, reared above his head. At his feet was a mosaic floor with garish Victorian flowers and blue swanlike birds. There was a reception office behind a glass pane on his left. The stillness was complete, and he felt like the only visitor in an urban museum. He waited in front of the glass where he could see a dapper man with a thin moustache, reading a copy of the Daily

Mirror, and leaning back in an easy chair. Luke pressed a finger to a plastic button on the counter and an angry buzz made the man leap and throw his paper down in one movement. Luke saw him rearrange his distracted face into a hasty smile.

- Good morning, sir. How may I help you?

A pleasantly toned, but obsequious voice, that carried the local accent, strangled under an odd version of Received Pronunciation.

- I'm the new Patient's Advocate. They told me I should report to reception.

- Ah, the new Patient's Advocate! Very good! Wonderful! I'm Brian.

He waited expectantly.

- I'm Luke. Luke Walker. It's nice to meet you.

- Hello Luke. Well I hope your time here will be long and fruitful! It's not a bad place really. I have a key to your office, and you can get one for the toilet on Jutland corridor from the Nurse Manager. You mustn't let the patients use it of course. To get to your office you need to go down to the main corridor, go left and follow it past Somme, Ypres and Verdun Wards, keep going, and the Advocacy Office is the first door in Jutland corridor on your left.

He beamed at Luke, and at that moment there was a muffled shout from the direction of a section of corridor that ran across one end of the reception area. A voice was raised in pitch to a yell, with others threatening, and the whole mixture rising confused like the dinning echo of a public swimming bath. There were running footsteps. A thin man in a brightly coloured dressing-gown ran into the hall, his head back shouting in some guttural language unknown to Luke, arms and legs flailing as though unused to running. A few seconds later, a man and a woman in jeans and jumpers appeared, moving faster. The dressing-gowned man ran towards Luke.

5

- Help me! They are trying to kill me!

The male nurse tripped him and he fell in a multi-coloured heap at Luke's feet. The male and female nurse lunged and landed on top of him.

- Come on sunshine, let's be getting you back.

The man resisted, wriggling his body so they couldn't get proper hold of him, but the two of them quickly suppressed him. Grunts of exertion and exclamations filled the air. The two nurses seemed to become aware of Luke. Brian beamed at them and said brightly

- Good morning! This is the new Patients Advocate, Mr. Walker.

Brian seemed oblivious to the squirming form pinned underneath the two nurses. The female nurse looked as if a sudden thought had struck her.

- He is on a section, isn't he?

The male nurse suddenly looked shifty.

- Er, actually I don't know.

They both looked at Luke, then back at each other, and loosened their grip on the dressing-gowned man, who scrambled to his feet and staggered towards the massive doors, pulling them open with difficulty and disappearing through them.

The male nurse looked again at Luke, this time a kind of glare, daring him to say something. Luke wasn't about to say anything. He was astounded by the whole series of events. The two nurses nodded to the receptionist, and he nodded back with a relaxed smile, as if nothing had happened at all. Then they turned and started to make their way back the way they'd come with a strange, forced nonchalance. When they had disappeared, Brian smiled at Luke.

- High spirits this morning!

Luke looked through the panel of a window to the side of the main door, where the dressing-gowned man was limping at a fair pace down the tarmac road away from Needleham, the multi-coloured coat-tails sailing in his slipstream on either side.

*

In the office of Augustus Tarpow, the Joint Executive Planning, Strategy, Management and Finance Sub Group (JEPSMFSG) was underway. Tarpow, known as 'Gus' Tarpow to the numerous enemies he had made on his rise from Nursing Assistant to Senior Unit General Manager, sat with his Nursing Manager, Moking, on one side of the great leather topped desk, while Professor Drogham and his consultant, Mr. Ellis, from the Professorial Unit sat on the other.

- Good gracious, one of the patients is escaping!

Frankly Professor Drogham was bored. He didn't really see why he had to sit in on managerial matters. He was a doctor, not a bloody accountant. He was glad for the distraction of a brightly coloured figure making its way at speed down the hospital drive. The others looked out curiously. Ellis, the younger man, broke the silence.

- Well I think we must rely on the nursing staff to deal with any er… situations. I'm sure they have things in hand. He's probably just going to buy some cigarettes.

Ellis was a little miffed. This was his first consultancy and he was keen to make a mark, but it was taking him longer than he'd expected to understand the complexities of life at Needleham. He just didn't feel the others took him very seriously. He felt uncomfortable with the formality of Tarpow's office, the huge portraits of early patrons and superintendents, the strait-jacket in its glass case. The others all looked dubiously out at the fleeing man. Patients were known to get desperate about their cigarettes but moving at such speed was unusual even so. Reluctantly, they turned their attention back to Ellis, who continued.

- As I was saying, I think one of our main aims for the next few months should be to set up a series of meetings to consider the implications of the National Service Framework, and what we need to do here at Needleham to implement it fully.

- The National Service Framework?

The Professor repeated the words slowly. Tarpow intervened to answer the Professor's query.

- The National Service Framework was introduced by the Labour government in 1999 to set standards for mental health care across the country. As you know mental health is one of the new government's key health priorities.

- Ah!

The Professor looked relieved. Tarpow remembered that they had received a shipment of several hundred copies of the tasteful lavender-coloured National Service Framework publication shortly after it was published eighteen months ago. He remembered the big boxes lining the corridor leading from his office. Actually they were still there.

The Professor seemed to have decided the matter to his satisfaction, at least.

- Well, we have our own systems here, so that won't really affect us too much.

It was Ellis' turn to frown.

- But these are Government directives, passed down from the Department of Health. It's a statutory requirement that we have to comply with.

The Professor shrugged.

-   O, we never bother with that sort of thing here.

Tarpow saw that Ellis was taken aback by this response. Personally it was old news to Tarpow that the Professor (and in fact all medical directors of mental health units he had ever known), considered it optional whether they took the laws of the land into consideration or not, but he was keen to move things on, and stepped in brusquely.

-   We'll certainly organise a meeting to look at that. Of course such matters concern the county council as well, and I was hoping that our senior social worker Miss Graytfell would be present. Unfortunately Julie is attending a conference today. So in view of that, I think we should move on. I think our more pressing problem is the financial situation. We are really going to have to shut down several wards very soon, probably the Day Hospital as well. We're closing Occupational Rehab more or less immediately.

-   Closing?

Ellis looked alarmed.

-   Well, no, not closing exactly. We're going to reprovide it. We'll redeploy the staff.

In other words, Tarpow thought, make them an offer so ludicrous they won't take it, and then pay them off. The Professor looked concerned.

-   Is the situation really as bad as that?

-   It's worse. We've got a financial black hole. We're going to have to take immediate action. It's not going to be very popular.

The whole financial situation was very unfortunate. Needleham, partly through Tarpow's connections, had been chosen as a pilot that allowed the hospital more independence over its finances, in fact complete control over its own budget. Although still technically part of the NHS, it was operating as an autonomous unit, investing and borrowing money. It was not tied by the constrictions that had bound hospitals until then. This was all to the good, except for the Financial Manager, a personal friend of the Chair of the Board and an excellent fly half, in fact an all-round good chap who had only one fault. He was completely useless with money. He had covered his mistakes finally by fiddling the finances. His whereabouts were currently unknown, but he was thought to be somewhere in Brazil.

- I hope the local press don't get hold of it.

The Professor's already lined face looked haggard at the prospect.

- We've only just got over that last enquiry. They took us to task over that.

- Well I suppose it _was_ their reporter who died.

Tarpow said this reasonably. Professor Drogham's face fired up with anger.

- How was anyone to know how susceptible he would be to anti-psychotic drugs? There was nothing anyone could do.

Tarpow said nothing. If a newspaper sent a reporter under cover pretending to be a patient to spy on the hospital then they had to bear some of the responsibility as far as he was concerned. The frown on Ellis' face made him look older than his years as he began again.

- We need to think of some way of presenting the cuts to the public so that the papers won't pick it up. We need a Modernisation Plan. I could bring some ideas to the next Strategic Board meeting. Of course we'll have to try and get the patients groups on board. What are the Patient and Public Involvement Forum like?

The Professor was looking at Ellis again in a startled way. Tarpow decided that Ellis was simply naïve and carried along by the force of his own thoughts, rather than deliberately provocative. The younger man didn't notice the look the others exchanged.

- The Patient...what?
- The PPIF, the Patient and Public Involvement Forum? The statutory body that replaced Community Health Councils? You know, the regulatory watchdog?

Luckily Tarpow had endured several hundred meetings in his Health Service career and was used to keeping his laughter strictly to himself. The moment Ellis said the word 'watchdog' in conjunction with the Needleham Patient and Public Involvement Forum, an image had come to him of a miniature terrier, the type that old ladies adorn with large pink ribbons. Tarpow struggled to gain control over his face before he spoke.

- Ah, yes, well it is rather at an early stage here in Needleham. We are planning to have a meeting about it. Of course, we do have a Patient's Council, which our Involvement Worker organises.

Ellis was impressed.

- Really, that's very forward looking.
- Yes, it's a very powerful body. Obviously I'm doing what I can to stop it.

The Professor at least chuckled at his humour, but po-faced Ellis just stared back at him like a frog in a blond wig.

*

Luke had been sitting in his office for an hour when he heard a shuffling and slapping noise in the corridor outside. He had reread his contract, his job description, the Patients Advocacy scheme literature, and finally the fire regulations and hospital notices pinned to the wall. He did not recognise the sound, as it came closer and closer to his door. He expected a knock, but the manifestation passed and continued down the corridor, which was a dead end. Perhaps a cleaner? At this stage he would have been glad to see anyone. Then he heard the sound returning. Again it grew louder as it approached his door. A double clap followed by a swishing sound of cloth on the plastic floor tiles. He was moved to step the two paces to the door of the small room and opened it up a crack to peep out. The corridor was brightly lit, with a long row of fluorescent tubes reflecting from shiny pale green walls. To his right he saw a bright green backside, and the yellow soles of a pair of slippers, disappearing round the corner on hands and knees.

He returned to his desk, overshadowed by high stacks of trays on either side of the old computer, and the looming tower of a grey, four-drawer filing cabinet. The Patients Advocacy Office was so narrow that with outstretched arms he could touch the wall on either side. The décor was a particular shade of off-white that is not a true colour at all, just what happens to white paint if you leave it exposed and unpainted for a decade.

The only window in the tiny room was at least two meters off the ground, and he had to climb onto the desk to look out. He could see dark woods just beyond a well-tended lawn, crossed by stone paths. Four benches faced into a little square with a fountain (not working). An old stone outbuilding sat beyond, on the edge of the wood, with a wrecked slate roof, overgrown by climbers and bushes. An arm of the main building away to his left showed three storeys of curtained windows.

Why had he ever thought this would be a good idea? He had come back to Myllroyd, the nearby town where he had spent his childhood, following his father's death the previous year, and somehow stayed. He had taken up volunteering at the local CAB, doing an outreach project at the local charity Mindfields, whose clients were mostly ex-Needleham patients, so when the advocacy job came up it seemed a logical extension. It had been a long shot from the start, one of those applications you fill in just to keep your hand in. He knew nothing about madness, or 'mental health' as it was now euphemistically called, but from the start of his interview they had seemed keen to overlook his shortcomings and give him the job. He wondered about the incident he'd seen. Was it his job to intervene in such incidents? 'Unhand that patient!' What were his rights? What were the patient's rights? He did not know. He should not be here. Was unqualified to be in such a position. It was a disaster. Again.

The first visitor came soon afterwards. Luke jumped at the tentative knock, and moved too quickly to open the door, smashing his knee against the wooden desk leg. The subsequent pain throbbed through most of the conversation that followed, distracting him. He found behind the door a thin man with the lined face of a Native American chief. He was old but quite erect and at least as tall as Luke, with thinning swept-back hair plastered to his scalp. He had bright blue eyes that regarded Luke with the intense indifference of a bird of prey, and he was wearing an ill-fitting black suit that still bore traces of original quality.

- Advocate.

He said gravely. It wasn't a question, more of a resigned statement. Luke ushered him into the little office, and the old man looked around in a slightly bewildered way.

- It's money.

He said, after Luke had introduced himself. Luke felt the blood drain out of his face and dash down to his heart, which started up in surprise at the sudden onrush.

- Money?

He repeated, uselessly.

- Yes, you see I get the twelve pounds a week allowance, but it's not enough you see. I smoke, and it's gone in no time!

The old man leaned in to Luke, though his eyes veered away, sweeping around the room, as if checking for hidden microphones, before locking back on Luke's terrified face. Luke felt some response was called for.

- Well that is the regulation amount. Everyone gets the same.
- But *they've* got some of my *own* money! I got left some money when my mother died! A lot of money! And they're keeping it for me! But they're not letting me have it, see! I've got to ask them for it all the time, and they only give me twelve pounds a week plus a fiver from me own, and it's not fair! It's my money! Why shouldn't I have it if I want it?

Luke pondered.

- I can't see any good reason. Let me just write some of this down.

He opened the fresh clean reporter's notepad on his desk, mainly to give himself time to think. He knew nothing about money. When he was a volunteer at the CAB he always passed on the money stuff to more experienced people. Money was like a strange substance that he knew had mysterious properties, like Mercury, or Sulphuric Acid, but he just hadn't been listening in the class when those attributes were taught.

- Let me just take some details. What's your name?
- Walter. Walter Whitehead.

Luke looked at him and noticed the little black-headed colonies around his nose and on the upper reaches of the deep folds that crossed Walter's cheeks and followed the contours of his mouth.

- And this money, this inheritance money. It's yours, right? I mean there's not a....... ward of court or anything? I mean you don't have to get anyone's permission for it, like a brother or a solicitor?

Walter looked at him curiously.

- No brother, no solicitor. It's mine, that money. My mum worked hard for it. She had a little shop, after my dad ran off, and she worked at it. And she left it to me, cos our Sandra, well anyway she's been passed away a good long while, so it was just me, you see, and she left it me, and it's mine by rights, you know, and they don't let me have any of it, but in small bits, that's no good to man nor beast, and it's not fair.

Luke wrote the words 'Sister Sandra', 'mother, shop', and 'check ward of court?', and 'man nor beast' underneath Walter's name and the date on the first page of his notebook.

- It certainly seems as though you have a case. Listen, I'll contact the ward and see what they say about the situation.
- They'll say I can't have it, I've asked them, that's the point see. That's why I want you to get onto them.

Getting onto them, that was the job of the advocate. You got onto them. They didn't like it.

- Right, I'll try and talk to them today, and I'll come and see you tomorrow and let you know how I got on.
- Thanks, mister.
- Luke. Just call me Luke.
- Cool Hand!
- It's funny how many people say that.

Walter clutched Luke's hand with both his own and beamed into Luke's face.

- I'm pissed off with them! You stick it to them.
- I'll see what I can do.

He left Luke, who found that his palms were sweating. The little room was intense with the weight of expectations.

His second customer came while he was still recovering from the first, and about to make the phone calls he had promised to Walter. He opened the door to a young woman with anxious eyes. Her hair was dyed bright red and long enough to hang down on either side of her face, half hiding it.

- Are you the new advocate?
- Yes, come in.

She looked back towards the main corridor as if expecting pursuit, and he had visions of the nurses reappearing, but all was quiet. When the door closed she sat in the only other chair there was room for, apart from his own, and burst into loud tears. He looked around for tissues, tea, anything he could offer, but there was nothing to hand but papers and files. He felt desperate. His week of training at Mindfields had involved Patient's Rights Under The Mental Health Act and The Principles of Advocacy, all described in a pleasantly theoretical way by his manager. The session on the role of an advocate had mentioned nothing about tears and the etiquette of dealing with the aforesaid in a tiny office. He waited until the sobbing subsided and she took the palms of her hands away from a face that was now blotched and tear stained.

- Sorry.
- Don't worry. That's fine. You take your time.

He marvelled at where these words had come from, certainly not his own frozen, frightened brain.

- Why don't you just start at the beginning and tell me all about it.

The advocate is not there to pass judgement

She poked at her nose and dabbed her cheeks with a tight ball of overworked tissue.

16

- I'm Anthea, a patient up on Paaschendaele Ward. It's horrible!

Her voice ascended into a soft wail as she bent her head and gave way to another gust of sobs.

- I think they are trying to kill me!

He should reassure her. He knew that feelings of persecution were common. He knew that however poor the care here was, they would surely not be actively trying to kill people.

The views of the patient must always be taken seriously, however unreasonable they may seem.

- Can you tell me a bit more about it?

At last the deep shudders subsided enough to allow her to speak again.

- This office is so small. I'd forgotten. It's tiny isn't it? It used to be an old storage cupboard and they converted it. It's where they kept those rainbow coloured dressing gowns they make the new patients wear.

Luke thought of the man he'd seen escaping.

- Why do they make people wear those?
- You're not going to get far in one of those are you? Can't exactly blend with the crowd. They put this office up here deliberately to be out of the way, so nobody can find it.
- You've been here before, then. Did you come and see the last advocate?
- Her head fell forward with another soft wail, and she cried quietly for a few more moments. When she had recovered sufficiently she said:
- I am the last advocate.

*

Maria Paraskeva, the Involvement Worker for Needleham Mental Health NHS Trust was walking along the brightly lit main corridor. A slim woman in her early thirties, she was going round all the wards in the hope of drumming up some interest in the Patient's Council meeting she was planning. She had already drawn a blank on the Somme Men's ward, and Verdun Women's. The corridor was several hundred yards long, with regular windows through which she could see the backs of other buildings, and occasional glimpses of the lawns and woods of Needleham. Every so often along the corridor's length was a long radiator and beneath each one a male body stretched out. Some were sleeping, but others eyed her cautiously as she passed. It was hospital policy to lock male patients out of their bedrooms during the hours between breakfast and teatime to stop them sleeping, so they came and slept under the radiators. Some were ragged, but others bore traces of fashion through the ages, velvet jackets with wide lapels, shell suits, bomber jackets in dirty denim, and duffel coats. One man wore a dinner jacket with a black bowtie and was snoring loudly as if sleeping off a wedding reception. She stopped to give a leaflet to each one awake, and all accepted, with varying degrees of comprehension and interest.

She slipped through a large green door to try her luck on Paaschendaele Mixed, where no patients at all were to be seen in the spacious dining room, the TV lounge, or in the corridors leading down to the bedrooms. Recently refurbished, the ward had the still air of an ideal home exhibition, with its as yet undefiled carpets and anodyne impressionist prints. Maria approached the nurse's station, where through a panel of thick green glass reinforced by wire mesh she could see shapes of people and hear raucous laughter. She knocked a little too loudly on the door. The laughter ceased abruptly. There was a pause, then the undrawing of a bolt, and a bearded, stern young male appeared. Maria saw the same expression on the laminated name badge on his lapel. She knew Nurse O'Price, from

18

sight anyway. As with many of the nurses, she felt that he had a certain contempt for her because she did not belong to the medical staff. She thrust forward her own plastic name badge with its picture of her own cheerful expression, and the details of her authenticity and uprightness in this den of illusion and altered realities. O'Price took more time to read the badge than was strictly necessary, given that the only writing was Maria's name and occupation.

- I've come to let the patients know about a meeting we've organised later for Wednesday. I sent everyone a flier about it. Did you see it? I can't see one up anywhere.

There was a derisive sound from behind the door, a distant cousin of a laugh, but one that had spent too long in the wrong company. Now that Maria was closer she could see that there were at least five people in the little room, as many filing cabinets, and a desk covered in papers and files. The bearded nurse took his time to say,

- We don't go much on fliers up here.

A female's voice chipped in, the same one Maria had heard laugh.

- You can put them up, but they just rip them down!

- Where are all the patients?

The man at the door motioned with his eyes to the door of the smoking room, and with a nod was gone. Maria heard laughter resume as she walked away. She pinned her flier to the blighted cork of an abused and neglected notice board.

She would need to approach the subject of spelling later, tactfully. Max was new on the 'Computing Skills as a Step to Social Inclusion Through Paid Employment' class, and his enthusiasm needed nurturing. Especially now that Arman had run away. The dining room-lounge in front of her was a huge room with a carpeted area of deserted armchairs to one side, the tiled floor of the dining area on the other. It was still and silent now in the pale sunlight that filtered in through the high windows on two sides. To the left of the notice board was a chipped yellow door, and when she opened it a cloud of billowing smoke poured out like an old pea souper lost in time, released after detention following some street altercation. At first Maria couldn't see into the room at all, but as the smoke poured past her, and the air cleared, she picked out two rows of chairs going away into the distance, each one with a smoker in it, an ashtray and a mug of tea on each chair arm. The room was much smaller than the dining room, or the TV lounge, more like part of a corridor, but there were at least sixteen people in there, and perhaps more lost in the fog at the end of the room.

-    Hey, Maria, have you got a cigarette?

A figure raised itself with effort from the wooden wings of an armchair and struggled towards her over the outstretched legs that occupied the narrow aisle between the two rows of chairs. Maria recognised Liron Shulman, the faded club singer.

-    Liron, you've got a cigarette.

Liron peered at the stub between his fingers, at the packet in his other hand.

-    I need more man!

Always Liron needed more, whatever it was. He threw his arms out and began to sing an old Barry White song.

-    I can't get enough... of your love!

A thick Needleham accent from somewhere behind him in the gloom yelled.

-    Fuck sake man, pu' a sock in it will you?

Then a female voice of protest.

-    Language!

Another male voice piped up, directed at Maria.

-    Hey, have you got any weed love?

-    No, I'm the Involvement Worker, I don't have any drugs.

-    O, sorry love, I thought you were the Social Worker.

Then a more querulous female voice, addressing Maria from the fug of the room.

-    Are you sure you're not the social worker?

Maria looked down at her pink cotton top, with its little mirrors and flower motif, her stone washed jeans flaring out to the buckled ankle boots beyond.

-    Do I look like a social worker?

- Actually, yes.

*

The staff canteen at Needleham Hospital was a large cheerless room in the main administration block. Recent decoration, prints of ladies with parasols wandering sunlit French gardens, and an expensive modern lighting system suspended from the high ceiling did little to disguise the fact that this was a big old warehouse of a room. Through the row of high windows down one long wall Luke could see that the day that had begun with promise had given up and was regressing into sullen greyness. He and Anthea Drell, the previous advocate of Needleham Hospital, were the only customers. Thirty little formica topped tables spread out, flanked by pert, plastic cheese-plants. Anthea, calm now, sat opposite Luke, sipping a coffee-coloured drink. Luke looked around.

- It seems very quiet in here.
- At one time there were two and a half thousand patients, so there was a huge staff team. Nowadays there's only about three hundred patients, so there's hardly any staff.

She gave him a hard stare.

- You all right? You look a bit ... Childe Roland to the Dark Tower Came!

Luke was startled. It was the very poem he'd been trying to think of.

- You know that poem?
- Of course, the gallant knight riding through the desolate landscape on his quest. Robert Browning. Do you like poetry?

He wondered whether to be honest.

- I hate it. My dad taught poetry.

He thought about the bags of poetry books in the hall at his father's house ready to be shipped out to Oxfam or Age Concern in Myllroyd High Street. His father had taught poetry at the local grammar school, and before he realised it was a hopeless struggle, forced Luke to memorise Tennyson and Hardy, Matthew Arnold and Gerard Manley Hopkins. Fragments would sometimes rise unbidden, like ghosts in a Victorian graveyard. Anthea was speaking again with that intense insistency.

- You have to understand poetry if you want to understand madness!

She looked at him very closely with those staring eyes.

- What exactly did you do before?

- I worked in an outdoors pursuits centre, at Llangsyffrin, in Wales. I used to help kids put on their boots and take them on walks, caving, a bit of climbing.

- And why did you stop?

A sudden inexplicable fear of heights; a sudden terror of enclosed spaces.

- Personal reasons.

The words dropped into the pool of the conversation like murder weapons, and like a guilty man, he felt compelled to over-elaborate.

- My dad died last Summer and I came back here to sort out his house. I just sort of stayed. I was brought up around here.

- Ah, you're a local! But have you ever actually done mental health work before?

He had not, other than puzzling about the intricacies of DLA or Housing Benefit for people discharged from Needleham. She appraised him coolly.

- I don't want to be funny but I think they'll eat you alive in this place.

23

Her red hair framed her face like a halo of fire. She seemed now perfectly clear and sane to Luke. What was she doing being a patient here?

- I can't believe my manager didn't mention that there was an advocate who became a patient. They didn't give me any reason why the post was vacant.

- I'm a source of deep embarrassment to them. Actually the whole project is. For the sake of appearing independent they had to get someone from outside the hospital to run the advocacy project, and Mindfields tendered for the work, but it's way off the beam of what they usually do. They don't really know anything about advocacy.

She was looking into space and there was a silence that Luke found uncomfortable. When she spoke again her voice had changed, as if Anthea had temporarily vacated the premises, and someone with a softer, older voice had replaced her.

- You know the Anglo Saxons used to call January Wolf Month, because the wolves would be so hungry they were brave enough to come into the villages then?

He didn't. She seemed to shudder.

- This place has ghosts. Do you know sometimes I can hear the hospital speaking to me?

Luke indicated that he did not.

- It's very sad, this hospital. Actually it wants to die. It was all right to start with, but now it's had enough. It didn't want all this happening in its name. It wants to close and be put out of its misery. When it's very quiet I can hear it.

Luke looked around at the plastic topped tables, the hatches on the right behind which morose kitchen staff clattered big steel containers preparing for the lunch time rush. This wasn't how he had imagined his first day would be.

- There's something going on. I don't know what it is but something's not right in this place. Arman, the one who escaped, had this theory that they are secretly killing the patients.

He was looking into her enlarged pupils, which now seemed alive with a terrible knowledge. Eyes should not be like that, he thought. Pupils should be small and watchful, guarded pinpricks around which you can admire the nice colours. Anthea's pupils were so large he could not guess what colour the irises might be. He let his gaze drop to the brown liquid in the white mug. The unpronounceable, many-syllabled name of an anti-depressant on its side gave him no comfort as she spoke again.

- There have been too many deaths.

It was as if the temperature had dropped suddenly. Luke looked at Anthea and couldn't take his own eyes away from those terrible doorways into the void. She was obviously completely mad. Why had he ever thought he could work in a place like this? He tried to think of a reasonable question he could ask but ended up just staring at her.

- Deaths?
- People die here all the time. From all sorts of things.

She lowered her voice and her hand came across the little table to grip the cuff of his jacket. She nodded slowly. She was his second client, perhaps one of the more sane ones. Why had he ever thought this would be a good career move?

- No wonder you got stressed out.
- I lost it during a Review Tribunal. I called the Unit Manager a fascist.

- I can see that wouldn't go down well.
- Well, he is a fascist in fact. Tarpow. You'll get to meet him soon enough. Everyone knows he's a bastard, but you're not supposed to say it.
- They can't say you're mad just for telling the truth!

She laughed again, long and loud.

- That's exactly why they do call you mad!
- So, how can......? Well, what can I do? I mean how can I help you? You know, what is it exactly that, as an advocate, I might be able to achieve for you?

His interview technique needed work. She leaned closer in, but before she could say anything the door of the dining room swung open, and three men came in talking in loud voices. Some kind of joke seemed to be going on, with two of them ribbing the third.

- Shit, it's O'Price.

Anthea hissed, and her head went down. She raised her cup as if trying to hide her face behind it. The tallest of the males glanced round as the three men moved towards the hatch, and his look fixed on the two people huddled in the corner. It was the nurse who Luke had seen earlier at reception, manhandling the man in the multi-coloured dressing-gown. When he saw them, he frowned and changed his trajectory, walking briskly over. Luke saw that he had a neatly trimmed beard and was dressed in what seemed to be the regulation nurse uniform of blue jeans and a dark coloured jumper, with the square laminated card of his identification badge flapping at his hip. He gave the impression of enjoying the walk across the room, and the chance to exercise his muscular body. He came much too close to the table, leaning over them as they sat.

- Now then Anthea, come on, love, you know the rules, you've been in this place long enough.

26

Anthea quickly drank down the rest of the brown sticky substance and spoke to Luke.

- Come on, we've got to go.

Luke stayed sitting, looking from one to another, as Anthea, flustered, gathered her bag up. Then they both looked down at Luke, as you would look at a child who has not been able to grasp some simple fact about the ways things are.

- Patients not allowed in the staff canteen.

Anthea explained.

- But you used to work here.

The nurse moved even closer to Luke, so that he had to look up steeply to meet the man's gaze. Luke noticed a spot on the man's nose, and that, although the mouth was set in a smile, the eyes were cold.

- And you are?
- I'm Luke Walker, the Patient's Advocate.

The nurses breathed an 'ah', and his mouth curled further into a stiff smile as his eyes flickered upwards for the briefest of seconds in the ancient universal gesture of mockery. He said, in a voice of exaggerated enthusiasm.

- The new patients' advocate! Well I'm very pleased to meet you.

He offered his hand, then when Luke reached out naively to shake it, withdrew it suddenly, saying in a much harder voice,

- THIS IS THE STAFF CANTEEN AND PATIENTS ARE NOT ALLOWED IN HERE. Come On Anthea. Out, NOW!
- Come on, Luke. Let's go.

Anthea said this anxiously. They were both staring at him. He slowly got to his feet. As he walked towards the door the nurse half shouted.

- It's just the patients who can't come in. You're alright.

Anthea had already disappeared through the door, and Luke turned to face him. The other two nurses had turned as well and were watching from the serving hatches. Even the serving staff were only half-heartedly ladling as their attention turned to the little confrontation being enacted in front of them. Luke wanted to say something cutting, some proud, decisive retort that would hang in the air long after he'd gone.

- No, I'm really not.

It didn't quite make it.

*

TWO: February

The first Superintendent of Needleham Hospital, General Cardew, had been, as an Oxford student, a keen follower of Kraepelin and his new ideas about treating Praecox Dementia, as schizophrenia was then known. However, Cardew had come back from active service in South Africa 'changed'. This was the word always used in reports and correspondence of the time, although no contemporary records could ever throw light on that ambivalent term. Rumour at the time had it that Cardew's incompetence had resulted in the failure of the ill-fated Jameson raid designed to seize the Transvaal from the Boers in 1896. Queen Victoria is reported to have said 'Cardew is a lunatic', which her advisor had passed on to the Army Board as 'Cardew should be in a mental asylum'. The subsequent report by a tactful administrator rendered this as 'Cardew's talents have wider application than the military, and our suggestion is that a position be found, perhaps as the superintendent of a large institution'. Since none of the more conventional candidates had any intention of accepting a posting to the further reaches of Yorkshire, Cardew was offered, and accepted, the posting of Superintendent of the new West Riding Pennine Pauper Lunatic Asylum, which he held until his death on the Somme in 1916.

A History of Confinement in West Yorkshire, Hubert Johnson

*

-   What are you reading?

Luke turned the cover of his book towards the woman who had just woken up by his side, who made a pouting, mock unhappy face at him.

- I can't see without my glasses - tell me!

They were in Susan's pink bedroom. Pale sunlight through closed curtains cast a glow over an overcrowded dressing table. Luke felt sudden warmth from the large body that curled towards him, one leg hooking over his own pair, pinning them down.

- It's A History of Confinement in West Yorkshire.

She looked up at him with blue slightly unfocussed eyes.

- Oh Luke! Tell me you're joking!

- What?

- Never mind 'what'! You poor deluded sweetie! It's Saturday morning. It's your day of rest.

She nuzzled against his arm, patting his belly.

- A day for recreation. You shouldn't be doing that stuff today.

- Did you know the money for Needleham originally came from wealthy financiers, who made their money in petroleum?

- No, and I don't care particularly.

As if to emphasise this point her head disappeared beneath the blankets.

- Apparently there were bi-products from petroleum the Rockefeller family thought could be used for drugs. It's incredible really - you think setting up a hospital like Needleham was purely to relieve suffering and all that, but actually they were trying to figure out how they could cut down waste and make more money. What's the matter?

- Don't stop, I was enjoying that.

Susan's reddened face emerging.

- Luke! For goodness sake!

She was out of the bed and flouncing towards the door pulling a dressing gown abruptly to her as she went. She could carry a flounce when she needed one. He looked around the room, unsettled suddenly by the rich evidence of femaleness, the bottles of many colours and shapes on the old dressing table with its panel mirrors; the pile of bras and underwear, and heaps of other pastel coloured clothes. They always slept together in her space now – she deemed his father's house "too creepy". He continued to read,

'Some contemporary patient's accounts refer to Summer 'culls' from 1907 onwards, when the wards had become dangerously overcrowded. Patients were reputedly sent to hide in the woods, and nursing staff acted as 'beaters' to drive them out across the lawn in front of the main building, while the General and other civic dignitaries fired on them from balconies, with .303 rifles soon to see duty in Flanders. These guns carried a bullet like a small shell. Few of the patients were hit, though it was mostly fatal to the ones who were. Although there is no written evidence for this practice, contemporary records do show a decline in patient numbers during those years, despite an overall increase in mental patients nationally, a trend that continued until Cardew's bizarre death several years later, single-handedly charging across no man's land dressed as Florence Nightingale.'

When Susan came back, bearing a tray with steaming mugs, her sleepiness was gone. She set down the tray before him in triumph. It had two bowls of yoghurt, concealing a nutritious cereal, the whole covered in fruit and seeds. Susan loved food, one of her many gifts to him, whether he appreciated it or not.

- You can't let work take over your life.

- No, I don't want to be a bore.

At this she hooted too enthusiastically, as if it was an especially good joke, as she climbed back in the bed and set about her breakfast bowl with relish. She was a woman of appetite.

They had met when Susan's job as a social worker took her to the Citizen's Advice Bureau in Needleham where Luke was working as a volunteer. She had found his painfully shy incompetence attractive after a recent failed liaison with a Complete Bastard and decided to take him under her ample wing.

-   My brother's going to get married!

She announced this after scraping her bowl with enthusiasm. Her eyes were bright and piercing like an owl's. Marriage was mentioned often. It disconcerted him.

-   The doctor? Who to?

-   I only have one brother. Yes, the doctor, Luke dear. He's marrying his girlfriend, strangely enough. In the Summer. We must go up and visit them or get them to come down here. She's a doctor too.

A momentary flurry of panic started up in Luke's stomach, but it was a vague threat. The time to start worrying would be when dates were mentioned. Luke didn't like the sound of Susan's brother, who she had variously described as "having a brain the size of a planet", "very good at music until he gave it up for his studies", "played rugby and cricket for the school".

-   You should try and get over your stuff about doctors, Luke. Your preconceptions. They have a really hard job to do. Where would we be without them?

-   Well the ones at Needleham seem a weird lot. Most of them are quite old, really stuck in their ways.

-   It's an impossible job. Are you getting on any better with the nurses?

- They're a bit standoffish.
- They see you as a threat. You need to build relationships. You've got to see it from their point of view. There've been a few Public Enquiries at Needleham in the past few years, and I suppose they're a bit sensitive.

That was Susan, he reflected, always prepared to see the other point of view. She shook her head.

- That incident with the pyjamas for instance, and the pig's head....
- Pig's head?
- I don't remember all the details. There was a big stink at the time. I think the media exaggerated it all.
- I think I heard Maria say something about it.
- Maria?
- The Involvement Worker.
- What's an Involvement Worker?
- No-one seems to know really. It's something to do with helping patients to take part in planning and decision-making, but it doesn't seem to quite work somehow. She set up a Patient's Council – I'm going to meet them this week.

Susan made a snorting sound.

- Patient's Council! People are very ill, how can you expect them to be involved in decision making? It's ridiculous, I think you're getting too involved. At the end of the day it's a job. You have to leave it behind when you come home. How do you think I've managed to go on being a social worker for all these years?

Luke wondered that himself. How did people do this kind of work? Take Tarpow, who he'd now met three or four times. Each time the Unit Manager dominated the conversation, and talked about how much they welcomed advocacy, how the hospital was entering a new phase, described the things they planned to do, the things they were already doing, a stream of initials and policies and benign welcoming sentiments, until Luke was dazed. And suddenly the Manager rose, and the interview was over and Luke had not even begun on the list of questions on his little pad.

- You've gone haven't you?
- Sorry, I was thinking.
- You think too much, you frustrating man. You know I just can't imagine you used to work as an Outdoors Pursuits Instructor.
- Too dreamy?
- I think 'puny' is more the word I was looking for.

She roared with laughter and patted him on the head.

- O I'm just joking! Men! Can't live with them, can't live without them!

She was out of the bed and carrying the tray with its bowls, not flouncing now, but with the practical bustle of a woman with a house to look after. He was left wondering about Susan, and the relationship he was apparently having with her. Good Susan, who had pulled him out of the mire; whose surprisingly rampant sexuality had brought him back to his senses; whose practical nature had made sense of his confusion; whose well-defined and strong opinions on all topics had provided a bedrock in the tempest; who had encouraged him to take this job at Needleham in the first place. Dear Susan who had plans for him and them.

He sighed.

*

Next day, in his office beneath the clock tower, Tarpow regarded the new Patient's Advocate. The view through the second-floor bay window was of the well-mowed hospital lawn, with dark woods flanking it, and the tarmac road back to civilisation winding away to the left. This view was relatively unchanged since the hospital was completed in 1901. The two men had shaken hands, and now the new man sat on the other side of Tarpows' large oak desk, looking rather thin and insubstantial in the spacious office with its portraits of benefactors, tasteful French prints and new lime green carpet. He was nervous, Tarpow noticed. Good! That was how it should be! The younger man's eyes flickered around the room, and his fingers played unconsciously with the edge of the foolscap pad on his knee. Tarpow let him stew for another moment, carefully putting away a file into a drawer of his magnificent desk. When the advocate had gone he would take it out again. At last Tarpow deemed it was time and followed the younger man's gaze to the large portrait of a man in military uniform with the hospital in the background.

- Cecil Cardew! The original hospital Superintendent. He ran the place with a rod of steel until he went off to serve in the Great War. We could do something of that spirit today, I think.

Tarpow, a corpulent man, who could nevertheless move quickly enough when he wanted to, threw the other a testing glance. The younger man met his gaze solidly and blankly. Not a good sign.

- I trust you are still finding your work with us enjoyable?
- It's fine thank you. I'm beginning to find my way around. I still haven't located a key to the toilet on Jutland corridor…
- Ah, you must find Nurse Manager Moking for that - the mysterious Nurse Moking! I rarely catch sight of her myself! I'll try and have a word.

Tarpow ostentatiously made a note on a pad in front of him. He actually saw Moking several times a day, but it didn't pay to give anything away cheaply in Health Service management. 'Get them by the bollocks and their hearts and minds will follow' was his private motto. Luke waited patiently. When Tarpow looked up his friendly expression was tinged with seriousness.

- We are very pleased to have advocacy functioning again at Needleham. It's an absolutely essential part of our service here, and indeed I think of the modern mental health system as a whole. It's intrinsic to our development plan. I think for far too long patients' views have been ignored. This simply wouldn't happen in any other sphere of medicine. We are utterly determined that the patients will have the very best care available to them, and advocacy is a key element of a modern service. It's especially important to us that the service is quite independent of the hospital. We considered having it directly managed, but then we thought, no, it must be independent, nothing else would serve the high standards we expect.

Actually Tarpow had fought tooth and nail to have the advocacy service run as an internal Trust department where he could keep an eye on it. He only gave in because of pressure from above, and because the Mindfields Manager had once been a nurse and could be trusted not to rock the boat.

- All our staff have been instructed about the advocacy service, and that their co-operation is required.

Staff had been told to say nothing, to give nothing away, to be utterly circumspect in their dealings with the advocacy service.

- I hope you won't hesitate to come and see me if there's anything at all I can do to help you in your job. Do you have any questions right now about any aspect of the hospital that I might be able to clear up?

- Well I do find it quite unusual that almost all the Trusts' work still revolves round Needleham Hospital. Most of these large old institutions in other parts of the country have closed, and other towns of comparable size have much more in the way of community services.

A wary look crossed Tarpow's face and was quickly gone. Tarpow's face was not the place to linger long.

- Well there are local circumstances here that make it a little different.

Having friends on the Regional NHS Planning Board, for instance was a great help, but he didn't want to go into that.

- It's true that perhaps we have been a little….behind the times here in Needleham. But we don't believe in change for its own sake. We just want what's best for the patients.

Tarpow had his sincere face on although it didn't suit him. Luke looked down at his folder and considered his next words carefully. He had heard about the family culture of Needleham, with generations of the same families working on the same wards.

- I did read about the court case last year.

- Well that was unfortunate.

Unexpected! The boy had done his homework. Tarpow made an internal note to keep an eye on this one. It was indeed an unfortunate case. The hospital had appointed the unqualified son of the charge nurse, against five G grade nurses who'd applied for the job. Luke had read about the case in the local *Akathadale Times*. It had all come to light, so to speak, when the nurse set fire to a patient's pyjamas. Very nasty, particularly since he was wearing them at the time.

Tarpow made an expansive, dismissive gesture with his arms, leaning back in his chair, and shrugging and laughing at the same time. It was an impressive, mesmerising performance.

- What can I say, you get the occasional bad apple. We've learned and tightened up our systems. In fact it's precisely because of such incidents that we've decided to prioritise our advocacy service.

And not in any way because of pressure from the Department of Health.

- Things have changed a lot around here.

They'd sacked that bloody squealer of a social worker who grassed for a start.

- We are in a new era! We have a new Labour government!

Did Luke detect a slight sigh of resignation in the way Tarpow said that?

- Who have, in their wisdom, decided to prioritise mental health! Surely goodness and mercy shall follow all the days of our life and we shall dwell in the House of the Lord!

Tarpow laughed a professional laugh that had no humour in it. It was like a clinical sample of a laugh that had been refrigerated and stored in a test tube for several years, waiting for the right moment for its use. It had a smell of ether about it. Luke smiled out of politeness. There were other incidents Tarpow could have told him about. The pig's head in the bed. The victim of that particular little piece of horseplay was still in Intensive Care at the Regional Secure Unit.

Unfortunate since he'd been quite a promising junior doctor until then. The human cannonball. He still shuddered about that.

- I'm sure we're going to get along fine.

Tarpow reached forward disconcertingly over the broad, leather covered desk. Luke resisted an urge to leap out of his chair and hide behind it. He found himself placing his own pale, thin hand into Tarpow's fleshy paw. It was hot and moist and surprisingly strong. It said 'I am being friendly now, but note well that should I wish to crush every bone it would be well within my power to do so'. It held on longer than was strictly necessary. It gave the impression it badly wanted to maim Luke's hand but was being restrained for now by the kindness of Tarpow's brain.

Which could be withdrawn at any moment.

When the advocate had gone Tarpow rocked back in his chair and looked out at the lawns. The advocate did not seem clever enough to seriously interfere, but still, he would require watching.

Closely

*

A curious silence followed Luke about the hospital in the early weeks. The patients treated him as if he were one of the staff, in other words they were suspicious of him. They would stop talking and look shiftily out of the hospital windows as he passed on the corridor, their eyes flickering back when he had passed. 'Pen pusher' was the general verdict, based on his paleness, his troubled academic air and the black plastic brief-case he carried around with him. Staff members were equally distant, sensing a threat, though he seemed so ineffective and innocuous that it was hard to see from where. To his face they were mostly as contemptuous as they felt they could get away with. He heard the phrase "you'll learn" several times on different wards, when he said something that showed how naïve, in their eyes, he was about mental patients and their devious ways.

He quickly learned that money was a source of much discussion among staff at Needleham Hospital. Consultant psychiatrists (who in their opinion, were the most important cog in the Needleham

39

machine) resented the fact that senior managers like Tarpow were more highly paid. A qualified and moderately experienced psychiatrist was paid slightly less than a middle manager, and so on down the dual hierarchy.

On the other hand it was a matter of deep concern to the psychologists that they were paid less, grade for grade, than the psychiatrists. (One bright D. Clin student undertook a research thesis that showed 87% of Clinical Psychology supervision sessions at Needleham at some point touched on feelings of inferiority psychologists bore towards psychiatrists because of this fact.)

There again psychologists were paid more handsomely than even the most senior of the nursing staff, which was something that often formed the basis of resentful conversations at the Needleham Staff Social Club, where the nurses tended to congregate. The nursing hierarchy ran from the Nurse Managers who oversaw several wards, to Charge Nurses and Sisters with particular responsibility for one, then to different grades of nurses down to the least experienced auxiliaries, and remuneration was ranked accordingly. (The one anomaly in the nursing payment structure was for the 'bank' nurses who came in on almost every shift from a local employment agency. Although technically the least experienced and skilled, these were paid pro rata almost as much as the Charge Nurses and Sisters, which was the one common feature that could unite all other nursing staff in bitter resentment.)

The nursing hierarchy ran parallel to that of the Social Work Department, where the Social Workers were paid by Needleham Council on a slightly inferior pay scale, and they could never quite get over this. They were locked in a perpetual regrading battle with their Council chiefs, but due to the high turnover in staff, this never seemed to gain any momentum. Below the great graded echelons of nurses and social workers were the office receptionists, porters, and cleaners, who earned just enough more than they would in the

Benefits system to make working worthwhile. The only paid staff lower than them were the catering staff, and no-one really knew how they survived on the wages they were paid, least of all the caterers themselves. Eventually when this dawned on them, they left to become well paid 'bank' nursing staff, so the kitchens were in a perpetual staffing flux, which some said accounted for the terrible standard of food.

However, the pittance of the lowest paid kitchen workers, the untouchables at the very bottom of the Needleham pay hierarchy, was still ten times the weekly allowance paid to the patients, and the only thing all assorted paid workers, from the highest manager to the humblest kitchen assistant, could agree on was that the patients ought to be damned grateful for what they got, and given that their board and lodgings were paid for by the state, £12 a week was more than adequate for their needs.

Nurse O'Price was certainly of this opinion and had just said as much to the Advocate git, whose name for some reason just would not stick in his head. They were sitting in the spacious office on Passchendaele Ward, O'Price's home turf, with its walls feathered with sheets of type written notices, and desks overflowing with trays and little plastic holders for pens and paper clips. He went on.

- What you people don't seem to realise is that we are dealing with very ill people here. If we were to give Walter access to his full money, he would just go out and spend it immediately, and then have absolutely nothing for the rest of the week.

The git just did not get it. He stared back blankly as O'Price was talking.

- But it's demeaning for Walter to come and ask a nurse every time he wants a cigarette. And anyway, it's not just his weekly money. The ward is keeping Walter's savings money. You don't have any right to keep it. In fact it's....

He seemed to swallow as though gearing up for some effort of will, like an underconfident horse approaching a jump.

- Illegal what you're doing.

The word dropped into the pool of the conversation like a black stone, and there was a pause as the ripples spread into the room. There was something about the advocate that intimidated O'Price. Not something physical, for sure. O'Price would have enjoyed breaking the other man's nose and rendering him unconscious with a single blow from a right arm trained in a thousand workouts. It was something else that daunted him. In particular it was the use of the word 'illegal'. O'Price had nothing against the word, nothing in fact against the concept, and even the reality of illegality. He had done many illegal things. He had revelled in most of them and would do many more. But the word took on a new dimension in the mealy mouth of a well-spoken bastard git like – what was his name?

Who might conceivably know what he was talking about.

On the other hand he might not. He did have the shifty look of a bull-shitter. The question was - was O'Price feeling lucky?

He was not. He threw his pen down onto the desk in an obvious gesture of irritation.

- It's not my decision anyway. It's a clinical matter for Mr. Ellis.

A classic response from the unwritten handbook of psychiatric nursing practice, 'when all else fails, deny responsibility and pass the buck'.

- Ok, I'll ask him about it. Anyway, I've brought you some leaflets about the Patient's Council. It's on Wednesday, in the Art Room.

Price snorted and did not offer to take the leaflets what's his face offered, so in the end the advocate placed them on the table.

- The patients know about it. If they want to come they'll come. If not there's nothing I can do about it.

- But you'll try and encourage people to come? I mean Maria seemed to think on some wards they organised special activities to clash with the Council.

O'Price considered. He could hardly say this was one of the options his superior, Tarpow, had suggested.

- We can't force people to go. It's a free country.

- I know, but you could make sure people see the leaflets.

O'Price gave the slightest movement of his head which might have been acknowledgement but could equally have been denial or a nervous tic.

- I'd like to see Anthea Drell too while I'm here.

O'Price stared at the other man coldly.

- I don't know if she's on the ward at the moment.

- She's in the Quiet Room – I noticed her as I came past.

O'Price knew this of course but giving nothing away was one of the principles of the game as far as he was concerned. When the advocate had left the nurse's room he turned to the student nurse, as he ostentatiously threw the leaflets into the waste bin, and said drily:

- The problem with our patient's advocate is that his arse is too close to his nose.

The young nurse grinned at him, having no idea what he meant, but aware instinctively that appreciation of the humour of one's superiors was a precondition of making any kind of career progress at Needleham.

*

Luke found Anthea kneeling by the skirting board, a book in her hand. She looked up at him as he entered and gave a smile that he thought was brave and weary.

- Happy Imbolc!

Luke looked bemused.

- It's an old Gaelic Festival marking the beginning of Spring.

Luke glanced out of the window where a sullen West Yorkshire morning was reluctant to lighten up. There had been frost on the playing field as he walked over from the bus stop.

- The Spring is coming. Imbolc was the time people would start to plant crops. The rising sun aligns today with the inner chamber of the Hill of Tara, where the old kings were crowned and the Stone of Destiny stands.

- Anthea, I spoke to Doctor Ellis about your drugs.

- Luke, I'm worried about you. You shouldn't work here unless you have a spirit guide. In Native American culture, they went into the wilderness and fasted and meditated, and at some point a vision of their spirit guide, an animal, came to them. My guide is a kestrel. You must have a spirit guide too, waiting to help you.

He thought about this. An image of Bagpuss came into his mind.

- What are you reading?

- I'm healing the hospital with poetry.

The room was a sterile chamber with nothing but thin emulsion on the walls, and a functional beige cord carpet on the floor. It was overheated, and dominated by three pieces of heavy new furniture, a lime green settee and two matching chunky armchairs all covered in a plasticised, easily washable material, with a strange motif of surreal leaves. There was a desperately unhappy cheese plant pleading in a corner near the barred window. Its own leaves were edged with dryness. It was on its last legs. Luke thought it was the kind of room you might rent in a sinister hotel, where a phantom team scrubbed away signs of clandestine happenings each morning. He perched on the edge of one of the big chairs, as if afraid if to relax into it. Anthea's voice rose in incantation.

- Poor captive bird! Who, from thy narrow cage,
  Pourest such music, that it might assuage
  The rugged hearts of those who prisoned thee,
  Were they not deaf to all sweet melody;
  This song shall be thy rose:

It made him uncomfortable. He sat politely until she finished and turned to him. Her voice was trembling with some hidden, mad emotion.

- Do you feel it? This building?

He listened. The ward was very still.

- I'm not sure.

- The hospital is sick. It's in pain. I can feel it. It's troubled. It's trying to say something but no-one can hear what it's trying to say.

The pastel walls, the new carpet, the painted radiators and windowsills could not disguise an atmosphere of unrest, as if a sheet had been thrown over a sleeping monster.

- I think it wants to die.

The words invaded the room like bank robbers, and everything else that might have been said in response fell face down on the floor and kept very still. There was a loud electrical buzz from somewhere. She pointed towards the double socket set into the skirting board.

- The hospital has a natural system like the human body. It's kind of lymphatic. The best way to heal it is to try and get something into the electrical system. There are wires that go

45

all round these walls, under all the floorboards, all over. If you can get some healing power in that way it will circulate through the whole place.

She paused and gave him a straight look. He looked back at her evenly.

You are not here to judge the patient's belief system.

- I'm going to try some Sylvia Plath.

He felt a wave of unease. She picked up another book from the pile at her side.

- This is a poem called 'Words' she wrote just before she died. It starts… "Axes!"

She stopped and began to sob.

- That is so fucking true! Words are like axes! People…ah…!

She put her head into her palms, dropping the book and began to howl quietly. He had known Sylvia Plath was a bad idea somehow, that poetry would lead to no good. He should know. Throughout his childhood books of poetry had stared at him from shelves and bookcases and much good had it done him. He tentatively reached forward and put his hand on her surprisingly bony shoulder. Her whole frame was shuddering. He couldn't bear her crying.

- Words can be good too. Words are healing, kind things, that's why you're reading to the hospital. Have you got any John Hegley. He's very funny, that will cheer the place up.

She started to cry louder, making rhythmic hacking distressed sounds, so he knew John Hegley had been a bad idea. Sometimes you're better with music at such times, he reflected. Without words, obviously.

*

At the Joint Executive Administration and Liaison Planning sub-group (JEALPSG), the Professor, Mr. Ellis and Tarpow sat around

Tarpow's desk. Nurse Moking was there with pen poised ready to take notes.

- Any apologies?
- Unfortunately Miss Graytfell, representing the social work team, is on a training course today.

Ellis frowned at this.

- That's a pity. Wasn't the patient's representative meant to be here too?
- The patient's representative?

Professor Drogham seemed genuinely puzzled, and Tarpow said quickly

- Ah, yes, she was, our Ms. Paraskeva, but she's unable to attend today. Please record her apologies, Nurse Moking.

It would not do to have that troublemaker at this particular meeting, Tarpow thought. Ellis looked disappointed.

- That's a pity. I was hoping to have her input for the discussion of our centenary celebrations.

The West Riding Pennine Pauper Lunatic Asylum had been completed in October 1901. They discussed the upcoming celebrations at some length. The idea of a Summer Fayre, which had been popular in the 1930s, and used to raise funds from the local communities, had been resuscitated. Ellis was uneasy that festivities were to be funded by a drug company, Toxico Pharmaceuticals, but in the current economic situation there seemed little alternative. The arrangements, for a reception, speeches, workshops, a performance by the Happy Days creative writing group, and a bouncy castle all seemed innocuous enough. Ellis cleared his throat.

- Of course we have to think about the patients.
- O, I don't foresee a problem there, we can confine them to their wards for the day.

Ellis frowned at the Professor.

- We can't confine patients who are not detained under the Mental Health Act! I was imagining they would be invited to the celebrations!

Drogham sighed. Inviting the patients! Had Ellis met some of these patients? It was political correctness gone mad. He wondered if political correctness could go mad. What would be the treatment? CBT was unlikely to work. Actually political correctness was more of a personality disorder, he reflected, and so unlikely to respond to treatment at all. His meditations were interrupted by Ellis, who clearly had a bee in his bonnet.

- Well we'll come to the centenary celebrations later on the agenda. I've been looking through our financial position, and I'm rather concerned about this problem we seem to be having with the Private Finance Initiative arrangements.

He was holding up a letter of several pages.

- I've checked the original contract, which states quite clearly that our repayment arrangements to the private company who built the Happy Days Centre are at a base rate of 3%, and yet now they seem to want repayment at 17%. I just don't understand this at all. They are threatening to suspend their services.

Tarpow took the sheets of paper across the table. The Private Financing arrangements meant that cleaning, maintenance, and repairs were dealt with by a private company. Nursing staff could not do so much as change a light bulb. Actually things generally took so long to organise, that suspending the maintenance contract would make very little difference, he reflected.

- Ah, I see the problem.

He said, after scanning the letter.

- The original contract was with the Venimo Health Company, with which, as you so rightly say, we agreed a 3% repayment package. But this new letter comes from the Toxico United Company, quite a different concern!

- I don't understand.

- Well, under the government rules for PFI, the companies are allowed to sell on their contracts to a third firm.

- To sell on? What on earth does that mean?

- Well in this case it means that we are now dealing with a completely new company, who are renegotiating the original contract. I wouldn't worry. They are just bluffing. I'm sure in the end they'll settle for 10% or so.

- But that's going to cost us hundreds of thousands of pounds.

Ellis was appalled. Tarpow shrugged.

- Rules of the game, my friend.

Actually Tarpow couldn't really be upset by this, since his wife had considerable shares in both the Venimo Health Company, and in its sister company, the Toxico United Company.

- I think a more pressing problem actually is the catering contract.

Ellis was frowning.

- Well I wanted to come onto that. The caterers have stopped doing lunches. The only available food for staff is from two dispensing machines. What is going on?

- I'm afraid it seems to be a loophole.

- A loophole?

- Yes, indeed, a loophole in the original contract. It seems that in our original contract we agreed to pay the Venimo Catering Company five hundred thousand pounds to produce meals for our staff for the current financial year. Now, apparently they are refusing to honour that contract.

- Well, presumably there are penalty clauses to cover this kind of thing?

- Indeed there are. Indeed there are.

It was Tarpow's turn to frown.

- However, through some oversight in the contractual arrangements, we can only reclaim three hundred thousand pounds.

- What! So in other words the company is going to get two hundred thousand profit whether or not they actually produce any meals or not?

- It seems that way.

- And is there anything we can do about this.

- According to our legal advisors, there is not. We are stuck with the current arrangements. Of course the contract is only binding for one year after which we can renegotiate the contract with a new catering company. In fact since the staff obviously need to be fed, we will be getting a new company in almost immediately.

The Toxico Catering Company, who had an impeccable record.

- So in effect we are paying two companies for the same service? This is terrible. No wonder we're in such a bad financial situation.

Tarpow breathed in deeply.

- It's certainly true that this new phase of development has not been without its teething troubles. But I think we are learning all the time. And I'm sure we won't make the same mistakes again.

Venimo Legal Services were definitely getting the boot at the end of the year, for instance.

*

Later that day Luke received a visit from the Nurse Manager. She spoke without preamble as he opened the door.

- Someone has reported that you have been leaving the toilet open.

She stayed in the doorway as if reluctant to enter the little room, a tiny bird like woman with darting eyes that bounced off Luke and all round the room as though she were a seaside landlady checking on the knick-knacks. Luke looked at her blankly.

- The toilet. Someone reported that you have been leaving it open.

She repeated as the same speed and volume. Luke made a vague pointing gesture to the left.

- The toilet here?
- Exactly. It is a staff toilet, and apparently patients have been using it. It has to be locked when you have finished with it. The patients have their own toilets. That one is for staff.

Luke considered.

- But does it matter?

This time it was Nurse Moking's turn to look blank.

- Matter? It is a staff toilet. The patients have their own toilets. They should not be using it. It must be kept locked.
- But I think I'm the only staff member in this part of the hospital. And there don't seem to be that many patients. I don't think really there's any need.
- I remind you that the Patient's Advocacy scheme operates at the hospital as a courtesy. We allow the use of an office, but

we expect that basic hospital rules will be adhered to. If you are unwilling to do this then I am afraid we will have to withdraw the facility.

- Withdraw the toilet?

- Withdraw the key. You would then have to go to reception and get a key in order to access the toilet. Are you with me?

- Of course. I understand perfectly. It is very important that the patients not be allowed to use the same toilets as staff.

He imagined he was resorting to contemptuous sarcasm, but it came over rather limply, like abject capitulation.

- It is a health and safety issue.

- Really? I'm very interested in that. Could you show me the health and safety policy.

Now she did look at him suspiciously.

- All hospital policies are available on request to the relevant authority.

- And that would be…

She considered carefully.

- In this case… me.

- So could you show me the health and safety policy?

- Mr…er?

- Walker.

- Mr. Walker, I am not intending to make life difficult here, but there are certain protocols.

- I understand.

- If you have any problems with any of the regulations I suggest you take them up with Mr. Tarpow.

- Thank you. I believe we have a meeting arranged, so I will talk to him when I meet him next week.

- Please do that. I'm sure you will find that what I say is true.

There was a pause while they stared at each other. Having won her battle she seemed reluctant to leave. Having lost his, he did not know how to proceed.

- Very well. I will say good day.

The door closed, as the pencil Luke was fiddling about with broke into two separate pieces.

*

The Patient's Council was held in a distant wing of the hospital, near the long stay 'continuing care' and geriatric wards, behind the Industrial Therapy Unit. It was so hard to find that some patients were of the opinion that the hospital buildings shifted around in the night. The little room was wreathed in smoke, which circled several times as if examining the occupants before finding its way to the slightly opened window and streaming out to freedom. Although it was the Art Room, there was little space, and the central table seemed to fill it. Various 'still life' paintings of misshapen fruit adorned the walls, along with more lively renditions of burning buildings and semi abstract disintegrating human figures with lightning forks emanating from their heads. Maria was fidgeting. She was small and dark-haired with the kind of uneasy energy that solves crime and makes scientific discoveries. She was an ex-patient of Needleham, and when the fashion for "user involvement" was at its height, the Mental Health Trust had taken her on as a poacher turned gamekeeper. The Patient's Council was her baby, albeit one that refused to put on any weight. At least this Wednesday there was the added interest of the new Patient's Advocate, although her first impression of him was that he was a bit too soft and middle-class to make much impression at Needleham.

She was sitting next to Max who had on a green woollen great coat, his long dark hair straggling over its collar. Max's overcoat was festooned with badges of many different kinds, sprouting like fungi all over the lapels and breast of the thick jacket. 'VOTE KAFKA' stood out in big red letters on a plate five inches across, next to 'TONY BLARE'.

- Shall we make a start? Remember our rule to keep the smoking down to one at a time please. Anthea is still..... not well. Any other apologies?

- Hubert is unable to attend. Apparently he's at home working on his latest masterpiece, which is to be a novel about the mental health system in the style of Jack Kerouac.

There was a moment of bemusement in the room. The speaker had neat, short hair, and was stylish in a black leather jacket. He had thick lensed glasses that made his eyes huge and spoke in a sombre cultured voice.

- Thank you, James. Hubert hasn't been for months anyway, I don't really expect him anymore. Max, Liron, just one at a time please.

Liron's habit of chain smoking made the one smoker at a time rule hard to stick to for the rest of them. Already he had worked his way through four, raising the crumpled roll ups to his mouth every couple of seconds. People looked at Maria with varying degrees of curiosity, balefulness, and indifference. She felt her throat constricting against the toxic air.

- Alex, did you manage to do the minutes?

A round faced bespectacled man looked startled, and started forward as if suddenly woken.

- Well I've been having some problems with my phone, you see.

- But what's that got to do with the minutes?
- They said they were going to come over and fix the line on Tuesday, so I didn't manage to get on with my notes which I'd left at my Aunt's, cause I was waiting, but they didn't turn up and that's not the first time it happened. A couple of months ago they were supposed to come in and put another socket in for my mother, and she waited days for them. They'll lose the business, I mean it's not like the old days when they were nationalised and people couldn't go elsewhere, I'll probably change to Orange, I think.

He waited expectantly.

- So, we don't have the minutes?
- No, in fact we don't really have them, no.
- Ok, well I think I have my old notes here, so I'll refer to them. Let's start off with introductions then. I'm very pleased to welcome Luke Walker, our new advocate who some of you have met.

Luke smiled uncertainly around the room. He had an ill-fitting jacket of a dark green colour that was at odds with his blue chinos. Maria thought that either he had no sense of colour, or no regard for appearance. In any case he looked a bit shifty.

- Do you want to say something about your work, Luke?

Luke drew a breath, and felt a rush of panic, but before he could speak a younger woman with heavy black make up, black clothes and black back-combed hair spoke.

- He's here to defend our rights. He's going to help us fight the fascist bastards.

Next to her, and sitting very close to Walter, an older woman in a flowery dress looked puzzled.

- Is it benefits?

Alex, the volunteer, answered this.

- It's more kind of support I think, he's not there to tell you
  what to do but help you kind of make your own mind up so
  you can have informed consent, at least that what I seem to
  remember Anthea telling me when she did that job, but I'm
  not really too sure.

A thin, erect woman with long, severely tied back blond hair and a
smart dark suit cleared her throat and everyone waited. She had a
certain bearing and seemed to belong in the offices of the
administration block, rather than at the patient's council. When she
spoke she had a strong Eastern European accent.

- The advocate is like the runner in your cricket game. The
  patient is the batsman with an injury, and the advocate must
  do his running for him, for he can only walk.

Liron began to croon gently in a ruined voice that still bore distant
echoes of the lovely tenor it had once been.

- And you'll n-ever w-alk a-lone! You'll ne---------ver w-alk a-
  lone.

- The advocate is here to bear witness. He is the Paraclete!

- The what?

They all now looked at James.

- From the Latin 'Paracletus'. Translated as the Holy Spirit in
  most versions of the bible, but originally meaning the
  'advocate', the comforter or intercessor. With luck he will kill
  the first-born of those continuing to promote the biomedical
  model.

There was a beat where no-one seemed sure whether this was
intended seriously, before the mad twinkle behind the thick glasses,
and the little smile made it clear.

- James, you do talk horse shit sometimes.

Max shook his long hair as he said this, and the massed badges on his greatcoat tinkled as they touched. No-one seemed to object to his language, least of all James, who smiled benignly as though used to being maligned.

- He's just here to help you with drugs and things.

Max concluded, and then they all looked around at Walter, the only one of the group who had not yet voiced an opinion, and he said quietly,

- Blessed are the peacemakers.

They all then looked at Luke. He coughed nervously and squirmed a little on his chair.

- Well, it's a bit of all those things, I suppose. I don't work for the Trust, I work for Mindfields, so I'm independent of the hospital. I'm here to try and make things more balanced. It's like there's scales and all the weight is on one side and my job is to try and balance it up.

He looked round. They all gazed back at him. He felt compelled to continue.

- I've been trying to meet as many people as I can in the last few weeks. I'm here to support people, so if any of you are having problems, say with your treatment or money or anything, let me know.

They all nodded approval, and he didn't know what else to say.

- He's been helping me with my money.

Walter said. They considered this.

- And has he sorted it out for you yet?

Marjorie asked.

- Well, no not exactly sorted it out, but he's trying.

- They looked at the new advocate again with varying degrees of interest and suspicion. The tall, blond haired woman spoke first.

- I understand you have been trying to help Anthea? I think I may be able to help you. Anthea has agreed that I come with you to accompany her to the next ward round. I know these doctors and their ways.

- So you must be The Countess? Anthea mentioned you.

Alex burst out laughing at this point, and Marjorie, the older woman sitting next to Walter, stifled a chuckle and quickly produced a handkerchief to bury her merriment. Luke looked around to find the others amused, apart from the Countess herself.

- I understand people sometimes do refer to me with this appellation.

She said coldly. Maria intervened, taking hold of the moment and guiding it back on track.

- That's great, we'll be working together. Now we should think about the centenary celebrations. I've been invited to a meeting with Tarpow about it. It was supposed to be this week, but I haven't heard anything yet. Anyway, the Patient's Council will have a stall, so I'm hoping everyone will take a turn and help us with that. And James tells me that the creative writing group will be putting on a play!

James held his hands aloft as if to quell tumultuous applause, although the room was silent.

- It's an opera actually.

There was a bemused moment of giggles, whispers and glances. Marjorie was particularly intrigued.

- An opera? What, with people poncing about and singing?

- Indeed Marjorie, there will be much poncing, and even prancing, and perhaps even the odd pirouette. To be honest it's more of a musical than an opera. My provisional working title is 'The Storming of the Bastille'. It's a metaphor for Needleham Hospital. Did you know that when the Bastille fell during the French Revolution, they found not only political prisoners but mad people in the very deepest darkest cells?

They did not know this. Maria was aware they were going off piste, but she liked to encourage political debate.

- They liberated the political prisoners, and then in the furthest reaches they came across..... mad people. The story is uncorroborated to be perfectly frank, but never let the truth get in the way of a good story.

They were all suitably impressed, and all volunteered to take part, while insisting that they couldn't sing.

- I can't sing for toffee, but I'll do the costumes or something. And we should make a part for Anthea, and try and get her to the rehearsals!

They all agreed with Marjorie, and Luke noticed the Countess' eyes gleaming, as though she'd had a sudden idea. When the hubbub had died down Maria resumed control.

- Has anyone got any other items for the agenda?

- Yes, I've got one.

The rest of the group looked at Walter sympathetically.

- Ok, Walter, what would you like to talk about?

Maria sounded wary.

- I know that my redeemer liveth.

He looked around expectantly, beaming at the assembled activists. Maria smiled at Walter, although something within her sank.

- OK, Walter, I'll put that under 'any other business.'

But Walter was in his stride.

- This is definitely the main issue confronting us at this time. Though I walk and I follow of the shadow, yet I fear no evil...
- I know but we can't really deal with that...
- His word doth comfort me.
- He's right you know. We don't pay enough attention to the healing power of Christ.

Marjorie, bespectacled and taciturn, would always support Walter, in whom she took an affectionate interest. The whole meeting was taking on the aspect of a revivalist crusade as Alex stepped in helpfully.

- That's true, Walter. This group should be about healing. We should be promoting the recovery model, whether it's the healing power of Christ, or some other way, which is for every individual to find his own path for himself, or herself of course if it happens to be a woman because as we know women are proportionally over represented in the mental health system. I was talking to my mother about this the other day. It's no good just being against things. We need to let everyone know what we're for! We need to be positive as well as negative!

Maria couldn't help thinking that this meeting was not getting off to a good start. Here they were faced with the ultimate oppression - electro shock, enforced drugging, a continuous daily lowgrade holocaust foisted upon an unsuspecting population by the vicious propaganda of the drug companies and their accomplices. And could they agree about anything? At least Alex' last contribution gave her the chance to get back in.

- Exactly! And that's why we need to respond to this latest
round of consultations that the Trust is having. They sent us
a letter here.

She produced a sheet of cream paper, nearly as thick as a place mat, embossed with the Trust's logo, and handed out photocopied versions of it.

Needleham Mental Health NHS Trust
Your mental health is our business

Consultation

Needleham Mental Health NHS Trust is undertaking a consultation about the future of the Gallipoli Centre for Therapeutic Interventions.
Please answer the following question by circling the appropriate option:
Would you prefer to:
a) Move to modern, comfortable, state of the art,
   purpose built facilities, which offer up to date
   mental health care in accordance with the National
   Service Framework (NSF) and guidelines from the
   National Institute for Clinical Excellence (NICE)?
Or :
b) Continue in antiquated, inadequate, unhygienic,
   cramped facilities far from the centre of town with
   poor public transport?

Please put any other comments in the box provided below.
Please return the form by April 1st 2001 to Needleham Mental Health NHS Trust, Depot Lane, Needleham, West Yorkshire. NH5 7S.

Max, who had been sitting against the back wall, balancing his chair on the two back legs, suddenly lurched forward and spoke.

- It's a farce. They already know what they're going to do!
They've already told the nurses they're moving.

- What?
- I went up the other day to see somebody on that Unit. One of the nurses said straight out to him while I was there, 'don't get settled in, we won't be here in May, we've had our marching orders'.
- So the consultation serves no purpose?
- It serves a purpose all right. They're fulfilling their duty under the law to have a consultation.
- But they've already made the decision?
- Exactly. They're not going to let a bunch of loonies tell them what to do, are they? And there's more!

Everyone looked at Max expectantly. His powers of getting the low down on what was going on at the hospital were legendary. That he was secretly the eccentric millionaire owner of the hospital was a rumour that had long been circulating, though only on the locked ward for the most disturbed patients.

- The Happy Days Centre is going to close.

Now everyone was taken aback. The Happy Days Centre was the limbo all in-patients at Needleham dreamed of reaching after the hell of the back wards.

- They can't close Happy Days. Where will people go?
- Don't ask me. They're in a mess. They're talking about closing Passchendaele, and Somme, and Verdun.

Max shrugged philosophically.

- Personally I don't give a monkey's. It's just less oppressive institutions. I say we should just have a big celebration!

He was an anarchist at heart, Maria reflected sadly, and spoke up to counteract his ultra-left tendency.

- We can't let them get away with it. We should protest in some way.
- Perhaps we should set up a campaigning group, get the newspapers involved, and have a demonstration?

Everybody turned to look at the new Patient's Advocate with new interest.

THREE: March

For many years there was a strong rumour that a section of the nursing staff was trained to bear arms during the turbulent days of the General Strike of 1926, and during the long Miner's strike that followed it. There were indeed reports of strikers being harassed by unknown and disguised bands of well-trained men in West Yorkshire. No clear proof came to light that nurses at Needleham were involved, although one patient did write to the hospital superintendent to complain that early morning drill sessions outside his ward window were keeping him awake. Sadly this patient died before he could be interviewed. The early 1930s certainly witnessed the formation of an elite group of nurses who could be relied on to drop everything and come to any situation that was getting out of hand. This happened several times a day, and young men running down the corridors was a familiar sight. During the 1960s, this group took the unofficial name of a TV police series, and was known as 'The Flying Squad', a name that has stuck to the present day. When The Squad were called, duty doctors, porters, cleaners, and other nurses all gave right of way and stepped to one side. The Squad were not noted for their gentleness, in fact broken bones sometimes resulted from their involvement. They were recruited by a process of osmosis. The job description was unwritten, the person specification obscure but containing the qualities of being male, having a certain attitude, and a particular physical presence. One day a promisingly spirited young male nurse would find himself drawn to one side by an older one, and from then on, he would be part of that special class of nurses the others revered, respected or feared, according to their leanings.

A History of Confinement in West Yorkshire, Hubert Johnson

Luke first saw Needleham when he was eleven, driving with his father among sheep and stone flecked hills. It was the Easter break, and they were coming back from his second term at the boarding school in North Yorkshire he'd been sent to, following the death of his mother. The speed of his father's driving alarmed him. In fact, most of the world alarmed him at that time. It seemed a strange, uncertain place. It was mysterious to Luke how other people could be so sure about things. For instance his father drove along these rural roads in the old Austin Cambridge estate, riding happily over the brow of a blind summit, round hidden corners, never doubting that the road would continue unravelling before them, with no oncoming traffic to impede their progress. How, the boy wondered, did his father know they were not about to reach the final summit, turn one last corner, and the car would fly off into black space and fall into nothing?

As if in response to this thought, after one blind corner, the sign had leapt out to meet them:

NEEDLEHAM
NO "MAD" DRIVING
PLEASE
DRIVE CAREFULLY

He had heard the word "Needleham" before. He lived in Myllroyd, a small Pennine town some miles away, and the name of was invoked throughout his childhood by other children, teachers, and even his own father. It was a word used to threaten and cajole, to intimidate and silence. It described what would be your destiny if you didn't stick to the straight and narrow path; the place you would end up if you didn't mend your ways. 'You'll get sent to Needleham' had the same grammatical form as 'you'll go to hell', a vague, apocalyptic state from which there was no return; the end of the line. But eventually he had realised it was an actual place, rather than an abstract concept like 'prison', or 'exile'.

As they drove into the little village Luke looked across at his father, who had the fierce scowl he always had while driving, in fact most of the time these days. It was impossible to say or ask anything that would bridge that enormous gap, so Luke turned his attention to the passing world and watched carefully. The village looked like any one of the well-kept stone hamlets that minded their own business in the folds of these Pennine hills. There were daffodils on the verges, blossom on the trees. The few people in evidence were going about their business with a studied normality. There was no hint of excess or unreason. He decided there must be another Needleham somewhere, the opposite of this one, where lost souls went. Either that, or he would have to admit the possibility that the seemingly solid nature of reality might crack open at any moment to show some other, more sinister, nature.

*

- The problem is, dear, that the poor girl really needs to choose her fights.

Marion Walmsley, aka the Countess, intoned this as she eased her Corsa onto the busy dual carriageway. It wasn't so much that she'd timed the manoeuvre badly, but her leisurely ten miles an hour contrasted starkly with the onrushing fifty mile an hour traffic. There was an ensuing moment to test the resolve, nerve and reflexive capabilities of several drivers.

- Why are people always pipping!

She sighed sadly. Several obvious replies suggested themselves to Luke and were rejected on the grounds that they would jeopardise the mission, and possibly his future relationship with the Countess. He unclenched his hand from the door handle.

- Are you alright, dear?

66

She turned her heavily made up large brown eyes, full of concern, on him. When he tried to speak his mouth was so dry he could only make a dull scraping noise.

- I'm fine. Please watch the road.

With her power dressing and strange accent, which drifted between the Home Counties and the more obscure parts of Eastern Europe, the Countess was the only one of the patient's council who could command the respect, if not downright fear, of the nursing profession. The rumour was that she was once married to a consultant, which had given her the language skills of the profession. When he proved unfaithful (the rumour continued), she had torched his car outside the lover's house, playing the Hank Williams classic 'Your Cheatin' Heart' at full volume through a large battery-operated boom box. It wasn't really that fact which got her admitted to the local mental health observation unit, but her resistance to arrest, and insistence that she had connections with the old Russian royal family and current Mafia, who would shortly come to exact revenge on all who laid hands on her. She had only spent a week at the unit, but it had turned her into a life-long campaigner for the rights of the demented. After that week a rather embarrassed man with a moustache and a strong Eastern European accent had arrived, and following private discussions with the consultant, she was released. The nickname stuck from that point on.

They had left the old village behind and came over the brow of the hill where the stone settlement of Needleham Hospital appeared in the valley. The rain chose that moment to dab and fleck the car windows, and in the dismal light the darkened buildings ranged away, layer on layer, wing after wing. The Roman numerals of the stone clock towered above roofs and turrets, chimneys and windows, a closed world of dark sorrows and unspeakable torments, and that was just the staff. The Countess pulled the car over into a lay by near the main gateway, where they could see the massive stone pile through the trees and across an overgrown cricket pitch. She spoke quietly.

- There were once two and a half thousand patients living here.

He tried to imagine mad people swarming across the landscape in front of them, the teeming corridors, long rows of beds side by side, separated only by a small bedside cupboard, the long queues for food, for drugs.

- Where did they all go?
- I'll show you where some of them went.

She drove gently back into the steaming traffic.

- For goodness sake would you stop pipping!

Some moments later they stopped again, this time by a bare field about a hundred yards long by fifty yards wide on the opposite side of the road from the hospital.

- What is this place?
- Look!

There was a stone gatepost with a small brass plaque.

This is the site of the old hospital graveyard which contains the remains of 2,898 patients who died at the hospital between 1907 and 1969

R.I.P

Luke was still confused.

- How could so many be buried here? This field isn't big enough.
- Mass graves, like paupers. No headstones, no names.

They stood for a few moments, but there was nothing to see, just the empty field with its tufted grass, a small stone derelict chapel, and the padlocked gate.

- I'll show you something else.

They drove back to the main gate, narrowly avoiding a bus, which to the Countess' surprise stopped at a bus stop. They veered round it into the path of a large articulated lorry with extremely good brakes. When Luke opened his eyes there were sheep grazing alongside the long curve of the drive, and soon they parked beneath the clock tower. No-one was around in the little glass fronted reception room as they entered through the main doors. A brightly lit corridor stretched in either direction. Under each radiator as they walked along a body slept, for it was still a cold Spring. Marion strode on purposefully until they came to a small corridor on the left.

- They always leave it open.

She pushed a heavy door and slipped out of view. Luke followed her and found himself in a vast dusty space, a room whose floor was as big in area as the field they had recently left. He realised it was the old ballroom he had heard about but never seen. The walls climbed to forty feet or more and then gave way to large dirty windows, which grudgingly let in discoloured light. Large dark portraits of benefactors and local politicians glared down from yellow walls. At one end of the room was a stage with ragged crimson curtains, and piles of chairs, boxes and machinery. The floor was wooden parquet, but uncared for so that it showed dark, stained areas. Someone had rigged up a badminton net in the middle of the space, but one of the supporting poles had fallen over, and it sagged to the floor. A small bird had somehow found a way in and flapped at the windows high above, making a distant distressed chirruping sound.

Marion turned to Luke.

- Shall we dance?

She began a circular dance into the room, holding an imaginary partner and dada-ing a demented tune that bore a distant family resemblance to the Anniversary Waltz.

- Every week the doctors would entertain! How are you my dear! So glad you could come! Please be my guest!
- Marion, I don't think we should.......
- The patients? O don't worry about them, they are safe asleep. We gave them extra doses so they would not act up. Yes, you are right to admire our beautiful fireplaces, four of them and all with raging fires. We would not want you to catch a cold! The patients saw the logs, it's good for their health! *Mens sana in corpore sano*! Keep the bastards busy!

There were indeed no less than four big stone fireplaces, their mouths boarded over now with hardboard.

- Please Marion. We've got to go and see Anthea!
- Ah, Anthea!

Marion stopped in mid waltz as if struck by a sudden thought as the door opened, and a small fierce woman walked in.

- Can I help you?
- Alas, we are beyond help, I fear!

From Marion, and Luke hastily said

- Yes! We have an appointment with Doctor Ellis. There was no-one in the office at reception and we seem to have got a bit lost.

There was a staring contest going on between the new woman, who was eyeing Marion throughout Luke's speech with one eyebrow raised theatrically, and Marion herself, who smiled back evenly.

- Please follow me.

The new woman said eventually, and they followed her out. Luke was sweating despite the coldness, and Marion winked at him as she passed.

Ellis was already talking to Anthea when they were ushered into the office that would have been spacious were it not so crowded with files and books. The woman gave Marion a final glare as she exited. Marion smiled sweetly.

- Come in, come in.

It was the first time Luke had met Ellis. Opinion about him was mixed among the patients. Some considered him to be a kind man, at least in comparison to the traditional doctors of Needleham. He didn't prescribe as many drugs as some and avoided shock.

- Anthea was telling me about your, er performance. It sounds very interesting.

He was looking at Luke, who looked back blankly.

- The play?

Luckily the Countess took up the cue.

- We have been practising hard for the centenary celebrations! It is a fine play, Dr. Ellis, a fine play. An operetta and a modern classic. There is a suggestion we might take it to Edinburgh next year.

The word 'Edinburgh' gave Luke a slight jolt. He just had to trust the Countess' method here, as they had decided. Dr. Ellis certainly looked suitably impressed. Luke tried to breathe deeply.

- And Anthea is essential to the play! We wish to take her out today to rehearse. We are very keen that people start to learn their parts and that we are fully prepared for the Centenary celebrations.

She said this firmly and Ellis looked puzzled.

- But the celebrations are not until the Summer Fayre!

- One cannot start too soon.

Ellis seemed to accept the Countess' vehemence, and turned to Anthea, who was staring sullenly at a glass paperweight with an alpine plant trapped forever inside it.

- But Anthea, you really haven't been well, have you? Your neighbours were very concerned about you. I'm just not sure you're ready for this. We've only just started the stabiliser. And to be frank you have been a little aggressive. Wouldn't you say?

Anthea's eyes blazed.

- I was manhandled by your nurses. I specifically said I didn't want to have drugs, and they forced me to take them.

Marion stepped in as things seemed ripe to go out of control.

- Dr. Ellis, we understand completely the difficult situation you are in. Each day the papers bring forth stories of the terrible disasters the psychotics wreak on an unsuspecting population. The stabbings, the pushings onto train tracks, even the leapings from churches and other high buildings in unforeseen acts of self-destruction and immolation.

Luke felt that Marion was possibly overstating the case a little here. She continued,

- How is it possible for a well-meaning doctor, a healer by trade, whose historic task is to do what no philosopher from the beginning of human consciousness has been able to adequately do, that is to define and understand the human mind itself, the psyche with all its weaknesses and delusions, its penchant for the irrational, how can such a person no matter how dedicated and well trained, fulfil all the demands an ignorant public would foist upon you?

Ellis looked for the first time uncertain, and could not answer the question. Possibly like the rest he was not sure what the question actually was.

72

-   You cannot, sir! It cannot be done! There is no accurate way
    of predicting which of the poor souls you discharge each day
    into this dog eat dog melange will commit acts of outrage
    and violence against the unsuspecting and innocent, or
    against themselves which as we know is statistically the more
    likely.

Ellis smiled thinly and nodded his head uncertainly.

-   So perhaps then the only answer is to lock them all up, as the
    brutal popularism of the tabloids would have us think! Keep
    them all under lock and key! Then at least you know the
    world is safe! That the people themselves, these poor
    benighted, demented souls, are safe.

Anthea glared at her at this point. Ellis struggled to fill the gap left
by Marion's dramatic declamation.

-   Well of course we don't wish to detain people unnecessarily.

-   Of course not.

-   We have to decide if people are genuinely dangerous.

-   Genuinely, indeed!

-   We have to allow people to take risks.

-   Ah yes, risks!

-   We are after all, not a concentration camp!

This was unexpected, even to Marion, and there was a pause as
they all took it in. Luke could see Anthea about to open her mouth
and wreck everything by insisting that this was in fact a concentration
camp, with drugs instead of razor wire, or some other comment
unhelpful to this situation. Marion got there first.

-   Of course you are not! This is not Auschwitz! There are no
    trains! We do not scrabble to eat insects or rats.

Again Luke could see Anthea poised to make some sarcastic remark about Needleham food, but Marion flowed on and didn't give her the chance.

- We know these things. And we know that you, like us, prize liberty, not even beginning to mention the fact of the terrible overcrowding, and the constant need for beds for the newly diagnosed mentally unhinged. So we have come to give assurances that for the duration of the rehearsals Anthea will be in the finest hands.

- Really, so do you have skills of the caring profession in your group?

- Indeed we do. Mr. Walker here, the patient's advocate, Dr. Walker I should say, although his doctorate is of the academic rather than the medical variety, you understand! Dr. Walker is a Gestalt Therapist of many years' experience and will be on hand for the whole performance and until we deliver Ms. Drell safely back into your caring hands later this evening!

Luke looked down at the carpet and concentrated on a big red flower.

- Really! Well I'm rather interested in Gestalt myself!

Luke dared a glance up and Ellis was beaming at him. He decided the time was against actually saying anything at this point, and just smiled and nodded in a way that he thought might be described as 'sagely'.

- He has for the moment given up his 'hot seat', if you know what I mean, to concentrate on theoretical study. The figure of his forthcoming work looms large against the background of his years in the field, so to speak.

Luke smiled steadfastly down at the red flower, while he waited for Ellis to pose the inevitable unintelligible question, as you would wait for the blade to fall as you stare down at the bloodied revolutionary cobblestones. But Ellis thankfully cut the conversation short.

- Well, now is not the time and place for a discussion.

Too damned right!

- The whole thing hinges on Anthea herself! Do you feel up to this?
- I'm much better today.
- No strange thoughts?

Anthea looked him straight in the eye.

- None at all.
- No voices, no thoughts of harming yourself, nothing at all out of the ordinary?

Anthea looked out of the window as if pondering, though Luke could tell she was just letting enough time elapse to give the impression she had pondered.

- No, doctor.

The Countess could not contain herself.

- She is an easily influenced soul who was temporarily unhinged by reading the works of dubious so called 'Romantic' poets.
- Really?
- Yes, aristocratic dilettantes with nothing better to do with their time than espouse fashionable causes. We will make sure that she reads no poetry in the next hours you can be sure!

Ellis was looking at her curiously now, in a way that suggested he was rapidly leafing through some cerebral version of the Diagnostic and Statistical Manual for a suitable category.

- Well, I've nothing against poetry.

He said lamely. A few moments later the Countess, Luke and Anthea were climbing into the Corsa in triumph. Luke felt a great wave of relief and euphoria. He turned to the Countess.

- How do you do it?

- It is simple really. I think of it as the tennis theory.

- Tennis?

- One stretches the opponent with a long forehand down the tramline, which was the statement of the extreme philosophy of detention. Ellis obviously does not want to be seen as espousing such an oppressive theory, so he has to chase this to the back of the court and counters by stating the view you wish him to have. This is the equivalent of a soft backhand return. You are by now standing at the net and able, by agreeing with everything he is now saying to drop the ball back gently just over the net. He is unable to counter this and cedes the point.

- But what was the bit about claiming I'm a therapist? 'Dr. Walker?' I'm not a doctor of any kind! Suppose he'd asked me some question I couldn't answer?

- It worked, didn't it? You have to learn to improvise, like a musician, Doctor.

As she turned the ignition key Anthea burst into tears behind them.

- What's the matter?

She put a hand against the seat in front and another against the roof of the car. Her face was crumpled with anguish.

- There's something wrong with this car.

They got out and examined the tyres, the exhaust, turned the engine on and ran it for a while listening for unusual sounds. There was nothing, and eventually they got back in and drove away. Three

76

days later the electrics packed up and it had to be towed away for a new starter motor.

*

Tarpow loved his room, and particularly, when he felt like a break, to walk from one end to the other, savouring his possession of such a fine working space. He would look at the wooden fireplace, inspect the big green aspidistra and cheese plants for signs of decay, glance out at the weather over the woods of Needleham, and revel in his good fortune. Today he had just completed a tour, when there was a tentative knock at the big oak door. He boomed a response and welcomed Maria into his office. She looked wary, Tarpow noted, almost uncomfortable. Good. He motioned her to sit down.

- Ah, Maria! How are you?

Tarpow smiled in a way he thought disarmingly benign. Maria experienced this as threateningly sinister.

- I'm fine. The nurses are still tearing our posters for the Patient's Council down on some of the wards, though.

- Really? I will have a word at our next Ward Manager's meeting.

Tarpow made a show of writing a note to himself on a pad he took from a drawer of his desk, although in fact the Ward Managers didn't have regular meetings, and in any case he had himself suggested the policy of tearing down Maria's fliers. He circled the little stick rabbit he had drawn and put the pad carefully back into the drawer.

- I was also going to ask you about the issue of proper representation on some of the Trust's Planning Groups. We did talk about this, and you said you'd look into it.

- I did indeed, and I have talked to the senior managers about it. I'm afraid they don't think it's appropriate.

- Not appropriate?

- Not appropriate.

What a lovely word. It was close to being Tarpow's favourite, he thought. For a start it had four syllables, which gave it gravity, and a sense of having been arrived at after due consideration and a careful weighing up of all available evidence. If you threw in the implication of morality, and the suggestion of carefully erected boundaries, then it became the perfect way of saying 'no', without having to offer any evidence whatsoever. Maria looked stunned.

- Surely it's a fundamental principle of our policy that people using the services are to be involved in all aspects of the Trust's work?

Her voice had become a little high and agitated, so Tarpow automatically went low and calm.

- Maria, you've gained a lot of respect since you started working here, but there's a feeling among some people that you're, how can I put it, a little bit over involved.

- Over involved? But I am the Involvement Worker! I'm paid to be involved!

- Precisely! You are our Involvement Worker. You are a symbol of how seriously the Trust takes the principle of service user involvement. This is a fundamental idea of a democratic National Health Service. We have taken on board the Government's views on this so seriously that we have created a post for Involvement!

- And surely my job is to ensure that service users are involved at all levels of the Trust's work?

- You misunderstand. Your job is the involvement. The very fact of our giving you a job within the Trust means that we are involving people, irrespective of what you actually do! Let me try and put it another way. We pay you to talk to the patients, and find their views, then you bring those views to the relevant meetings.

Maria glared at him.

- But it doesn't seem to change anything! What about the consultation about the Gallipoli Centre for Therapeutic Interventions. People are very concerned about the proposal to move it from Needleham Hospital to a site on the industrial estate. Is it true that the decision has already been made about this?

- There is no truth in that rumour. The consultation we are currently having with staff, patients and members of the public is bona fide, and our final decision will be based entirely on the findings of that piece of work.

- But the new unit has apparently already been completed, fully decorated, and is waiting for them to move in!

Tarpow looked wary.

- Well, the point is that there actually is in fact no viable alternative to the plans the Trust have put forward for that unit, so we thought it best not to waste any time. We have performance management targets.

- But doesn't that make the whole thing a farce?

- It is not your job to criticise the decisions managers make. Your job is….

- Yes?

- To be involved, that's all. You're an Involvement Worker, you get involved. We make decisions. Clear?

The two glared at each other. Tarpow had not meant to get into it with this junior worker. It undermined that sense of himself of a judicious handler of people, but there was no doubt that Maria was a pest and a nuisance. Who did she think she was wearing that shell necklace? And since when did tie-dye come back into fashion? He took a deep breath and straightened some papers on his desk.

- That will be all.

*

The Patient's Involvement Worker was not invited to the Joint Executive Modernisation and Development sub group (JEMADSG), which met some days later. Tarpow had assembled Professor Drogham and Mr. Ellis. Moking and Nurse O'Price were there to represent medical staff, and Trevor Blenkinsop, a coroner from Dewsbury, on behalf of the Hospital Board. Tarpow had been hoping to get the local authority social workers on board too, so he was disappointed that the senior social worker Miss Graytfell was on annual leave. Of course, he was chairing the meeting.

- We should start. We have a full agenda, but just to get it out of the way there is a small item not on the agenda I wanted to bring your attention to, a proposal to extend the drilling licence in the hospital grounds to Abetter Gas and Oil Company. It's rather a formality really, so I thought we could deal with it quickly and get onto more important things. A little background - as you know the whole valley was once a coal mining area. In fact pit workings go right underneath some parts of Needleham. It seems that we are sitting on top of shale rock, from which experts think it may be possible to extract deposits of natural gas. Abetter has been drilling some exploratory shafts, and now want to extend this to other parts of the grounds.

They all thought it sounded a promising idea. Only Ellis looked thoughtful.

- Won't it be rather intrusive? I mean for the patients?

80

- The drilling won't be near the wards currently in use. They'll be drilling in the grounds, and under parts of the old hospital.

- So they'll just be drilling?

- At this stage basically just drilling, yes. Well, drilling and testing. It's rather an ingenious process, which goes under the technical name of hydraulic fracturing. Apparently they send down water under pressure into the old mine workings and it forces the gas up to the surface to be collected. Very simple and safe. It goes without saying that if there is gas down there, since the hospital is a foundation trust, and financially independent, then we could be sitting on a small fortune.

They all looked very impressed apart from Ellis who still had that sullen frog look.

- We already have problems of subsidence at Needleham. Are you sure this won't make things worse?

Tarpow laughed.

- I have every confidence in Abetter. They are very experienced in these matters and are an extremely reputable firm!

He wasn't lying, he reflected. Abetter did have a good reputation. They had done well in keeping that Namibia scandal out of the headlines. Only industry insiders, and a few canny others like Tarpow, were aware of the worst mining accident in that poor country's troubled history.

- And they will just be using water, under pressure?

- Just pure simple honest water.

A fleeting memory leapt into Tarpow's mind. Apparently there were certain other chemicals that would be used, in highly diluted quantities, of course. The words 'mercury' and 'uranium' had been mentioned and seemed innocuous enough. Only when the words 'hydrochloric acid' and 'formaldehyde' were mentioned did he have a moment's doubt. This doubt had pirouetted in an attention seeking way until a more substantial thought, involving banknotes of the realm, grabbed it by the collar and flung it from the stage.

- I should emphasise that the extra finances from this venture will be essential to the Trust over the next twelve months, quite apart from whether anything of substance is found.

- And how much will the contract be worth?

Trevor could always be counted on to look for the bottom line. Tarpow mentioned a substantial figure and they all nodded happily. That seemed to quell young Ellis's queries. Of course Tarpow didn't mention his own fee – an equivalent amount to be paid into a private account for 'consultancy fees', which had not influenced his decision in any way, and so, clearly, was not necessary to mention. It was simply and obviously what was known in the business as a 'win-win situation'.

*

The entrance of the HAPPY DAYS project had been designed by local art students to resemble the front of a huge American car. Luke was pursuing his Outreach Policy. He had decided to visit every unit at the Hospital to tell staff and patients about his work. It was beginning to pay off and he was seeing a trickle of patients who had heard that the Advocacy office was occupied again. This was his first visit to the HAPPY DAYS Day Hospital, which was the large house near the gate he had passed on his first morning. He walked between two big headlights at either side of the front door, pushed against the radiator grill painted on the door panels, and stepped into a room that was meant to be the heart of America in the 1950s. There beyond the reception desk was a coffee machine that had been decked up like an old time Wurlitzer jukebox. The kitchen and eating area had been done out to resemble a diner. The male staff wore leather jackets and quiffs, and the women had ponytails with long cotton skirts and wide belts.

Luke signed in without disturbing the frantic typing of the bespectacled woman with a beehive wig who was punching away at an old PC. He walked into the main seating area where several people were reading newspapers or simply staring. James smiled and nodded to him from an armchair, wearing his habitual black leather jacket, even though the day was mild and the room warm. James' eyes seemed huge behind his heavy framed spectacles, and their brightness gave him a wild look. A large TV was showing a pugnacious man interviewing a sweating, uncomfortable woman in front of a studio audience.

- So basically what you want us to believe is that you shouldn't have to pay back the £50,000 debt you racked up just because your doctor claims you have a bi-polar disorder? I mean come on! Do you think we're stupid or something! Anyone could say that!

The legend at the bottom of the screen said:

'Mad? Bad? Or just having us on?'

The enthusiastic jeers and yells of the TV audience were in marked contrast to the forlorn atmosphere in the room. Luke sat down on a bright red leatherette couch, next to a rigid man in a vivid green jumper with large red spots on his neck, who was staring not quite at the television. He seemed tense and every few seconds he rocked forward and slurped from a pint glass of thin looking orange crush.

- Hi.

The man turned to him slowly, and it seemed he was having trouble focussing. He took another drink from the glass and rocked in his seat.

- Get thirsty with the drugs. Got to keep drinking.

- O, sorry about that. I'm the advocate.

- Bloody drag. Good job Jesus is looking after me. Is Jesus looking after you? What's your name?

- Luke.

- Like Cool Hand Luke?

- Ha, yes, that's it. Or Gospel According To!

The man's expression had creased into a sudden frown. Did he think Luke was insulting his religion?

- Fuck off!

The man with red spots on his neck got up huffily, picking up his pint glass and walked out. There was a silence when the other occupants of the room looked at Luke with cool interest. James rose carefully and crossed the room to take the seat the first man had vacated.

- I apologise for Jeremy's behaviour. He isn't himself today. Actually I've never known him be himself so I probably wouldn't recognise him if he was. Welcome to Happy Days! We were expecting you.

The voice was like dark chocolate, deep and apparently enjoying the taste of itself. Luke looked into the dilated pupils that met his. Thick-lenses made the eyes look far too near. The look was sharp and unselfconscious

- You were expecting me?

- Your word goes before you! We benighted denizens of this psychiatric underworld were given advanced notice of your pending arrival, with the chaser that we be circumspect!

- They told you not to talk to me?

The other man looked around the room, a surreptitious look, mock frightened and worldly. No staff were present. He raised both his eyebrows in gentle outrage.

- My dear sir, perish the thought! They would say no such thing outright. Merely say that it was implied.......

He drew out the last syllable into a long wavering bass note, while at the same time dropping both eyebrows, so that now he was peering at Luke sternly. It was so hard to know when mad people were joking.

- I see. I thought people were a bit... aggressive today.
- O don't mind Jeremy. He's a Christian.

He left the remark hanging in the air. It seemed that pulling it down might be complicated. Instead Luke considered James. His black leather jacket was studded and multi-pocketed, and he wore blue denim jeans and polished, black Doc Martins. He had a certain neatness and style which made him stand out amongst the other patients who seemed to be dressed randomly in clothes belonging to people of other sizes, generations, nationalities and gender.

- What did you do before...
- Before I was mad? I used to work in the theatre.

James said this rather grandly.

- Really? That sounds exciting. What did you do?
- I worked in the theatre bar. Actually I got the sack. I couldn't really concentrate on the job.

James looked at him conspiratorially over the dark frames of his stylish glasses.

- Too much talent! All those beautiful actors! I kept giving them the wrong drinks. In the end I made a bit of a pass at one and they sacked me.

Luke looked around. The TV show was reaching a climax, with the audience baying, and an angry husband shouting at the tearful debtor.

Several people were sitting in the huge armchairs that curved around the screen, three overweight men and two nervous women. Eyes veered away from his as he met them. A male nurse walked in briskly, switched the television off and clapped his hands. Apparently it was time for the news quiz. People didn't seem enthusiastic. James regarded him closely.

- I'm going outside for a smoke. Would you like to join me?

It seemed like an offer he should not refuse. James had already leapt up and Luke followed. They went through a corridor, past closed doors on either side, to the smoker's doorway at the back of the building. From here they could see an expanse of grounds with the main hospital block on the right and woods on the left. The sky was grey and the air brought fresh rumours of rain. James was already studiously drawing on a roll up. Luke spoke first.

- It seems quiet today. Apart from the TV, I mean.

- It's quiet every day. 'Quiet sleep feels no foul weather' is the
  motto of the Happy Days Centre I'm afraid. 'Days' spelt 'D-
  A-Z-E' obviously. I come here for the creative writing group.

- You're not an in-patient?

- Used to be. Apparently I have a schizo-affective rapid cycle
  bi-polar disorder, with paranoid tendencies, which my doctor
  thinks is genetic, despite my assurance to him that research
  on dizygotic, indeed any twins, in fact all genetic research, is
  utterly flawed in its very conception.

There was a gallant bitterness in his voice. At that moment Max came up to the door in the green civil defence overcoat and lit a dishevelled roll up. Luke noticed a new small white badge that read 'THE SOUND-BITE IS DEAD'. James welcomed the newcomer warmly.

- Max is an artist and philosopher, a key member of the Happy
  Days writing group. Max, how did you get on with
  Krishnamurti?

86

The new man looked pained.

- Not very well. You can't understand what he's on about, and he contradicts himself. I think he's a bit of a wanker to be honest.

- Good lord, man! Please don't say that Krishnamurti is a wanker!

- He says, like, "Don't follow any teachers", right? But he's written the bloody book in the first place, so what's that all about then, eh? It doesn't make sense.

James waved his cigarette into the moist air.

- Well, it's a paradox. That's part of his point! That it's thinking itself that gets us into these difficulties! It's the mind, or rather our lack of understanding about the mind. The point is simply to be aware and just let those thoughts pass through your mind. Thought produces conflict, and paradox. The very act of it. As soon as you begin to think you are in conflict.

Max looked dubious. Luke was struggling to keep up. James carried on.

- Krishnamurti emphasises the need to understand our minds, the very subtlety of our thinking.

He waved expansively at the buildings of Needleham, the woods, the universe in general.

- We think we are aware, but do we ever really look at anything? Do we ever really see anything other than our own preconceptions?

Max and Luke looked suspiciously at the surroundings, then exchanged a look. Max spoke in an Eric Morecombe voice.

- There's no answer to that.

A young nurse with a thin beard of stubble appeared and lit a ready-made cigarette, puffing on it furiously.

- Now then lads, what are you up to?

There was a pause, then simply to fill it, Luke said,

- Discussing Krishnamurti.

James shot him a warning look. The young nurse burst into a snigger that was half coughing.

- Krishna-who-ti?

- Krishnamurti. He's ....a thinker, I suppose.

The nurse seemed to find the thought enormously amusing, and he continued to smile delightedly, as he attacked his cigarette with two or three swift intakes.

- Krishnamurti, eh? And what conclusions did you arrive at?

He said this with the air of his expelled smoke. Another pause, then Max spoke.

- He's a bit of a wanker.

This delighted the young nurse even more.

- So, Krishnamurti's a wanker! Well, it's good to know that you professors have sorted that one out!

He seemed to relish the thought. Luke had a picture of the story being repeated in the staff room.

- And is our leader, the divine Janet, here yet?

James enquired, giving Luke the distinct impression he was moving the conversation on rapidly.

- Yes. Creative Writing will be starting in five minutes. I understand you are working towards a piece for the centenary celebrations?

- Ah yes, 'A Hundred Years of Platitudes' was my suggestion for a title, but Janet didn't seem to like it for some reason.

The young nurse looked bemused now.

- Well, keep on writing.

He took a final swift four tokes on his cigarette and squeezed it out against the wall, throwing the stub into a tin bin by the door. Luke had never seen a cigarette smoked with such gusto.

- Write on. As they say. Write on, professors!

He gave them a manic beam and disappeared back inside the building. The three men looked at each other. Then James said.

- Utterly mad, like all the rest of them. It's best not to talk too much in front of the nurses, about ideas and such stuff. They don't like it. I think they have rather an inferiority complex. Are you coming to the writing group, Max?

- No, I'm going to do some cutting. I've nearly finished the hospital!

This comment puzzled Luke, but James seemed to find it quite intelligible.

- Nice one! What about you, Luke. Are you going to come in and introduce yourself?

- Do you think Janet will mind?

- Not sure, only one way to see.

The Happy Days Creative Writing group took place in a small room reserved for creative purposes, being the smallest in the building, and with no windows. Pictures of a young Elvis and a sneering Gene Vincent hung on the walls in clip frames. James and Luke were the first in the room.

- What did Max mean he was going to do some cutting?

- Well Max may talk, and occasionally act, like an oaf, but he's actually a rather good artist. He makes these fabulous models from single sheets of paper, by making cuts and folding. It doesn't sound like much, but he manages to do amazing things. The Sydney Opera House?

Luke checked James' expression to see if he was joking. He wasn't. Then Janet Mayfield, who was the Assistant Manager at Happy Days and group leader, walked in and greeted them cheerfully. The ponytail really did not suit her, Luke reflected, but she was happy for him to stay and talk to the group members. One by one they ambled or slouched, dawdled or meandered in. The group was fifteen minutes late starting. Luke knew Alex, Walter and Liron from the Patient's Council meeting. Several others he was meeting for the first time, and glad to be with James, who was clearly held in some esteem. After his brief introduction and a few questions Luke was preparing to make his exit when there was a terrible metallic racket. Luke covered his ears, and after a few seconds dimly recognised the Star Spangled Banner, which due to hideous distortion bore an uncanny resemblance to the controversial Jimi Hendrix version.

- What is that?

None of the others looked in the least concerned. James answered affably.

- It's the alarm bell. Don't worry. They test it this time every week. Either that or it's the Flying Squad.

- What's the Flying Squad?

Luke asked, but the others just shook their heads.

- You don't want to know.

And since no real conversation was possible at that point, he didn't find out then.

*

Nurse O'Price of Passchendaele Ward was an enthusiastic member of the Flying Squad, and on this occasion, he was the one to call it. The door of the nurse's station had burst open, and O'Price glared at the young student nurse who entered so abruptly. He frowned a strong question, and the breathless young man replied

- It's Max, he's got a knife. I was just walking into his room and he turned round with it in his hand. One of those fucking Stanley knife things.

O'Price continued to frown and laid his Stephen King novel on the desk in front of him after carefully folding back the corner of the page. He reached for the phone and dialled reception.

- Hi, Henry. Yes, yes I'm alright. Yes, look, Henry.......Henry, stop a moment, ok! I want you to put out the word for the Squad to get to Passchendaele right now. We have a knife incident.

He replaced the receiver, picked some keys off a hook and threw them across the room to a distracted woman who caught them one handed and reluctantly put down her Sudoku book.

- Prepare some aquaphase.

He moved to the door with the student in his wake, and down the corridor towards the bedrooms. He didn't like Max Ernest at all. Not that he was anti-Semitic, or anything like that, not publicly anyway, although some of the Squad he could name were extremely so. As far as he himself was concerned white was white. He just didn't like the arrogant way some of them were so up themselves, and this one in particular. Thought he was a bit of an artist, always down at OT and spouting about some wanky theory or other. He was due, that was for sure.

- Ok Max?

He shouted through the door. There was no reply, and he waited until a couple of the guys had run onto the ward, and the aquaphase was handy. Then he opened the door and stepped in. Max Ernest turned around startled from throwing water on his face in the little hand basin.

- What's going on?

Without replying O'Price walked across the room and got hold of Max at the wrist and upper arm. He pulled him away from the washbasin sharply so that one of the other men could get hold of his other arm in the same way, and they marched him across the room to the bed. Max was protesting now and his voice rose with alarm and anger. His face glowing red from the effort stared into O'Price's. They paid no attention to his cries, and threw him face down on the bed, O'Price kneeling on him and holding his arms up his back. A nurse pulled down the pyjama bottoms and pushed a needle full of soothing poison into the clenched buttock. Max screamed as the needle went into the tense muscle, like a screw-driver going through balsa wood. Then he went limp and was silent. O'Price spoke.

- Put him in seclusion, and we'll see how he is when he wakes up.

The others left the room, taking Max. Now alone, O'Price looked round and found the blade on the window-sill. It was a vicious little number, one of those craft knives with a chunky handle and a tough short blade, most likely brought back from OT, who would get a right bollocking when he caught up with them. The knife was next to a sheet of white A4 paper out of which a curious structure rose. It was a model of Needleham Hospital. Tiny representations of the buildings and the clock tower had been carefully sliced out of the single sheet of paper and folded up to be stuck together to form the familiar roofs and chimneys. Little windows had been cut carefully out of the walls of the buildings, and a picture of the clock, set at midnight, drawn in careful ink on the main tower. Here was the administration block and the wing where the elderly wards were; there at an angle to the main body of the hospital was the long wing, a later addition, and currently housing the acute wards. There were small outbuildings set apart from the main building, out towards the edges of the white rectangle, representations of buildings which had been wards, but were now disused and becoming overgrown. In Max's model they were as pure and crisp as the main building itself. There was even a tiny paper cross over the little chapel.

O'Price marvelled for a moment at what he was seeing. He turned the paper this way and that, examining the ten thousand incisions that had made a world, the world of Needleham, rise from a single sheet of paper. Then he carefully retracted the blade into the body of the craft knife, whispered the word 'bollocks', before picking the sheet up, screwing it up into a tight ball, and throwing it into the metal bin.

FOUR: April

The chapel at Needleham was built in 1910 and one of its most striking features is the presence of 25 carved mice, which can be found hidden in various places. These were created and placed there by Nicholas Bosket, a talented wood carver who was a patient at the hospital between 1905 and 1915. Bosquet was also responsible for carving the oak panels on the front door of Needleham Hospital, including the notable "ship of fools" panel, which drew the admiration of John Betjeman. However Bosquet resented being made to work on the chapel, being an atheist, and apparently placed the mice as a kind of revenge on the authorities who sought to make use of his talents. Often the mice are in lewd poses.

A History of Confinement in West Yorkshire, Hubert Johnson

Susan was frowning at Luke, and he felt intimidated. He tried to sink back into the mock leather of the pub seat, and focus on the half pint of beer on the table in front of him. They were in what he felt was a rather synthetic wine bar in Leeds, an environment full of the glittering lights of quiz machines, noisy TV screens and chrome surfaces that reflected everything back in an alarming way.

- You can't just go around doing things that aren't part of your job description!

He knew this didn't really have anything to do with his job. It had started with his honest appraisal of the film they had just been to see, which Susan had for some reason taken a personal affront to. The film had been two hours long, and as far as Luke could make out was about a block of flats in Eastern Europe where very little ever seemed to happen. And more to the point, it didn't happen in black and white, and with sub-titles.

- Well nobody checks up on me. As long as I'm doing my job, I can't see why they would bother if I do….extra things.

They had argued about what film to see in the first place. Susan had made a disparaging comment about Luke's preference. She had read a review and seemed to know the entire plot, with its strengths and (mainly) weaknesses, as well as the admittedly good performances from some of the actors (though others seemed to be resting on their laurels, and one in particular was abysmal). She could furthermore place the film's historical significance within its genre and by the time she had finished giving her opinion of why it was a bad choice, he felt he knew so much about it that there seemed little point in actually watching it. But the tower block was undoubtedly worse. He just shouldn't have said so. Now Susan was saying:

- It's just not the job of an advocate to go round helping people to organise demonstrations.

Luke sighed.

- Well people are very upset, and they don't really have much of an outlet for it. That bloke Max I was telling you about is only just recovering from all the drugs they gave him. They had him in solitary confinement for a week.

- Don't be silly. There's no such thing as solitary confinement.

Luke thought it better not to argue. They might call it 'seclusion' these days, but the white room, devoid of furniture, with its small reinforced window and concave mirror high in one corner, so the person inside could be seen wherever they were in the room, was the same thing. Anyway Susan was continuing.

95

- It's a mental hospital for goodness sake! You can't let people wander about with knives!

- I know that. Anyway I'm just going to a meeting, that's all.

- In your work time!

- Yes, true, in my work time, but it is advocacy in a way. I'm supporting an initiative from the patients. The patient's council want to have an independent campaigning group, and I said I would help.

She looked at him drily.

- Quite the liberationist, aren't we?

She scathed well. She also couldn't leave an itch unscratched.

- I can't believe you couldn't see that it was a feminist film.

- Well, I know what you mean, but the blokes were victims too, weren't they?

- VICTIMS!

He marvelled at her ability to get an edge of lacerating viciousness into a mocking laugh.

- Anyway, I'm completely bored with this whole conversation.

Susan took in a huge intake of breath with a loud sighing noise and a theatrical shaking of her head as she picked up her large glass of white wine. She turned her head pointedly to survey the rest of the room. When she tipped back her head to drink he admired the fine features of her face and neck, a thin silver earring pointing to the earth like a compass needle, as the head tilted at an angle. Her expensively cut blond hair fell away in layers over her ear and stopped abruptly at the nape of her neck. Below he could see the edge of a bra strap across an open apron of skin, and lower still her breasts pushed against the dark cotton of her dress. He imagined his hands cupped over them, a pleasure which might well be receding this evening unless some action was taken to rectify the situation.

- Anyway, how is your mother?

She turned to glare at him with an expression so full of contempt and anger that he thought for a moment she was going to throw the glass of wine over him.

- My mother is fine.

*

Unit Manager Tarpow and Nurse Manager Moking were looking down at a squat machine, which had just been delivered to Tarpow's office. Tarpow had a certain affection for Moking, although he did sometimes suspect she came from another planet. She was rather an intense woman who he suspected adored him, or at least could be counted on to do everything he suggested, which was just as good.

- Here it is, Nurse Moking. My PAL!
- Your pal, sir?
- My PAL, indeed. This machine was carefully built to my own specifications. You've heard of the Patients Advice and Liaison Service?
- Of, course. It's part of the government's plan to make the NHS accountable. Each Trust was meant to set one up four years ago, but we....

Her voice trailed off uncertainly.

- Yes, Nurse Moking?
- We...haven't got round to it yet, sir, due to....other priorities.
- Well we have now, Moking! This is it. This is our PAL service!
- But it looks like a shredder sir!
- Ah, but it's a shredder with a difference! Watch this!

Tarpow took a sheet of paper from his desk.

\- This is from this morning's mail.

He waved the paper above Moking's head. She could make out the words 'outrageous', 'disgusting'.

\- This is a complaint from an angry customer. Watch carefully now!

Tarpow fed the sheet into the long straight shark's teeth of the machine. There was an angry whine as the steel blades chewed ravenously. Tarpow beamed.

\- See this scanner here.

He pointed to a thin screen just above the cutting edge of the machine.

\- These are PAL's eyes. He is carefully reading the letter and taking relevant information from it.

The whining stopped; the mechanism satisfied for a while.

\- Now watch.

Tarpow adjusted a setting at the top of the machine, then pressed a button at the side. A quieter tone filled the air, a conscientious printer doing its efficient work, and enjoying being of service. Tarpow took the new sheet that emerged and passed it to Moking. She read:

Needleham Mental Health NHS Trust

Depot Lane
Needleham
West Yorkshire
NH5 7S

Your Mental Health Is Our Business!

Our Ref: digam/01
April 21st 2001

Dear Mr. Flanaghan
It is with deep concern that I read your comments in
the letter dated 23rd March 2001.

I have made initial enquiries with the people
concerned and can assure you that your complaint will
be dealt with as soon as possible in a thorough and
professional way. I will be writing to you again in due
course.

Yours honestly

Augustus Tarpow
Unit General Manager
Needleham Foundation NHS Trust

- That's very impressive. You haven't even read the letter.

- I don't need to. The machine scans the name of the person,
  date, everything you need. In a month's time, without
  prompting, it will automatically generate a letter that says we
  have looked thoroughly into every aspect of the complaint
  and amended our policies accordingly and this will never
  happen again, thank you for your concern.

- But suppose you need to refer to the original letter? I mean
  didn't you just shred it?

- It never happens, but if it did, there is a copy stored in PAL's
  memory. We can regenerate it.

- Well that's very clever. What's the significance of 'Our Reference – digam'?

- 'Digam' is something to do with the operating system, but I think of it as 'Do I Give A Monkey's'. PAL saves money, Moking, that's the main thing. We're in a market situation. PAL doesn't need a pension, or holidays. Just a yearly maintenance and he'll be fine.

- But suppose people want to speak to someone over the phone.

Tarpow beamed at her, and reached across to punch another button. His own slightly muffled voice emerged from a tiny speaker in the machine's side.

- This is the Patients Advice and Liaison Service. Please choose between the following eleven options. One, I have been a patient of Needleham Mental Health NHS Trust, and I want to compliment staff on the treatment I received. Two, I have been a patient of Needleham Mental Health Foundation NHS Trust and I wish to enquire about an article of my property which was mislaid. Three..

Tarpow spoke over his own recorded voice.

- There are several layers to PAL's call centre function. It takes people at least three minutes to get to the stage where they can leave a message. If they get that far, my secretary will pick up the messages and someone will get back to them....at some point.

- It's very clever.

- Thank you Moking. Apart from saving us money, we can market this design and who knows? The whole NHS might be running with it in a couple of years and Needleham will be sitting on a goldmine.

Just then the phone on his desk rang and he frowned. The receptionist was under strict instructions not to disturb him unless it was very urgent. He picked up the receiver.

- Yes…yes… yes… look Henry!… Henry!...Henry, stop for a moment. Just put me through, will you? Yes just put me straight through and let me speak to them on Passchendaele Ward.

There was a pause while Tarpow drummed his fingers menacingly on the desktop.

- O'Price? What the hell's going on down there?

There was a long pause as Tarpow listened, and his fingers stopped drumming.

- What? But we just got over one enquiry for God's sake!

There was more of what sounded like insects squeaking to Moking's ears. Then she heard Tarpow boom.

- Do nothing. Do absolutely nothing, do you understand, til I get there!

He slammed the phone into its cradle and glared at Moking.

- For God's sake the whole of Passchendaele's been poisoned now!

- Poisoned?

- Apparently there's a bloody fleet of ambulances ready to take people away to the Infirmary. It's one bloody crisis after another.

He rushed out, and Moking followed in his wake like a leaf caught in the draft of a passing gale.

*

The Merry Prankster was a student pub really, James reflected. It wouldn't have been his first choice for the inaugural meeting of the campaigning group, but for the fact that it had a good selection of European lagers. It was the haunt of the slackers that 'attended' Needleham Art College, but now in the Summer months, stripped of the financial gloss of those middle-class darlings who came to slum, it reverted to its shabby truth. Only James, Luke, Maria and Anthea were present for this first meeting. Anthea looked pale and drank only water. She was nervous and haunted, looking around constantly, and starting at sudden sounds. She was still technically a patient, though no longer a detained one, so she could come and go as she pleased. The four of them sat at a small pub table at one end of the room. At the other there was a raised platform where in busier times a duo would be elbow to elbow. James was holding forth on the most outstanding issue of the new campaigning group, its name.

- We definitely don't want to be 'Needleham Service User Forum' or anything boring like that. We need a name that is memorable, humorous, striking. I've been thinking about this, and I think we should call ourselves after a Dostoevsky novel.

- The Idiots?

- Yes, very funny, Maria, very sharp. Mind you don't cut yourself. No, I was thinking of 'THE POSSESSED'.

He announced his suggestion in his best bass imitation Hollywood voice over, which rolled out into the beer-stained room like the voice of God. Disappointingly, the others did not look impressed. Anthea seemed shocked and stared at him with dilated eyes. Maria looked as if she was still enjoying her witticism. Luke looked mildly approving, which was almost worse to James than downright opposition. It was Maria who found words.

- Well I think it's ok, but you know how religious Marjorie and Walter are. They're not going to like references to demonic possession.

She didn't ever expect herself to be defending Marjorie and Walter's religious beliefs, but she wanted the group to be credible.

- What about 'Madvocates'?

Luke suggested. Yes, Maria thought, of course he would approve of a name that contained his job title. James butted in, full of expensive lager, and himself.

- 'Madvocates' is good, but people will think we are an advocacy group. There's also 'Mad Lib', which is clever, but I fear has already been used. If not 'The Possessed' then I prefer 'The Irredeemables', after Pinel, who first identified *manie sans delirium*, in other words 'that group of patients who are beyond redemption'.

They liked the rebel implications of his latest suggestion but felt that it was too obscure. Anthea spoke for the first time. Her voice was softer than the rest, wavering, as if coming from someone unused to speaking.

- What about The Off-Beats?

James raised his eyes to the ceiling.

- The title of Hubert's new novel. A homage to Jack Kerouac. I've read part of it and it sucks. Supposedly a racy bohemian take on the mental health system, only instead of hip young Americans, the heroes and heroines would be contemporary mental patients. Instead of Beats they would be Off-Beats. He envisages being the founder of the Off-Beat Generation. He wanted to call it "On The Ward", but I told him no one will get your reference to Kerouac's post-war hitch-hiking classic, and in any case, the point about mental patients is that they don't really do very much, let alone anything that will inspire anyone else to do anything but run a hundred miles from them. I think the whole thing is doomed.

- Well, why can't we be "The Off Beats"?

Anthea's voice had a quiet insistence. The others looked sceptical at first, but they wanted to be kind to their friend, and they couldn't think of an actual objection. One by one they came round to thinking it wasn't such a bad idea. Maria said:

- We should let Hubert know.

They agreed that "The Off-Beats" would be the working title of their campaigning group. Maria then produced four photocopies.

- What's this?

- It's a statement from Survivors Speak Out. I thought we could adopt it until we get a constitution of our own.

- A constitution? This is getting a bit formal!

James felt mildly outraged by the idea of a constitution, but clearly no-one was with him, so he let it go. They examined the sheet of paper in front of them.

> **Statement from Survivors Speak Out following Edale Conference 1987.**
>
> The right of self-advocacy among recipients of psychiatric services is now being accepted in tandem with the increasing evidence of the oppressive and damaging effects caused by the implementation of the medical model.
>
> The claim that resources are not available is untrue. What is needed is a redirection of those resources to provide benefit rather than medicalization imposed as a result of dubious psychiatric theories.
>
> As survivors of the psychiatric system, we make the following demands:
>
> 1 The right to choose. The right of individuals in time of emotional distress to choose freely what kind of help they want. The provision of the fullest range of services and information about them to enable such choices to be real.
>
> 2 Sufficient social security benefits, housing and employment opportunities without the usual stigmas, to enable real rehabilitation from psychiatry.
>
> 3 A proper spectrum of resources for self-advocacy groups and facilities for self-management, based on a real acceptance that recipients are competent, creative and caring.
>
> 4 A positive response from official bodies to practical proposals put forward by recipients. The opportunity to make our skills and experience effective.
>
> 5 The right to be valued for what we are and what we might become. Not for what we were, or were thought to be, either in recent times or in this or proceeding centuries.

Luke was impressed.

- It's very strong, as a statement of intent.

Anthea too liked what she read.

- It's good. What was the Edale Conference?

Maria explained.

- It was a get together of mental health survivors from all over the country at a Youth Hostel in Derbyshire to try and thrash out a national strategy, and this is what they came up with.

James had an objection.

- I don't think all medicalisation is bad. Obviously what happened to poor Max is really abusive, but it is possible to have a chemical imbalance...

James was thinking of his own self-medicating, but Maria cut in.

- Chemical imbalance is drug company propaganda! How could you know what chemicals are in a brain unless you cut it up to see? They just want to sell more drugs to 'balance the chemicals'. It isn't chemicals that drive people "crazy", it's the conditions people have to live in! It's capitalism that drives people crazy!

There was a deep grunting rumble, and instinct made Luke reach protectively for his glass of lime soda that was close to the edge of the table. Having cleared his throat, James spoke.

- I have to disagree. That's far too simplistic. All societies have recorded people who are different, from the ancient Greeks with their melancholia and hysteria, and even before that traces in other ancient civilisations. It seems there have always been those who don't fit, who don't experience the world like the rest. Some people are just born with skins too thin.

Anthea had been fidgeting, waiting for James to end and now she launched in.

- Yes, people have always been different, but up until the rise of science people would be tolerated in their communities! The basic problem now is we've lost touch with nature. Look at an animal, a cat, say. It doesn't feel separate from its world. But we've become separate. We've tried to be above nature, and dominate it, instead of realising we're part of it, and now our whole society's crazy. We're just the ones the looniness spills out of.

She threw up her arms to include all present in her judgement. Luke looked pained.

- That's the trouble! Three people, three different ways of seeing it. And you're all on the same basic side. On the other side there's the bio-medical model, and even they disagree with each other. Then there are the psychologists and the psychoanalysts, and all the other therapies people believe in. The mental health system is like the Tower of Babel.

James looked thoughtful.

- That's not a bad image! Babel came about because the human race was getting too uppity, trying to build a tower to God, so He put the kibosh on it by making them speak the different tongues of the world we know today as languages. Perhaps for modern man he sent madness for similar reasons?

- O, for goodness sake!

Maria couldn't contain herself any longer.

- God has bugger all to do with it! It suits the rich and powerful to have a pool of no hopers they can point to and keep everyone else in order! "Do your work and don't ask too many questions or you might end up like them!" We're serving a useful social function. They ought to pay us!

- They do pay us!

Maria turned to glare at Anthea.

- Well they ought to pay us more!

- And capitalists are people too you know!

Maria was about to turn on Anthea and lambast her for being a feather-brained, air-headed hippy bimbo, but luckily James got in first.

- C'est bon de tuer de temps en temps un admiral……

There was a pause while the others tried to take this in. None of them had paid much attention to either French or History classes at school.

- Pour encourager les autres!

He said triumphantly by way of explanation. There was a further pause, and a possible early schism in the Off-Beats was averted, as Luke tried to summarise the subtleties of the various arguments.

- The point is we all think the current way of doing things is bollocks.

- Yes!

- That's right!

- That's a reasonable summary!

The others agreed with his assessment. There was a hiatus, during which Maria looked thoughtful.

- The question is what can we do about it?

Maria, James and Anthea fell silent, each in their own thoughts of what they could do. It was left to Luke to break the silence.

- We can protest! We can organise a demonstration.

They looked at him in surprise and recognition. That wasn't what they were thinking, but it sounded right.

*

When Tarpow arrived breathless with Nurse Moking at the Nurses' Station on Passchendaele Ward, the scene resembled a disaster area, with clumps of people strewn throughout the day room and along the main corridor. As a large team of green suited paramedics attended to prostrate patients, O'Price tried to explain.

- It seems that the fridge in the patients' kitchen had been undergoing routine maintenance. The mechanic had replaced some of the refrigerant gas from the works.

- Gas? From the fridge? The fridge is bloody electric man!

- Yes, sir, quite, but it seems that fridges use gases that are cooled in a compressor and liquefied. The idea is that as they warm up they absorb heat from the surroundings and that's how they provide the refrigerating effect. It's really rather ingenious actually when you come to think of it.

- For God's sake will you tell me what happened?

- Yes, sorry. Well, apparently the particular chlorofluorocarbon in question was bright green, and the student nurse, he, well, it seems..........

- Will you tell me what the fuck happened?

- He thought it was lime juice sir, so he gave it to the patients.

- For God's sake!

- Mostly they just got really bad stomach ache. It was just Jeremy.

- Jeremy, do I know Jeremy?

- Jeremy Williams, sir. He was the one who stole all that Haloperidol, sir, and took it all at once. We had to take him to Accident and Emergency. Stiff as a board he was. Do you remember the trouble we had getting him in the car? Anyway, he had four glasses of this stuff, sir.

- And is he going to be all right?

- Well, it depends how you look at it, sir?

- What do you mean?

- Well, his earthly sufferings are over, sir, in that sense. He's dead.

There was a terrible silence broken only by the sound of the second hand of the plastic office clock placidly doing its round.

- We do need to think about what to do with the body sir. We are keeping the other patients out of the dormitory but it is making them rather anxious.

A sudden look of horror crossed Tarpow's face.

- O God, he's not black is he?
- No, sir, he was from Slaithwaite.
- Thank God for that.

*

James couldn't believe how banal and embarrassing the service was. It seemed blasphemous, on Easter Saturday, with the risen body of Christ apparent in every pure exploding blackthorn, to listen to the badly miked local vicar tiptoeing his way through niceties that had little to do with the blighted life of poor Jeremy Williams.

- Jeremy had a wonderful sense of humour, and despite the ah affliction of his mental illness ah, the schizophrenia which ah had affected him since being a teenager, he always maintained a cheerful ah disposition.

Had the vicar got the right person? Was he at the right service even? The white-haired lady in the front row who was presumably Jeremy's mother had a look of puzzlement, so perhaps he wasn't. As the vicar droned on, James noticed the soft sunlight falling over the swirling knots and grain of the pews, and over the seven people who sat among them. As it entered the chapel, the sunlight was mediated by stained glass, which showed among the mediocre saints with their dusty haloes a depiction of Jesus, casting out a legion of evil spirits, and depositing them into an innocent troupe of wild pigs. The Son

110

of God did not show much sensitivity to those poor porkers. The madman fawned with rolling eyes and gratitude at the Saviour's divine feet, while the pigs positively gavotted off towards the horizon, where a rocky precipice presaged their doom. A snotty looking Lamb of God was looking down at the scene from a nearby crag with a superior look on its serene and stupid face.

-   Man born of woman hath but a short time upon this earth.

And Needleham Hospital didn't help, in fact generally could be relied upon to make one's time even shorter. James felt he needed some distraction or he was going to lose it and start yelling out. Next to him Anthea was looking dreamy and red eyed. He nudged her thigh and pointed down to the small mouse nestling behind the red velvet kneeling rail. Anthea leapt and gave a shrill squeak. The tiny wooden rodent, half hidden behind the wooden post of the pew in front, was sitting back on its haunches with one paw held up towards those seated. Was it really holding up two claws? The vicar paused, the other five people in the room turned round. James stared impassively ahead and whispered to her.

-   It's wooden.

She was breathing heavily.

-   Bastard.

He raised both eye-brows in protest, and she looked fierce, then dissolved into quiet tears. He put his hand on her shoulder. The vicar paused momentarily, and looked vaguely in their direction, before continuing in that peculiar voice, beginning each sentence on a high, almost falsetto note, and falling away to a kind of resigned sigh.

-   "I know that my redeemer liveth."

So the question must be, why then do you not instruct your fatherly God to send down destructive fire and brimstone to destroy every last stone and damn Needleham into eternity? Come on, if you're a real god! Let's see what you're made of. I challenge you! You can't do it, can you?

Max, who was sitting in the pew in front turned and caught James' eye. He still looked bleary and unwell from his recent medicinal experience on Passchendaele Ward. He looked as if he were about to say something, but at that moment they were invited to pray, and the little congregation bowed their heads and mumbled incoherently. When James looked up the coffin was still standing on the little trolley between the pews and the pulpit, like afternoon tea. Soon the vicar would throw back the sheet and Jeremy would pop up with iced buns in either hand. 'Just fooling, guys'.

But he wouldn't.

As the strangely chopped discordant chords of the hidden organ swelled to signify the end of the service, and the coffin was carried out, James fell in step with Max, who whispered fiercely.

- Jeremy would have hated this. I was talking to him once about dying. He said he didn't want all this piousness.

James nodded in agreement. He'd only met Jeremy a few times, but insofar as he made any sense at all, he seemed like a non-conformist. Liron was walking behind and joined in their conversation.

- He said he didn't believe in an afterlife. If he died first he wanted us to celebrate, not mourn. He said if he ever died he wanted me to dance on his grave.

James smiled at Liron, and then was struck by the terrible image of what he'd said. He put it out of mind. Not even Liron was that crazy.

They walked the rest of the way to the grave in silence, with Anthea dabbing at her eyes, past gravestones that were sinking into the landscape, leaning at odd angles, ancient bunches of plastic flowers on some, the area mostly going to weeds. The air was light and fresh with scents after the long dead months. James wondered whether Jeremy had any family other than his mother. Only Moking and Maria from the hospital staff were there. Moking looked distant and awkward, pressed reluctantly into overtime no doubt. Maria had barely said a word all afternoon.

At the graveside there were more words from the vicar but they seemed more palatable in the open air. With some difficulty the four pall-bearers lowered the coffin to its final resting place. They had to take the weight and move carefully on the loose clay and mud around the hole. The box seemed to be straining at the ropes to get down into the hole.

Moking looked uncomfortable and picked up the tiniest piece of clay to throw down into the grave. Maria stepped forward to throw a handful down onto the varnished box, and James remembered what she had told him once, when she had visited Jeremy's ward, trying to recruit people for the Patient's Council. Jeremy, as mad as Ajax in his multi-coloured dressing gown, had pledged his undying love and proposed to her.

Liron also stepped forward, as if to throw a handful of soil, and stood for a moment, towering over the earthen lips. James had a sudden premonition and put his hand up to his face as he realised what was about to happen. Before any of the pallbearers could move, Liron half leapt and half slid down into the hole. His boots made a solid thud on the thick wood of the coffin. Mrs. Williams let out a single high-pitched wail as Liron threw his hands up and jigged along the length of the hole.

- Let's not have a sniffle, let's have a bloody good cry!

Liron once had a sweet voice and you could hear traces of it in the suddenly still air, a kind of debauched Tony Bennett, at the end of a long night of clubs and brothels. But he was singing with an angry edge now. The sound of his boots clumping on the solid oak of the coffin made a terrible frantic noise as though the corpse had woken and was panicking in the darkness.

-   And always remember the longer you live, the sooner you bloody well die!

Liron was throwing his hands into the air. It certainly looked like a rather rusty disco routine to James, more of a geriatric pogo-ing. The four pallbearers moved forward as Liron sang at the top of his voice.

-   Look at the mourners, all bloody hypocrites!

Two of the bearers leapt into the grave and grappled with him, as he shouted.

-   It was what he said he wanted!

He appealed to his friends, but they could do nothing. They stood there, and as the hefty men wrested Liron out of the grave, James could see that tears were rolling down his face.

FIVE: May

Electro-convulsive therapy or ECT was a feature of treatment at all the great asylums in West Yorkshire since its development in Mussolini's Italy during the 1930s. It was hailed at the time as a great breakthrough in treatment, although since the emergence of patient's rights groups, these claims have been questioned. Professor Bolt, the predecessor of Professor Drogham at Needleham claimed one hundred per cent success over a number of years. His method of monitoring and evaluation to reach this result was to ask patients if they had recovered or not, and if not, to give them more ECT until they thought it had helped.

'Fear and Loathing in Acute Day Care', Hubert Johnson
(unpublished document)

The flower child wore a cowboy hat and was smiling into the camera, holding up two fingers for peace. She wore a long frock with a pattern of exotic flowers that might have been peonies, or from some planet the Starship Enterprise had visited. She had several sets of wooden beads and gaudy bangles. Had the photo been in colour there would have been a lot of it, if not clashing then at least seriously vying for attention. Her smile said that she was a dancer, a dreamer, a dandelion clock that one breath of wind would lift and send flying. But in the eyes of that fragile face was a look that was clear and determined. It was a face that hinted at wildness waiting to be released. It looked as if it liked listening to Bob Dylan and reading the Bhagavad Gita, could roll joints and wasn't embarrassed by sex.

She looked like Janis Joplin's elder sister, Luke thought, as he looked at the photograph of his mother. The photo wasn't great, and the detail was blurred, but he thought he could see kindness and intelligence in it despite a lot of dark make-up. She had a high forehead under the wide brim, and the hand that wasn't gesturing at the camera was holding a roll-up or small joint. Some kind of white blossom was pinned to the front of the hat. She was sitting in a group at what might have been a festival, and was clearly with the longhaired, bearded man who sat on her right, smiling ahead and away from the camera.

At least he recognised his mother, but the man next to her made no sense to him. His mother looked like an earlier version of the woman who would later dance in the kitchen to Eton Rifles and tell him wild stories. The man was Luke's father. There was no mistaking the combination of facial features, despite the full beard. But the man who was Luke's father had hair cropped back into a featureless men's non-style that bore no resemblance to these luxuriant locks. His father would never have been seen dead in the flapping paisley patterned flares that spilled out below hands cupped around knees. More than any of these superficial things, the young, carefree face in the photo could never have belonged to the frowning man who prowled the house of Luke's childhood.

There were a few other photographs that included his father from the same time period, some clearly at the university where he had been a student, but the box he was looking in seemed to be dedicated to his mother. She was a 'townie', a Leicester resident he met at a Zombies concert. Luke knew that his father's family had disapproved of his relationship with the common shop-girl, but his father was nothing if not stubborn. There were colour photos of the wedding, which showed the two sides of the family awkwardly thrown together, then more of the house by the river at Myllroyd where the couple moved when his father came to work in, and eventually head, the English Department of the local grammar school. There were pictures of her nursing a baby that must have been himself. She was older now, more tired, the beads and bangles gone.

It was among these photographs that he found a letter addressed to his father with the stamp of Needleham Mental Health NHS Trust. It gave him a jolt to find the present intruding into his reverie about the past, and a further one to see the postmark carried a date only 6 years ago. What had either of his parents to do with Needleham? He pulled out the letter curiously and began to read.

Needleham Mental Health NHS Trust

Tannenberg Unit
Depot Lane
West Yorkshire
NH5 7S

Our ref: Digam/ac239

April 13th 1995

Dear Mr. Walker

In confirmation of our telephone conversation yesterday, I can confirm that Mrs Lucinda Walker died peacefully in her sleep on 11 April. I offer my sincere condolences and look forward to seeing you at your convenience, where her belongings will be available for collection.

yours sincerely,

Herman Robertson
Secretary to the Unit General Manager

Luke read this letter several times. It was a surprise to him, since he had always believed his mother had died of cancer in 1979.

*

Mental Health for A New Millennium

The Strategic Plan for Needleham NHS Mental Health Trust (May 2001)

Executive summary

As we move into a new millennium new concepts of mental health care are appropriate. The following paper is the result of a wide-ranging, cross-cutting consultation with key stakeholders.

Taking an over-arching approach, and in accordance with modern principles of clinical governance and accountability, services will be provided in a seamless way, underpinned by single assessment, effective sign posting, clear triggers for appropriate interventions and transparent pathways for specialist services. This will be a step in, step back service as required. We will put the right interventions in and leave the wrong ones out. Preconceptions about service provision will be shaken all about.

Standard activity data and monitoring information will be collected in line with agreed parameters, and new systems of accountability and engagement will be developed by securing buy-in from partners across different sectors. We look forward to a proliferation of local policies, focusing on different policy implementation silos. The modern service we plan will be based on the Recovery Model, where individuals will be encouraged and empowered to take responsibility for their own mental health. We will identify holistic approaches and aim for a maximum of social inclusion in our rehabilitation programme, so that care can be provided where people are most at home, in their communities, by the people who know them best, i.e. themselves and their closest friends and relatives.

We will integrate financial and cost information into Care Pathways, as well as quality indicators and clinical outcomes, in order to deliver and monitor quality improvement and cost reduction. The key-notes of this plan will be Quality, Understanding, Innovation, Delivery and Sensitivity.

The Professor looked puzzled.

- But what does it all mean?

Ellis was triumphant.

- It means that we close all bar one of our acute wards within the next three months, with a massive saving on staff costs.

Tarpow felt himself drawn to admire the younger man's audacity.

- So basically, we withdraw our service?

- Indeed, we do, in the interests of recovery and social inclusion!

The Professor was not convinced.

- But what will people do?

Ellis smiled at him with the kind expression of the inheriting son visiting the nursing home.

- The National Association for Systemic Therapeutic Interventions has done research to show that the average acute ward is not conducive to recovery from mental illness. People need to be in the community, among their friends, doing normal things, so we're just making that possible. We call it the Recovery Model.

- So we're just going to leave people without treatment?

- Drugs, Professor. There will be drugs. Our job will be to monitor them.

- Well thank goodness for that! I thought for a minute you were going to tell me we were getting rid of drugs!

They all chuckled over that one. Then a worried frown again came to the Professor's face.

- And shock? Are you getting rid of that too? That really works for some people you know!

119

Ellis reassured him.

- Business as usual for shock. It costs very little to administer, which of course is a key issue here. And with the Trust's new Green Policy we will be getting our electricity from renewable resources. The Unit at Needleham will carry on as normal. In fact we'll maybe even be expanding it. The hospital will still be here for those who need it, but we'll be encouraging people to get help in their communities and supporting them to stay in work.

- Supporting people to stay in work? That's not really our job, is it?

- Well, what I mean is they'll lose their benefit for several months if they lose their jobs, so there's shall we say an incentive to keep at it.

- I see. And this……Recovery Model. It seems to me it's just letting people do what they want.

- Absolutely not! The Recovery Model is challenging people where their lifestyle is harming their mental health, like for instance drinking, or taking street drugs. Anywhere in fact where we don't like what they're doing.

- And what if they want to challenge us by saying they don't want to take the drugs we want them to have?

- In that case they lack insight, and here again the job of our workers will be to challenge this and ensure compliance.

- In other words we can challenge them whenever we feel like it, but they can't challenge us? It seems to be the same as the system we already have.

- Exactly. The Recovery Model is the perfect radical, innovative, forward-looking theory which allows us to proceed just the same as we always have. In any case new legislation bringing in Community Treatment Orders will soon require people to take their drugs in the community, so if they don't want to recover on their own, we can make them recover.

- Really? You mean we won't have to section people and drag them into hospital?

- No, the government is panicking about the tabloids campaigning against Community Care, and claiming too many mentally ill people are being let out. They are proposing Community Treatment Orders which will give us the same powers we have in hospitals!

- Goodness. So really the whole of society will become one big psychiatric unit!

For the first time, the older man looked at the younger with grudging admiration.

*

Luke had a machine in the advocacy office that was more than a typewriter, but less than a computer. It was bulky and self-important, like a typewriter that had spent time in the gym. It had a little screen where typed words appeared and could then be saved. Later, if you were lucky enough to master the internal directories, you could find them again. It had no internet access but did have a little low-grade printer with two fonts, both ugly. One Thursday evening at about 6.30 Luke was laboriously using it to write up case notes on people he'd seen that day. He often worked late these days, feeling sometimes more at home at the hospital than at his father's house. The last call had been two hours before, so when the phone rang, he jumped. He considered letting the answer machine do its job, but instead picked up the receiver. The voice that spoke was a woman's voice, quiet and uncertain.

- I wasn't expecting anyone to be there.

It was hard to know how to respond to this, as so often.

- I'm not really here. Just writing up some files.
- I see. (There was a pause.) I was going to leave a message on the machine. It's just there's a patient on Somme Women's I think you should see, a Maltese woman.
- Maltese?
- Yes, she's called Francesca. I think she needs to see an advocate. She's rather unhappy. Can you come as soon as possible? Her doctor wants her to have electric shock treatment, and she doesn't want to.

Luke had assumed shock had disappeared years ago, either before or around the time *One Flew Over The Cuckoo's Nest* hit cinema screens in 1975. He thought it had been condemned to the 'oops' category of treatment - things like insulin shock and immersing people in freezing water that seemed like a good idea at the time but on reflection had more to do with the madness of the carers.

- Are you a friend?

There was a silence on the other end of the line.

- No, I'm a nurse.
- Can I have your name please?
- I don't think you really need to have my name.
- It's just a formality for the record.

There was a pause, then the phone went dead.

The next day Luke visited Francesca, a woman in her thirties with long black hair, prone to strikingly explicit street language. She had a melodious Mediterranean accent, with sudden lapses into guttural West Yorkshire. Her depression seemed reasonable to Luke, given her move from the bright island of her birth to Heckmondwike; the subsequent breakdown of her violent marriage; her husband's philandering; her father's death; her problems with the benefits system; the racist graffiti and the taking of her child into care. Her "illness" seemed to manifest in a fertile creative ability to insult her consultant. She suspected that shock treatment was punishment for upsetting him and was terrified at the prospect of it. She paced the floor of the visiting room constantly while she talked to Luke, like a panther at the zoo in a too small cage.

- I do not wish this treatment! I wish to return to my home, taking my child with me. They do not have the right to force me to do this, the arseholes!

Luke had read the guidelines and was inclined to agree with her. They suggested that ECT could only be forcibly given in situations where the patient would die unless something drastic was done - catatonic patients who had refused to eat, drink or talk and were withering away before the eyes of the concerned staff. Luke looked at the healthy individual energetically pacing up and down, a picture of fevered vitality.

- It's that fucking prick face shit head doctor. He doesn't like me.

- I talked to him. I found out that they have to get a second opinion and I told him.

- What did the shit face say?

Actually the doctor had laughed, but Luke couldn't tell Francesca that.

- He said he would take that into account and arrange that.

After he had stopped laughing, thrown a heavy folder of case notes on the desk and shouted something about "rights gone mad" that brought his secretary to the door.

Over the following days Luke's pleas on her behalf to the consultant, nursing staff and the hospital authorities were not successful. He tried to make contact with Julie Graytfell, the social worker involved, but she was presenting a paper at a conference in Ireland. The doctor appointed for the second opinion came and went, agreeing with the first. The following Wednesday, with the May sun making a sudden, brilliant appearance, and the trees all around Needleham exploding with blossom, each hosting a joyous chorus of birds celebrating how they had survived another winter, Francesca had her first "treatment".

Luke had agreed to meet her afterwards and set out to visit the 'Electro-Convulsive Therapy Suite' (or the 'Shock Shack', depending whether you talked to the nurses or the patients) for the first time. He found it in an underground corridor below the clock tower and the administration block. An unmarked door led to a nondescript corridor with more doors and a stone staircase. One high window lit the stairs but hadn't been cleaned for some years and the light it allowed was exhausted by the journey. At the bottom was a realm of strip lighting and walls glossed with the ubiquitous green paint that was Needleham standard, so they reflected bright flashes of blinding light as Luke passed. Cables and wires ran along the corridor, and mysterious doors had no explanatory labels. As Luke walked through a scuffed glass and rubber door, onto the Unit, one of the nurses Luke had met on Francesca's ward greeted him jubilantly.

-     She's much better! It really worked for her!

Luke walked on into the little recovery unit alongside the clinic, and in the overheated room Francesca was smiling at a daytime TV programme about cosmetic surgery.

-     Hi Francesca. Are you ok?

The young woman looked puzzled, then seemed to reach for a word.

-     Okay.

Yesterday she had been agitated, angry, upset. Now she smiled at him placidly. Luke sat next to her in a similar massive armchair. Finding that if he sat back, he sank into an almost reclining position, he pulled himself forward and perched on the front of it.

- You seemed very upset yesterday.

- Okay today.

It seemed the nurse was right. A troubled, unhappy person had magically become a contented one, as simple as that. It was scientific magic, the quick fix which had such a bad press, coming good. Francesca looked at him carefully and a doubtful expression flickered over her face.

- Who are you?

*

Tarpow's room seemed designed to intimidate. The heavy gilt frames round the paintings and the dark portraits within the room set Maria on edge. The sunlight entering the room through the high windows seemed qualified and reduced by the stone casements it had to pass to get there. The lime green carpet glowed in such an unreal way it brought back for Maria unpleasant memories of an experience with magic mushrooms. Tarpow made her wait while he read her report of issues raised at the Patient's Council, which she had sent him a fortnight before.

- Still getting these reports of gas in the water taps I see? I have had words with staff about this.

This had been an issue ever since the drilling operation had started in the hospital grounds. Patients had produced plumes of flame by putting a match next to the taps on certain wards. Tarpow had indeed had words with his staff about it. He had encouraged them to give more medication to the patients who complained.

- It's still a problem. I've seen it myself. It's all the wards that are close to the drilling operation.

- O, I'm sure it's nothing to do with the drilling. This kind of effect has been associated with mining regions for centuries. It's the methane, you see, it seeps up. Nothing you can do really.

- Well, you could stop them from drilling. One of the patients was quite badly burned.

- Ah, they will play with it you see, that's the trouble.

They both knew that the incident in question was a nurse's prank that had gone wrong. Tarpow changed the subject.

- How are the consultations about the Strategic Plan going?

- No-one can understand it. We'll need a patient friendly version if you really want people to be involved, but that will take time to produce, and some of the things seem to be already going ahead anyway.

- You were going to tell me what people thought about the new publicity for the Gallipoli Centre.

She looked down at the glossy leaflet in her hands.

- It's not so much the words people are unhappy about. It's the images.

Sitting across the broad expanse of his desk from her, Tarpow considered this.

- Really? I think they look very attractive. They seem perfectly acceptable to me. What's the problem?

Maria opened out the double folded paper and looked again at one of the photographs inside. It showed a smiling group of well-dressed people, sitting around a circular, pine table. An air of peaceful bonhomie radiated out from them. Their clothes were neat and sober. They were the epitome of well-adjusted citizens.

- What happened to the photographs of people who actually go to the Gallipoli Centre? You got everyone to sign a form that they could be photographed, then a whole morning getting a photographer down there, then you didn't use the photos.
- They didn't come out well. They didn't really seem to give the impression we were hoping to create for the new Gallipoli Centre for Therapeutic Interventions.
- So who are these people?
- They work in the offices at the South Yorkshire Trust. We thought they seemed more …welcoming somehow.
- They're Trust workers?

Tarpow shrugged and smiled in an annoying way. Maria continued.

- And the opening hours have been cut down. It used to be open six days a week, nine o'clock in the morning til five at night. Now it's reopened in the community it only opens on Tuesday afternoons and Friday mornings – that's only four hours a week!
- The rest of the time people are encouraged to engage with the local community.

There was a pause. Tarpow seemed to consider that his last remark closed this particular topic. Maria knew that boxes of the leaflets had already been printed and delivered so there was no point in fighting this particular battle. Tarpow refused to be ruffled. He had a new growth of moustache, which for some reason irritated her even more. When he spoke, his voice was measured, deep, calm, infuriating,

- Since our meeting in February I've given thought to your ideas about patient representation. I trust you've seen my paper about the new Foundation Advisory Group we've set up to oversee the consultation process? The Advisory Group as I see it is a fundamental cornerstone of the new Foundation Trust. It's a way of making sure key stakeholders are involved in the running of the Trust, and the proposed changes. I thought you would approve!

He said this last comment because Maria was frowning at him, and he spoke in a theatrical, hurt tone that invited a smile of complicity, but Maria either didn't notice this, or chose to ignore it, so he continued.

- We have members of the public, carers, and, especially, those people closest to your heart, the service users themselves! They will be invited to the Advisory Group, to inform our policies!

- But not to the Executive meeting, where decisions are actually made?

- It would be too unwieldy to invite people to the Executive meeting. And they probably wouldn't understand the intricacies of what gets talked about there. It would be very stressful for them.

Tarpow didn't mention his masterstroke – Maria would find out in due time. The Advisory Group and the Executive Group would meet at exactly the same time, so the Advisory Group would always be reacting to decisions that were three months out of date, when issues had been resolved and no-one could remember anything about them anyway.

- Why does it have to meet in such a remote part of the hospital? Last time it took some people all evening trying to find the place! Apparently someone had moved the signs around.

Tarpow laughed indulgently.

- Some of these patients, the things they get up to.

The nurses too if they're tipped the wink.

- One bloke was missing for fifteen hours and his wife reported it to the police. They found him sedated in the seclusion room on Passchendaele Ward.

- Well he had been very distraught!

- Because he couldn't find the meeting!

- Exactly. I think staff were justified in thinking he was a patient from one of the other acute wards.

- People are really worried that you're intending to close down a large part of the hospital.

- The service will be reprovided!

- Reprovided how, and where? There's nothing about that in the plan. What are the plans for reprovision?

- There will be community services. Workers will help people to....integrate into the community. I thought you were in favour of a person-centred service? Well, that's what we're trying to provide.

Tarpow glared across the desk at Maria. She was supposed to be a poacher turned gamekeeper, but she still had a salmon or two in her bag. It was time to deliver his main agenda item for this meeting, and he felt a thrill of anticipation.

- As you know the Strategic Plan will be launched at the Summer Fayre. Of course, we'll want the service users to be involved in this.

- Well, they will be involved in the play that members of the Happy Days Writing Group are putting on.

- Ah, I wanted to talk to you about that.

Tarpow's tone was regret itself, the Platonic form of it, from which all earthly manifestations were as pale copies.

-   Unfortunately we've decided there won't be time for the play now that we're including the launch of the plan.

Even Maria, used as she was to unexpected shifts of hospital policy, to sudden appearances of hitherto unseen policies, or the equally sudden disappearances of long-established ones, who ought to have been prepared for anything, was taken aback.

-   But people have been practising!
-   I'm sorry, there simply won't be time.

Tarpow had got wind of the irreverent tone of James's script from one of the nurses at Happy Days, and no way was the centenary celebration going to be used as a platform for that kind of nonsense.

-   People are going to be very disappointed.
-   Alas, it wasn't what I wanted. I'm afraid I was outvoted.

Tarpow smiled such an openly dishonest smile that Maria knew it had been his decision. She felt stunned, and surprised that the Hospital Manager still had the capacity to stun her after all this time. When he had shown her out of the room he went to the window reflecting on how well the meeting had gone. He would have liked to go out onto the stone balcony as he imagined General Cardew had done before him, the night before the first Superintendent had set off for France in 1916, when apparently he had addressed the mass of staff and patients congregated on the lawn outside this very room. ("Thank you, thank you! No really that's quite enough applause. Please, please, enough!") But the stone was no longer deemed safe, so Tarpow contented himself with staring out at the woods and humming softly to himself.

*

The pavements were littered with small leaves and dying blossom. The rain had pummelled them from limes that lined the streets in this part of town. Luke and James were walking through the wooded valley that led down to the lake in the municipal park. Since discovering that his mother had been a patient at Needleham, Luke's relationship to the Hospital was changed. He had already felt an empathy with the patients, but now it was personal. He tried to talk to Susan about it, but she was so outraged on Luke's behalf that his father had kept the truth from him, and seen it so clearly as an issue about patriarchy, that he felt there was no room for his own mixed emotions. He had told the other members of the Off-Beats group. His meeting with James was ostensibly to discuss this group, but as so often, James had theories to expound, particularly about the implications for Luke of his discovery.

-   The one thing you mustn't do is to think that this means that you yourself might be mad. Whatever your mother's diagnosis was, it doesn't mean anything about you. Genetic theories of madness are just bunkum.

-   Surely there must be some connection?

-   Well what about road kill?

Luke just stared back at him, feeling the beginnings of a headache coming on. James continued.

-   Road kill has nothing to do with genetics! When a rabbit gets run over, does it make sense to look for and blame a genetic predisposition to risk-taking behaviour? To getting run over? To a suicidal gene? Or is the real reason centuries of industrialisation, man's contemptuous disregard for his fellow creatures, the lethal nature of the motorcar, et cetera?

He paused to take in Luke briefly and took the look of distant abstraction as encouragement to carry on.

-   Remember when they found that people dying of lung cancer just happened to be smokers? Did people look for evidence that they all had a genetic predisposition to die of lung cancer, and the fact that they smoked was completely irrelevant? No, but somehow we don't think there is cause enough in the injustice and brutality of our current societies to cause people to be mad. We have to go looking for genetic connections.

They were walking through an old wood with oak and silver birch trees, and a new growth of wild garlic and delicate white wood anemones beside the path that would eventually lead to a coffee bar by the lake. Luke was struggling for comprehension.

- But maybe people have a disposition to be, for instance, addicted? And if it's not all genetic, surely at least part of it is? It does seem to run in families.

- For the sake of argument, let's accept there is a mad gene. Just think for a moment, that gene has survived for thousands, perhaps millions of years. Doesn't that seem to suggest there is some survival value in it? Otherwise wouldn't the so-called healthy creatures have slowly become the vast majority, and gradually the genetically defective have died out?

- So you think there may have been mad amoebas, crazy primeval tadpoles, loony amphibious creatures, dinosaurs and apes?

- Indeed. The mighty gamut of creation, with madness a necessary part of that wondrous spectrum. Unless lunacy has some survival value then those with a mad gene would be slightly less likely to survive than those with purely 'normal' genes, whatever that might mean. But is that the case? Apparently not! Clearly there is more and more madness with each passing decade. Madness is positively blossoming. It used to run in our society, but now it positively gallops!

- Did you make that up?

- Cary Grant in 'Arsenic and Old Lace'. Let us for a moment meditate upon the intriguing idea that there is indeed a survival value in madness! Imagine one of our dear ancestors faced with a world that was nasty, brutish, and shit. There he is, trapped by a wild animal, with no way to flee it, no way he can fight it. If he tries either of those 'normal' reactions he's buggered. So at this moment of impending termination what happens? He loses it big time and throws a wobbly. The adrenaline's pumping and his primitive brain is all over the place reframing reality to account for this unpalatable, unthinkable fact – that he is about to die! He's in overdrive, and produces a strange new version of reality, a new dimension where all kinds of lateral thoughts are suddenly available to him, with the wild energy to carry them out.

- The caveman has a breakdown?

- If one can use that euphemism of the over civilised mid-twentieth century to refer to the experience of a wild man of primeval times, yes. He goes bonkers. He loses his marbles. A kangaroo goes amok in his top paddock.

- And he escapes?

- No, he gets eaten – that time. But here is the beauty of it! Statistically over hundreds of years, every so often the mad caveman does survive. He does something so outlandish and strange that the bemused sabre tooth is totally thrown and our man escapes. It may only happen one time in fifty, but over the centuries it is significant! Mr. Normal, who has only the two doomed options of fighting or fleeing, is eaten every time. So the mad gene gets passed on enough times to survive.

They had reached a place where the trees parted to give a view of the ruffled surface of the little municipal lake.

- So now you're basically saying that I do have a mad gene, but that's it's a good thing? You've changed your argument!

James shrugged.

- My soul is expansive, why should I not contradict myself, as Walt Whitman once said when put on the spot.

By the shore below them, willows were being pulled about in the Spring breeze, and several ducks had abandoned the water for the shelter of the bushes. James seemed hardly to notice, as he continued to develop his theory.

- I don't think there's a gene at all. I'm just arguing the point. The position is even more interesting if you are a creationist, and don't give a monkey's for evolution. Because then God in His (or Her) infinite wisdom must have created madness and known about it all along!

Luke had a feeling that things were spiralling out of control. It's true that he was searching for some explanation but talking to James made him feel he was trudging across some frozen tundra with a storm rising and nowhere to camp for the night. Now his overexcited friend was pointing at the sky where turbulent clouds were massing.

- The Chinese apparently have a way of describing a storm. They say: "the sky is ill". But it's a metaphor! It doesn't mean we start firing drugs into the clouds! We've been trapped by an image! Trying to find a medical cure for 'mental illness' is like to trying to find the genetic cause for unemployment or homelessness.

They reached the tea bar at the lake just as the big drops of rain swirled down out of the mad sky. It was a little wooden shed with eight Formica topped tables set in two rows in front of a counter, behind which a bored young man reluctantly put down his copy of the Star as they entered. The place felt very intimate after the open air, and Luke tried to judge which of the tables would be furthest from the counter, but actually there was nowhere in the room where, in the absence of background noise, you couldn't hear everything that was spoken in any other part of the room. They chose to sit with their teas against the window where they could look out across the choppy lake, to the woods and hills beyond the far bank. Luke was troubled by the conversation. He was struggling, a man out of his depth, too polite to wave.

- What about people who are really....you know, out of it. It's okay for people like you. You're educated, and you've thought your way out of it, but some people really suffer, you know, really bad voices, telling you to kill yourself. Horrible self-loathing thoughts and delusions and hallucinations. What about them?

- I would never want to be a smart arse about other people's suffering. But I think you just have to treat every person as unique, with kindness, and thoughtfulness and really try to love them. Don't label them, treat them as individuals, as whole beings. Get to know them deeply and then you'll be able to see what troubles them. You'll begin to love them. I think there'll always be a place for soul healers, and wisdom. But these technicians scare me.

James looked out over the lake where the wind was rearranging a dozen grey shades. The bored young man was wiping down the shining machinery and glancing over at them curiously.

- You don't think there'll always be a Needleham, then?

- Please God I hope not! No, the days of Needleham are over, but what comes next is not clear. Needleham is going to sink into a hole in the ground sooner rather than later.

- A hole?

- The whole hospital is apparently built over disused mine shafts. Haven't you noticed the cracks?

135

- Yes, come to think of it there are big cracks down the wall in the reception hall.

- In the days when mining was big round here they didn't care too much which direction they were going in, or what they were tunnelling under. We can only hope.

James brought his hands together in mock prayer, and looked up toward the polystyrene tiles of the ceiling. Luke smiled politely, but took advantage of a rare gap in James' output to say what was really on his mind.

- My mother was on the Tannenberg Unit. Apparently, it closed down about three years ago. I'm going there with Anthea tomorrow.

- I've heard of it, but I thought it had been knocked down.

- Anthea says it's still there, one of those overgrown buildings on the perimeter.

- Do you really want to go?

- I don't know. I'll find out when I get there.

A sudden gust of wind boomed around the little cafe, and they stared out at the lake and fell into their own silent meditations.

*

Anthea loved the way nature had started to reassert itself over the outlying abandoned parts of the hospital. The weather had settled and produced a bright Spring day. Now they were outside the old Tannenberg Unit, where in the 1970s experimental psychosurgery had taken place until a series of "poor operational results" ("deaths", in common parlance) had forced its closure.

A rambling rose had taken over an entire wall of the old building. Other bushes had grown up, elder and hawthorn, and a solid patch of rosebay, on the point of flowering, had pushed its five-foot high stalks up where the ground had been broken by the bed of an old flower garden. Anthea paused to take all this in, and to give Luke the chance to catch up to her.

- You can still change your mind you know.

The building stood in the sunlight with its original white rendering turned off colour by the years. Anthea could see that the plaster was cracked and broken, weathered to a kind of pale yellow. The door of the old ward swung open, jammed into its new place by a growth of flowering grasses and dandelions. Above it a discoloured sign, screwed into the brickwork, still clearly said 'Tannenberg Unit'. The windows were divided into small oblongs that were opaque with dust and webs. A chimney pot lay on its side in the long grass.

- Do you want to go inside?

- I don't know.

She waited for him to make his mind up, knowing that he would go in, having come this far. He nodded and they moved towards the shadow of the doorway. Flies buzzed around where the bright light crossed into darkness, and the two people hesitated as their eyes became accustomed to the gloom. Inside the air was cool and they walked down a corridor where light green paint peeled from the walls, as if melted in some previous great heat. A line of doors opened out onto square rooms with barred windows. Anthea felt chilled by the sudden change in temperature. She turned to Luke, who was staring intently into one of the rooms, which was completely empty, but for a mouldy brown cord carpet on which old leaves had died.

- Do you think these were cells?

- Like seclusion cells? No, they're too big, I think. These were probably offices. Look, there's the mark where a desk was against the wall, and a filing cabinet there.

- Offices with bars on the windows?

- Standard. Maybe there was petty cash or drugs?

137

They walked into a larger room, where green light filtered in from both sides. He walked over to examine the iron grilles that were flaking and rusting behind the dirty glass.

- This would be the dining room.

Anthea walked to the middle of the room and threw her arms out as she turned slowly, as though she were a dancer in slow motion, reminding him of the Countess when they visited the ballroom. The ceiling sagged with water damage, and here and there they could see slats and beams exposed where the plaster had come away completely. Bare wires hung down from several circular fittings. Anthea seemed restless, and he followed her through a doorway at the far end of the room and down a further corridor. There was less light here, and a row of heavy doors slightly ajar. Each door had a thick glass panel, and when they peered round they looked into a tiny cell. Only a small high barred window let any light into this space at all. Luke whistled and spoke in a quiet voice.

- Makes the advocacy office look like a palace.

- These are the cells. Imagine!

- I'd prefer not to.

Six doors on either side of the corridor stretched away from them, each one clean but for the decaying debris of leaves. Beyond this corridor were more rooms. They did not spend long in this part of the old ward. The lack of light made them hurry back into the old dining room. Anthea took from her bag seven pink roses and laid them on the floor.

- What are you doing?

She looked patiently at Luke.

- I'm just going to do a little healing ceremony.

She took out a glass jar and half-filled it from a bottle of water she had brought. She placed the flowers in the jar and stared down at them as she squatted on the dusty floor. He watched from the side of the room as she took several little willow sticks from her bag and placed them in a circle around the jar of roses. Then she closed her eyes, and for a long time the room was very quiet. He felt uncomfortable with the silence. He tried to imagine how it would have been when there were people here, but he could not visualise how these patients, doctors, nurses might have behaved towards each other. It was like trying to imagine people from ancient history. His mother had been one of them. He was startled from his reverie by Anthea, who began to intone in a strange, quiet voice.

- Mighty spirit which moveth through all things, giver and taker, hear this blessing for all those who passed through these walls, those still living and those who have now passed on, let their souls be in peace, and let the healing power of the universe move through this space and cleanse it of all harm and bad feeling

He had a sudden, almost uncontrollable urge to laugh hysterically. This was so embarrassing. Anthea had said they should mark the occasion of the visit in some way, and he should have realised that she didn't mean simply the reading of a few thoughtful lines from some deluded romantic poet, but this crazy hippy shit. Her voice went on, incanting a strange improvised chant about the Great Goddess, and the Wholeness and the Oneness until his urge to laugh changed into a deep irritation, and he was going to have to say something, to shout something, because this was his day, his visit, and she had no right to take it over like this and put her weird stamp on it. This was his mother for god's sake! Words formed in a congealed mass in his chest and throat and face but when he opened his mouth to say

not words,

carefully chosen in neat lines, logical, dependable…

not calm, rational sentences,

proceeding in an orderly fashion...

not considered thought,

   restoring order, reducing chaos to symmetry...

instead   a break   in the wall of an old dyke,
a swollen canal   pouring through   in   a   torrent   of
sluicing green turbulent water
a trap door   into an ocean whose waves towered not
over but through him dissolution   as if something had
burst   melted or exploded
an artery fatally loaded with the semtex of fat giving out at last
a moment of panic then no option
but a cat
firmly and finally
out of a bag
among the pigeons

and big fat sobs squeezed themselves out of his chest, into his throat and out through his mouth.

He fought against it, clenching all the muscles in his upper body to hold himself in, but couldn't stop it, or the waves uprooted from somewhere at his centre. Tears escaped through the palms of hands that he'd put over his face. They poured past his nose, circumventing his mouth and dropped off his chin, eager to follow gravity and the natural law at last. Thick congealed memories of disappointment and grief, released, rushed into and clogged his nasal passages and stopped him breathing. He cried in a way he hadn't since he was ten years old. The overflowing canal broke all its banks and ran into new spaces, exploring, breaking fences, washing everything along in its path. Everything went, the whole neighbourhood, the town, the county. Whoever could climb up to them sat on their roofs and waited for rescue, while the brown flood took everything it could carry. When it eventually subsided it left him exhausted, trembling

   strangely peaceful...

Anthea had gone quiet momentarily when she understood what was happening. Now he became aware of her. She had come over to kneel next to him with her eyes closed. She now opened them, and stared at him intently, then took his hand and led him out into the sunlight.

SIX: June

Professor Drogham came to Needleham in 1980 as the youngest Professor at any NHS Professorial Unit in the country. He brought a reputation for research into the causes of schizophrenia, which he was convinced was a bio-chemical disorder science would soon validate. His main line of enquiry was a recent discovery that the urine of schizophrenics contains more DMPEA, a substance related to tannine, than 'normal' urine. He was certain that this showed either that DMPEA was itself the cause of schizophrenia, or that there was some other factor, as yet undiscovered, that caused both the excess of DMPEA and schizophrenia.

He experimented throughout the 1980s, but the link proved elusive. Then during tests it was noticed that the Sister on the professorial ward at Needleham, part of the control group, had herself extremely high levels of DMPEA. After investigation, the only thing that came to light was that the Sister drank large quantities of Yorkshire tea, which was known to be stronger than in any other part of England. The same was true of all the schizophrenics who had taken part in the research. Drinking tea was their main occupation, more popular than even masturbation. They drank at least a gallon of tea every day, and this was the cause of the preponderance of DMPEA in their blood samples.

Drogham was apparently shattered by this, believing as he did that he was on the verge of a breakthrough that would place him alongside Kraepaelin and Bleuler as a pioneer in the study of schizophrenia. His reputation never recovered, and he gave up research work shortly afterwards, although he has continued in his role as Professor at Needleham Hospital ever since.

*

Susan would no longer stay in the dark old house by the river.

- It's creepy, all those books. Just get someone to come and take them away!

- I just have to sort my father's papers then I'll clear the house.

- I don't know why you don't just bin everything. You've been very weird since you found out about your mum. I don't know why you had to go visit that place where she was a patient. It's macabre.

They were speaking late at night on the phone. They tended more and more to see each other only at weekends, at Susan's flat in Leeds. She was right, he knew. The house did feel dark and empty, cluttered with the possessions of a man who would never use them again, who had been a stranger to him in life, and was a greater one now he was dead. Still he was compelled to stay here, as if the house possessed some secret only he could unravel.

- And getting so involved with these mental patients. It's really starting to affect you. You're getting very paranoid, you know that?

He hadn't gone into details about what had happened when he and Anthea had visited the Tannenberg Unit. Since that time, for the last few weeks, he had felt a strange disorientation. Was it paranoia? Something indefinable had shifted. He thought of the letter he'd received that morning, which he also hadn't mentioned to Susan. She wasn't sympathetic to his thoughts about Needleham, and he knew he could not talk about it to her. He told her less and less about his day to day work. The things that Anthea and James said which sounded so amusing or interesting to him during the day became sinister or foolish when he tried to tell Susan about them. She referred to his friends as 'clients' and did not understand why he had to be involved in the Off-Beats group. Actually she didn't want to talk about Luke's work at all, but about the upcoming wedding of her brother

- Which I hope you're not going to chicken out of?
- I won't know any of those people.
- It's a chance to get to know them, you annoying man.
- I'll think about it.

She wasn't pleased. When he put the phone down he looked out of the bay window of his father's old sitting room. Outside it was an overcast but warm evening. He picked up the letter that had slipped so innocently onto the mat by the front door that morning and read again the neat hand-written note.

> Honeysuckle Cottage
> 17 Dalesedge Way,
> Needleham
>
> Dear Mr. Walker,
> I was interested to find out through Maria Paraskeva about your role as an advocate at Needleham Hospital and learn of your interest into historical practices there. Until four years ago I worked as a staff nurse at the hospital and I would be interested to meet you. Some of the things I witnessed in the hospital have continued to trouble me and I would appreciate the chance to talk to you about them. Please contact me at the above address.
> Yours sincerely
> Margaret O'Render.

A few moments later he let himself out of his flat and walked through the terraces, and into the woods nearby, down to the lake's edge, where he'd walked with James some weeks before. The wind was ruffling the surface of the lake, and he stayed there a long time. He wondered again about Anthea's idea of a spirit guide, but no animal came out of the gathering darkness, powerful and familiar, and when the night and the rain began to dispute about which was the more serious about falling, he made his way home. The streets of Needleham seemed quiet and sad, everybody at home watching the same programmes behind closed curtains.

That night he dreamed he was in the sitting room of his father's house, but instead of two doors into the kitchen and the hallway, there were three. The new, third door was set into the long back wall, and above it was a sign he'd seen in the administration corridor at Needleham Hospital.

'Patients Not Allowed Beyond This Point'

It was a big, sturdy door, not unlike the front door to the hospital itself, though instead of carvings, it had smooth lacquered panels, below which the swirl and grain of the wood seemed bright with internal light. He turned the big brass knob and the door at first resisted his touch. When he tried again it was as if it had made a decision to allow him to enter, and it swung open.

He was in a toyshop.

He walked from room to room searching for something, and eventually came to a storage room, which had shelf after shelf of soft toys. There between a teddy bear and a rabbit there was an old pink cat, a replica of an animated cat from children's television. The striped cloth of the cat seemed to glow. Luke approached it. It was clearly second hand, unlike everything else in the room. It had worn patches on its back, and some of the stitching that made up its nose was missing. Nevertheless, the beaded eyes had the curious intensity of enlarged pupils. When Luke was standing over it, he heard a voice that seemed to come from inside his own head.

Hi Luke, you took your time. I've been expecting you.

Luke wanted to reach out and touch the cat, but he dared not. There was a long silence in which cat and human regarded each other.

- I know it's a disappointment. People tend to want eagles and stuff, but the thing you've got to understand is that bears and birds were natural for Native Americans because they lived with them. To folk who live in an advanced industrial society, the Guide will take different forms.

Luke considered this.

- It's not that I'm disappointed. It's just that, well I was expecting, you know, a real animal.
- O, reality! That old chestnut!

Bagpuss scoffed.

- You have to take help anywhere you can get it.
- The other thing was, I didn't expect such a well-known public figure.
- Celebrity! It's just another trap. I was used, like we all were in those shows back then. Look at any of those big names, most of them crashed. Dougal, Muffin, The Teletubbies – they all got big addiction problems.
- What happened to you?
- I went that way for a while. Then I met a guy who pulled me out of it. Postman Pat. All that walking and meditating on his rounds, he figured something out. He helped me anyway.
- And now you're going to help me?
- I'll do what I can.
- I really didn't expect you to have an American accent.
- Sign of the times.

Luke woke up sweating. It was four o' clock in the morning. The room was already bathed in daylight.

*

Anthea did not want to meet Luke in the old converted chapel on Needleham's main street. 'I hate Starbuck's', she said to him, 'it's disrespectful the way they have the prices for their cappuccinos and lattes hanging where the hymn numbers used to be.' So instead on a bright morning they walked through the door of what looked like a cake shop.

The Chi Café had a special significance for patients from the hospital. It was run by two 60s hippies and had an air of laissez faire. Local artists displayed their work on its walls. None of the furniture, cutlery or crockery matched. James maintained that the café had magical properties and took on the character at any particular moment of the people who were drinking tea and eating buns there, absorbing and amplifying their energy and feeding it back through complex psychic loops. At the moment the only other customers were an intense well-dressed older couple, and the café seemed rather like the set of Brief Encounter, so perhaps James was right, Luke reflected.

He walked with Anthea past a glass counter where a young woman in a white hat was taking a burnished tofu pasty from a bright display case. In the back was a small white room with half a dozen wooden tables, four chairs to each one, all different. They were the only people there, and Anthea chose a table towards the back of the room. There were bad sketches of famous people in frames on the walls, for sale. Ostensibly Luke was meeting Anthea to discuss her upcoming appointment with her consultant, but as soon as Luke joined her she pulled a well-thumbed book from her purple shoulder bag.

- The I Ching! Remember I said I would do you a reading!

She had lost the uncertainty of a recent mental patient and was energetic and animated. She had taken off her red beret, and her long hair fell forward, so that the glittering chameleon brooch on the lapel of her corduroy jacket came in and out of vision as she moved. She began to throw ten pence pieces on the varnished table top, where they bounced with a sound like hailstones on glass. A flowery scent, honeysuckle or geranium, washed around Luke. One of the girls who had been working in the front came and took an order for teas while Anthea barely checked her coin throwing. For her part the girl seemed to take it all in her stride. Anthea scribbled circles and dashes in a little hard backed notebook with doe-eyed spaniels in the corner of each page. Then she leafed through the pages of the Book of Oracles. Its spine was shattered, and many pages were loose. It looked like a favourite teddy after several generations of careless love or abuse. At last Anthea found what she was looking for.

- Chung Fu! Understanding! That's a really good one! Chung Fu means a time of confidence and sincerity. 'The wind ruffling the surface of the waters of a lake'. It says 'pigs and fishes'. Does that mean anything to you?

Luke considered, and said that it did not. The older couple had moved closer and were holding hands under the table, he noticed.

- Well, sometimes you only understand these things afterwards. 'The superior man carefully avoids litigation'.

- Litigation!

- That's what it says.

- Show me!

- There, look. And this is interesting! 'A crane is calling amongst the water grass. Her brood responds. I have delicious viands. I will share them with you'.

She looked at him hopefully. He frowned, trying to recall. The last time he'd seen a crane was some ten years before on a trip to Flamingo Park. He was currently trying to go vegetarian again.

- I can't say it rings a bell. Do you think we should talk about this appointment?

She hunched her shoulders up and shivered ostentatiously.

- Tell me about your dreams.

- I don't really dream much.

- Everybody dreams.

- I don't remember them...

He stopped, remembering Bagpuss.

- Actually, I did have a dream. About a door.

- A door? What kind of door?

Her eyes took on a wide-pupiled look that made him uneasy. He felt a little uncomfortable altogether with Anthea these days. The need for him to be her advocate had subsided once she had left the hospital, but still they seemed to find excuses to meet. They seemed bound by a mutual belief that the other could be rescued.

- In the dream I was living in a big house, that was and wasn't my father's house. My father had said that the one thing I must never do was to open this particular door.

She had put her hand to the side of her head and seemed to be trembling with excitement. He paused.

- What kind of door, though?

- Well, an old oak type door. I just remember these old wood panels. Come to think of it, it was a bit like the door to the hospital.

- GWALES!

This exclamation coincided with the young waitress bringing in a tray of white cups and saucers. The girl did not seem to think anything strange in Anthea's cry, and calmly put teapots, spoons, and little metal tubs with white sugar and milk onto the table. Luke looked at Anthea questioningly. She was looking into the air above his left shoulder.

- It's an ancient story. A group of warriors was travelling back from a disastrous adventure in Ireland. Meanwhile the queen,

149

the cause of all the trouble, was so distraught at what she'd done that she killed herself.

- She killed herself? How?

- It doesn't tell you how. It doesn't really matter.

- I was just interested.

- Anyway, only seven warriors survived to return. They had the head of the king with them, and when they were talking to him....

- He could still talk?

- It's a magical story. Anyway they found that while they had been away their own kingdom had been taken over by invaders. At this worst moment, when everything had gone wrong, they came to a hall at a place called Gwales, overlooking the sea. Inside there were two doors open, and a third one that they must never open. As long as they didn't open that door, they forgot all the bad things that happened. They lived there for eighty good years, quite content with their lot, but one of the knights forgot the rule, and opened the door.

At this point Anthea paused theatrically. Luke grew uncomfortable.

- What did he see?

- He saw a beautiful expanse of ocean.

- That doesn't sound too bad.

- The problem was that the terrible memories of all their woes came rushing in on them. They remembered the awful battle, and the death of their queen, and the fact that their kingdom was now in occupied hands, and every friend and relative they'd lost. They were overcome by terrible anguish. It's you!

150

When you cried in the Tannenberg Unit. You opened the door! Now you'll remember everything.

She poured the tea.

- Then they had to bury the king's head.

- Why did they have to bury the king's head?

- I don't know. It started to go off.

Luke felt the need to re-establish some context to this conversation.

- I have to go soon. I'm supporting Liron to appeal against his section this afternoon. Should we talk about this appointment you have with Ellis?

She waved her hand in the air.

- Don't worry about that. I've brought you a necklace with a rune I think you should wear when you go to work. It will be a protection for you. What was that?

She brought out a leather thong, then stopped at an unfamiliar sound that came in loud and clear through the open window.

- I don't know.

They listened again, but there was no repeat of the unmistakeable sound of the steam whistle of an old locomotive, a sound unusual in these parts, since there was no railway line for twenty miles. The older couple had gone.

*

It was Luke's first Manager's Hearing, and he felt more nervous than Liron. Actually it was the first Manager's Hearing Needleham Hospital had ever seen. After his visit to the Tannenberg Unit Luke had thrown himself into his job with renewed vigour. He had discovered that patients detained under the Mental Health Act were allowed to appeal to the Hospital Managers, a fact that seemed to surprise the managers when Luke told them about it, and that he wanted to arrange a hearing for Liron. They stalled and prevaricated until their solicitor told them the advocate had his facts correct.

Now Luke and Liron had been sitting in the dark corridor for over three quarters of an hour, waiting for the solid door to open. The panel of Hospital Managers was meant to represent an independent view, but they had been locked in with the doctor and nursing staff for half an hour now and seemed to be getting on very well. Luke felt disturbed by the sounds of laughter that occasionally could be heard. It didn't sound like they were exactly strangers in there, and it also didn't sound as if they were reading the reports. He himself, as Liron's advocate, had received these reports only fifteen minutes beforehand, and had read them as carefully as he could. The nurse's report seemed to be wildly incorrect and to contradict itself at several points; the social worker's was vague and gave the impression that the worker had difficulties remembering who the client was, and the doctor's was written in complex jargon with unusual and idiosyncratic grammar and spelling.

Now, as the scheduled time for the Hearing came and went, and still the door remained closed, Luke could not concentrate any longer on the texts. He reflected that the corridor would be less forbidding without the big cardboard boxes that lined the whole of the opposite wall, blocking any possible light from the windows on that side of the corridor. He peeped inside one. It was full of copies of the National Service Framework. Liron was happily tapping his feet and humming to himself, confident of success, apparently. Luckily the corridor had a side door from which he could smoke every five minutes or so, or perhaps he wouldn't have been so calm, Luke reflected. Liron's indiscretion at the funeral was now far enough away to be reframed as an extreme reaction to grief. Luke had already briefed him on what to say and, more importantly, what not to say, to achieve their aim, which was discharge, and freedom from detention. There was nothing left but conversation.

- So you used to be a singer, Liron? What was it like, singing in the clubs?

Liron smiled back at him, and instead of speaking, sang very softly

- Thank you for the music, the song you're singing!

It was true he had a cultured voice, melodic and controlled. It filled the little corridor like the scent of a flower in a fetid underground chamber.

- Thank you for the daa daa, the joy you're bringing! Thank you for the music, for giving it to me!

- That's fantastic! I could be listening to Frank Sinatra, with a West Yorkshire accent.

- Ah, Frankie!

Liron's brown eyes went distant, and a rueful smile came over his lined face.

- I could tell you a story or two about Frankie! He sang at the Mecca in Leeds, just turned up one night, says 'Liron, can I have a go?' and I says 'Course, Frankie, go for it, boy', and you know he never looked back? Took the bit right between his teeth, he did. He was nobody until then.

At that moment the door opened and Nurse Manager Moking's head appeared in the gap. She looked at them both carefully before saying.

- You can come in now.

Meeting Room One was a big square headmaster's study with heavily framed prints on each wall showing the construction of Needleham Hospital, and a lush green carpet like a well-kept lawn. A solid wooden table dominated the rest of the heavy furniture, behind which two men and a woman Luke had never seen before were looking gravely at him. Moking had resumed her seat opposite them, in a little row of chairs with Nurse O'Price, and Liron's consultant, Mr. Ellis. There were two high backed chairs reserved for Luke and Liron.

- Please come in and join us!

The grey haired, bespectacled man behind the table said affably.

- I'm Trevor Blenkinsop, the Chair of the Hospital Board of Trustees, and these are my colleagues on the Board, Elizabeth Fielding.....

He motioned to the pink suited woman at his side, whose grey curls were immaculately cut and looked solid as marble.

- Who brings the wealth of her experience as a retired social worker.

Elizabeth stared coldly at Luke as his clothes shrivelled around him, the sprouting hairs on his unshaven chin elongated, and his hair became greasy and unmanageable.

- And this is Mr. Downing, the lay member of our panel.

The plump man on the other side of Blenkinsop smiled at Luke and Liron, though his eyes did not. He looked uncomfortable, unlike the other two, and like a car salesman more used to the cross questioning of the sales forecourt.

Blenkinsop introduced the other people sitting in the room.

- I'm afraid that Miss Graytfell, the social worker in this case, is unable to attend today. Julie is apparently attending a Training Day. But we have her report here.

He waved a sheet of A4 paper.

- Shall we begin? Let's consider the nurse's report. Nurse O'Price?

O'Price pompously cleared his throat and reiterated the main points of his report, in a strangled, formal voice. When he had finished Blenkinsop looked kindly at Liron.

- And is there anything you would like to add?
- Liron looked hopefully at Luke, and Luke spoke, as they had planned.
- We did want to query some things. For instance, the paragraph on page 2 where the claim is made that 'the patient reported that he thought he had insects in his stomach'.

There was a shuffling of papers as six pairs of hands found the relevant section. After a few seconds Blenkinsop said carefully.

- Well, it seems very clear to me. It must have been a very frightening experience, and obviously a sign of great disturbance.
- The incident in question happened just before the ward round. My client, Liron....

Liron beamed at him, and then around the room in acknowledgement.

- Was asked whether or not he felt nervous. He replied 'yes, I've got butterflies in my stomach'.

O'Price butted in.

- Are you saying that a butterfly is not an insect then? I'm no expert in ornithology, but I think I can safely say it is!

He glared at Luke.

- And I think you will find, Nurse O'Price, although I am no expert in hagiography…

He paused. They seemed to be looking back at him in alarm. He definitely had them worried. Himself too. There was certainly a word that meant 'the study of language', but he felt sure it wasn't that particular word.

155

- .... that we are in fact looking here at a metaphor, an image to describe a physical experience, not to be taken literally!

The look of alarm gave way to blankness, apart from Ellis, who was smiling. Luke pressed home his attack.

- Similarly, here on page 4 of the Doctor's report...

The sound of pages being turned, and now it was Ellis' turn to look alarmed.

- This reference to 'brain-worms', which is interpreted as 'the delusion that creatures were inside Mr. Schulman's head'.

Ellis felt the need to clarify and leaned forward.

- Yes, interesting! Mr. Schulman talked at great length about the brain-worms. Even though he didn't seem particularly troubled, it did seem an unusual, and potentially frightening, phenomenon.

He smiled ingratiatingly at Blenkinsop, who nodded back at him. Luke produced a photocopied article from his case, with the stamp of 'Leeds Reference Library' at a jaunty angle across its top.

- Can I direct your attention to this, a recent article from the *Journal of Psychiatry and Neuroscience*? I think from the title you will see its relevance. "Earworms: The Compulsive Nature of the Modern Soundscape". It's a study about how prevalent it is that musical people are prone to hearing repetitive little bursts of music. Apparently it's been noted for centuries, and is quite a normal thing, or at least affects many thousands of people, none of whom can be said to have a mental illness. With the advent of the modern 'jingle', which is actually intended to stick in your brain, it's become much more widespread.

There was a pause while Blenkinsop leafed through the article, leaning towards Elizabeth Fielding, who looked on sternly. Ellis, obviously taken aback, turned to O'Price, and whispered something. Liron leaned in towards Luke.

- No, but these really was real worms, right there in my head, squirming around.

- Liron, just let me handle this, ok?

When the attention in the room settled back again, he continued.

- And here again in the Nurses' report, where you refer to the 'patient's delusions and ongoing flights of fancy', quoting his 'insistent claim that he was personally acquainted with Gene Pitney, and had even sung with him on occasion'.

O'Price looked for support from the panel, who gazed back at him rather unpityingly.

- I don't think it's an exaggeration to say that Liron is a bit of a fantasist.

Luke produced a poster from his brief-case. Its dated appearance, and the worn corners and general grubbiness attested to its authenticity. The date was February 22nd 1976, the venue Batley Variety Club. Gene Pitney's name was at the top, but there at the very bottom, was the name LIRON SCHULMAN. O'Price went red and looked furious. The panel leaned forward in interest. There was no way they were going to let this lunatic out of the hospital, but they liked a bit of intrigue.

And so it went on. With support from Liron, Luke challenged the discrepancies, blatant mistakes and heavy-handed misinterpretations in the three reports. The nursing staff and doctor defended their positions stoutly. For an hour the discussion went back and forth. At last the doctor and Luke were allowed a final statement. Ellis was in no doubt that Liron was suffering from serious delusions, auditory hallucinations, and in no fit state to be discharged.

The final word was granted to Liron himself, who had behaved impeccably throughout, the model of sanity and rationalism, caught up for several years in circumstances beyond his control, but now well and ready to resume life in the outside world.

- And so Mr. Schulman, is there anything else you would like to say before we consider your appeal?

Liron looked around carefully, and his eyes met Luke's. Luke had a terrible premonition and gave him a pleading look. Liron winked and began to sing very softly.

- And now I've had a few, but then again too few to mention!
  I did what I had to do! I saw it too, without convention!

Liron had said very little until now. He had sat calmly as the conversation had ranged about his various strengths and faults. The others had almost forgotten he was there at times, engrossed in their verbal combat. But every eye in the room was on him now, and he seemed to respond to this. His voice rose in pitch and volume.

- I plant each carted cross,
  Each careful step along the bi-way!
  And more, much more than this,
  I did it my way!

- Thank you Liron. Let's be going now.

But Liron was gathering his breath for a final assault, and had clambered onto his seat, and thence onto the big oak desk, while the three hospital managers shrank back, as if fearing a Frankie Vaughan type kick. Liron walked along the table, trampling the paper reports, kicking over a glass of water, from which the liquid leapt to freedom.

- And there were tunes, I'm sure you knew,
  when I broke off more than I could chew.

O'Price was shaking like a car in gear with the handbrake on. He looked ready to spring at Liron, but caught between his urge to get his hands on a legitimate target for oppression, and wanting to let the fool damn himself completely.

And through it all when there was doubt,
I broke it off and spewed it out!

THE RECORD SHOWS

AND THERE SHE BLOWS

I DID IT

MYYYYYYYYYY WAYYYYYYY.[1]

He stood down to a deafening silence, broken suddenly by clapping from Mr Ellis, which was quelled by a glance from Elizabeth Fielding.

Mr. Trevor Blenkinsop smiled a thin smile at Luke as he gathered his papers.

- I think that will be all.

*

The bank holiday weekend at the end of May brought bright, hot weather, auspicious for the first ever demonstration of The Off-Beats campaigning group. The little demonstration stood at the gates of the Hospital to contest the launch of the Trust's Strategic Plan. There were about twelve people in a tight group on the verge by the blue sign that said Needleham NHS Foundation Trust. Someone had made an addition in thick black marker pen below it, so the strap line read "Your Mental Health Is **none of** Our Business". As the large, black car neared the gates of the hospital from the main road, Tarpow could see from its comfortable interior the makeshift signs the little crowd had erected.

---

[1] My Way, written by Paul Anka, Claude Francois, Jacques Revaux, Jules Abel, Gilles Thibaut, © 1968, and published by Concord, BMI and Suisa.

Disconn ECT!
SAY NO TO SHOCK!
MAD LIB!
100 years
Of pyschitric oppression!

- Don't they teach literacy at OT anymore?

The signs ranged from neatly printed to hand written scrawls. One, saying 'A Century Of Torture' was written in red gloss that had dripped when the board was prematurely placed upright, and the ensuing drips gave it a ghoulish, bloody aspect. Ellis, who was driving, seemed genuinely puzzled.

- Who are these people?

By now they were slowing to take the turn into the drive that would take them within feet of the protesters. Tarpow answered him patiently.

- Mostly disgruntled ex-patients. The kind that would complain about anything, on principle. It's a kind of symptom for some people. There's that Jew artist chap, Max what's name, and that troublemaker, Broussine, and a few patients they've dragged into it. Look, that's the advocate chap, poncing around. Who does he think he is, Nelson fucking Mandela?

- Doesn't he work for us?

- You're joking! No, he's employed by Mindfields. Independence you see, very important in advocacy.

- But the CEO of Mindfields is on our Board?

- He is indeed. Independence has its limits like everything else.

Tarpow smiled to himself. Mild mannered John Turbot was a walkover. A Lothario with a past he'd rather forget, and more to the point, would rather Gus Tarpow forgot, which was unlikely this side of dementia. Get them by the bollocks. By now they were riding up the drive, and the demonstration was receding in the rear-view mirror. Ellis looked puzzled.

- So who is the White Rabbit?

Tarpow looked back. Two or three of the little crowd were waving V signs at the back of the car. But there, behind them, shrinking down but clearly visible now, nonetheless, was the oversized head and long ears of a white rabbit suit. He shook his head from side to side as if to clear it.

- -Ellis, you learn not to ask.

*

When the car bearing the two managers passed the demonstration there was a brief outbreak of animated booing, but it soon faded. In truth the picket had turned out to be a little bit boring. For a start, not many people so far had been enticed out to the relatively remote site for the poorly publicised launch. The cars had been sporadic, and generally had studiously ignored the little band.

- Do you not think this is a bit futile?

Marjorie was ever unafraid to say what others might only think.

- Yes, but you've got to make the gesture!

Walter said. Then the White Rabbit said something.

- What?

Maria pulled the head up far enough to speak out under it.

- I said it's bloody hot in here.
- Maria, you could take it off now if you want. You've made your point.
- The trouble is I haven't got anything on underneath.

They agreed that they'd made their point and since the launch was due to start in fifteen minutes, they packed up their demonstration and started to walk up the drive to the hospital with a view to asking some awkward questions.

*

The audience was getting restless, not that this was in itself a cause for concern to Augustus Tarpow. If people submitted themselves to be present at the public launch of Needleham NHS Trust's Strategic Plan, in their own free time, without pay, then they deserved what they got. The meeting was grinding on into its forty-second minute, with Mr. Ellis doing a fine opening statement in the time-honoured regional tradition of Geoffrey Boycott. No-one had been allowed to ask a question yet. The air was drowsy with heat, and the haze of words from the platform had begun to assume the lulling backdrop of insects on a hot day.

The windows of the meeting room were thick with paint, and barely able to open, like most of the windows at Needleham. There was a fan that stood in one corner, but it seemed tired as it swung from side to side and made almost no impact on the solid body of heat in the room. The room itself wasn't big enough for the forty people who were arranged in neat rows before the panel of officials behind their oak desk. When Ellis paused to look down at his papers and cleared his throat to begin again, that bloody advocate had risen to his feet and was taking his chance.

- Obviously it's very difficult to take in such a big document, especially since it was only made available this morning, but from a quick look, it seems that you're intending to close down the Industrial Unit. But as far as I can see there are no plans for a service in the community to replace it. Can you explain?

Trevor Blenkinsop spoke into the microphone before Ellis could answer, in that polite voice which contained just enough coldness to discourage further interruptions.

- As I have already indicated, there will be time for questions following Mr. Ellis' presentation. If you could just wait until the end, I'm sure your questions will be answered.

Ellis smiled ingratiatingly, then continued to elucidate the strategic view, outline the underlying principles, and delineate the direction of travel which would underpin policy and give therapeutic justifications for the Trust's 'new vision of mental health services'.

From the sidelines Tarpow looked on seriously, though he was smiling inwardly at Trevor's consummate skill as Chair. The start of the meeting had been delayed of course, then Blenkinsop had made such a meal of introducing the panel of Ellis, Moking and Elizabeth Fielding that they had eaten well into the allotted time. Of course there would have to be time for questions in the last twenty minutes of the session, but Trevor would make sure that the people chosen to put questions would be from the Innocuous Brigade, either on-message nursing staff, or the tame mad or their carers who could be relied on not only not to rock the boat, but not even to recognise it was a boat, rather than say a van or a wheelbarrow that they were dealing with. He was rather put out by the size of the turnout though, considering there had been such short notice of the meeting. It was disappointingly good really. The audience was made of Trust employees, like O'Price and other nurses; some worn out cases Tarpow recognised as carers, the broken mothers and fathers of these wretches; some patients; Paraskeva and her crowd were here, of course; that trouble-maker the advocate, and the rest of the Mad Trots had all filed in together late. The only person who seemed to be missing was Graytfell the senior social worker, who was on a training day.

At last Ellis wound up his talk, but before Blenkinsop could make a request for questions that damn fool advocate was on his feet again, and speaking.

- I notice that the proposed redevelopment plan involves most of the wards at Needleham moving out into the community, but there seems to be a discrepancy. The seven wards that you are shutting have about a hundred and fifty beds, but the three units you mention in the community only seem to have about thirty. Can you explain this a little more?

Tarpow had been expecting this very question. Actually the Modernisation Plan did not go into details about bed numbers, and he knew the actual figures were something like a hundred and eighty beds lost at Needleham to twenty to be provided in the community, so that idiot advocate had underestimated the bed loss, but let that ride. Ellis was primed to deal with this and spoke in his benign consultant's voice.

- Modern thinking about patient care suggests that people are better cared for outside big units, so we will be trying to support people within their homes wherever possible.

- But won't the programme of redundancies interfere with your ability to do this?

Where did he get this stuff? They hadn't even let the union in on that one yet. Tarpow could see Ellis was floundering and stepped in from the sideline.

- We are considering voluntary redundancies, but nothing is definite yet. This is in keeping with maintaining a modern fit for purpose workforce. Some people may not be able to make the transition from working in the hospital to the community, so we are giving people the option to leave, and we will recruit new people for the new jobs.

Particularly since the old timers, with their annual increments, were on an alarmingly good screw, and could be replaced by untrained, dirt-cheap dossers from the dole queue.

- Any more questions?

Blenkinsop's voice was slightly too hasty. Maria and Alex put their hands up. He chose Alex who began at a distance from his subject, then qualified his opening remark with a series of tangential clauses that meandered like an ancient sage further and further into the wilderness, until finally he came to a standstill in mid-sentence and looked round hopefully. Blenkinsop shuffled his papers and Ellis, having left a respectful pause, closed proceedings.

As they left the hall Maria fell into step with Luke.

- I feel like they always get away with it.

Luke nodded in agreement.

- We just need something they can't deny. We need a skeleton to drop out of the cupboard.

They both laughed at that, then Maria looked suddenly thoughtful.

- Maggie O' Render, that ex-nurse…did she ever…?

Luke was startled because he had the exact same thought.

- I'm going to see her tomorrow.

*

There was a picturesque row of cottages at the edge of Needleham village where the road disappeared into the hills that would eventually take it over the moors and into Lancashire. Roses twined around the gateposts, and over special arches built to show them off. Most of the gardens were full of the bright blues and reds of summer flowers. Of the dozen or so cottages, only the one Luke stood in front of seemed to be neglected. He pushed, with some difficulty, a flaking iron gate that had almost lost its top hinge, and walked up the little path to the door, with trailing grasses swiping at his calves. Within seconds of his knock, a florid face appeared, and with it, a woman wearing a big comfortable looking green cardigan, with jeans and house slippers made to look like little labradors.

- Nurse O' Render?

- Just call me Margaret. And I'm not a nurse any more, of course.

He followed her through a dark hall, crowded with shopping bags, umbrellas, shoes, folded chairs, bags of coal, coats overburdening a row of hooks, and into a room crowded with ceramic cats. They teemed over the hearth and mantelpiece and thronged onto ledges that seemed specially made for them at various heights around the room. There was one huge Persian sitting on its haunches in a corner, surveying all with its superior gaze. There was a posse of tiny white kittens on top of the television, draping their little paws at various angles down towards the screen. There were gingers and blacks, tabbies and piebalds, some realistic, some fanciful, with waistcoats and top hats. The walls were similarly decked with photographs and posters, all of cats.

- Louis Wain!

She said, following his gaze towards the print of an abstract electric pattern that resolved itself into the shape of a cat's head as he looked.

- A great artist, mad as a hatter, and all he ever painted was cats.

- You do have a lot of cats.

It was a rather lame thing to say, but she beamed at him. Now he could see that she was probably in her sixties, red cheeked, with hair that was greying and thinning. Her eyes were blue and hazy, with no hint of malice or artifice. It was the open smile of a woman gone happily to seed and rooted now where she belonged. There was the faint, heavy, medicinal smell of stale alcohol. When she had ceremoniously made him tea, and they were sitting, she in the armchair, he on the matching settee, both with the same design of frolicking cats, he looked at her expectantly. She cleared her throat noisily.

- It was Maria who gave me the idea to write to you. I'm glad you get on with Maria. She's not always easy.

- She's very…committed.

- Committed, yes, committed!

Margaret gave an unexpected little titter.

- Rather a funny word to use in this context!

- O God, yes! I wasn't thinking. Anyway, she's…very principled!

- O come on, she's a pain in the arse.

- I wouldn't say that.

- Because you're too polite! You're too well brought up. But you might grow out of it in time, with luck.

She laughed again, a good natured, inclusive kind of chuckle. A real black and white cat moved nervously from behind her chair and disappeared into the kitchen.

- Don't get me wrong. I love Maria to bits. She was one of the few compensations when I worked at Needleham. She kept me going. But she was so serious! She kept giving me pamphlets and all sorts to read.

- Did you read them?

- Well you know, I had a look at them. They were a bit extreme. I couldn't really see the link between Needleham Hospital and the Russian Revolution to be frank. Anyway, I saw her in town one day and she told me you seemed serious. I thought you would be interested in some of the things I saw when I was at Needleham, and could possibly ask some questions.

She was looking at him expectantly.

- About?

-   TORVILLE!

She yelled at a white cat, which had appeared and started to gnaw at the curtains. It bolted into the kitchen, and she turned back to him.

-   About the deaths.

Luke remembered his first day in the hospital, the runaway patient shouting something about them *trying to kill us*, and then Anthea saying the same thing.

-   There were things that went on at Needleham that trouble me. And I have reason to believe they may still be happening.

He wanted to get away, out of this room, into the sunlit garden.

-   Things?

-   All kinds of things actually. All kinds of the usual bad practice that happens in a big closed institution and has been written about since Erving Goffman.

-   The horse's head?

-   That was a particularly bad example, but all of it really. I worked on an elderly ward and at mealtimes they put the dessert on top of the main course to save having to wash up two plates, that kind of thing. 'They don't know the difference anyway', they'd say. They used the patient's money to buy themselves expensive booze at Christmas, and any other time truth to tell. I'm better off out of it. They offered me early retirement and I went.

-   When did you retire?

-   Well I kind of was retired, if you know what I mean, about three years ago. I didn't really have an option. I made a complaint. They don't like that sort of thing.

She looked at him with a sudden bleak expression, then seemed to recover herself. When she spoke again her voice was brisk and business-like.

- Anyway there was more than just the usual unpleasantness. You may have noticed that the incidence of mortality at Needleham is high?

- I've heard people talking about it. There have been several deaths since I started work in January, but none of them seem very suspicious. Old age and accidents. And the suicide rate seems to be low for a big institution, according to reports.

- That comes from having the local coroner as the Chair of the Board.

Luke looked at her blankly.

- Mr. Blenkinsop! Didn't you know? Yes, he's the local coroner – very handy! You may have heard about the new government setting targets to cut suicide rates in 1997? That was when he was co-opted to the Board. What do you think is the easiest way to reduce suicide levels?

- I'm not sure. Be more careful about the drugs you prescribe? Special teams to support people with depression? Put fencing on the bridges?

- Yes, all those things are very worthy, but they would all cost money! The correct answer is… redefine the term! If you start to call suicide 'misadventure' instead, bingo, you've solved the problem at a stroke! Suicide rate plummets at no extra cost! Government happy! Trust Board happy! Everybody happy! A win win situation as they say.

- But people are still committing suicide? Presumably they're not happy?

- Well of course the patients don't win! That goes without saying. They go on jumping off high buildings, standing in front of trains, buying poison, whatever! But they are no longer suicides! They are "misadventures", the lot of them, so that's alright!

Luke sipped his tea while he took this in. A ginger cat came round the corner of Margaret's chair and glared at him, while she continued.

- The suicide rate at Needleham is indeed artificially low. So you would expect the death rate at Needleham to be low too, and instead the death rates here are…well check it out yourself. I think they are among the highest in the country. How do you explain that?

- I don't know. Why are the rates so high at Needleham?

Margaret O' Render gave Luke a long look.

- This is confidential?

- Of course.

- You're not going to quote me on anything? I'll have to deny it all if it gets back to me.

- You've got my promise. I'd just like to know.

- The thing is, I had to sign a form to say I wouldn't go public with anything I knew about what went on at Needleham, as a condition of getting the pay-off that paid for this house. I know it's shameful, and I'm not saying I feel good about it. But there are things that still trouble me, and I can't do anything about it.

She looked at him candidly.

- But you can.

There was a high-pitched skirmish in a corner, and a long - haired black cat leapt past Luke's shoulder onto the window ledge and was gone through the open window into the sunlit garden outside. Despite the brightness, the thick walls of the cottage made the interior suddenly seem cold.

Luke had never before been to Leeds Reference Library, a room of high ceilings and dark wood that perched several floors above the main public library in Leeds. The tiny lift had been out of order, so he had to climb a series of staircases that started very grandly up to the first and second floors with their art and music libraries, then grew narrower and darker to the third and fourth floor administrative offices, where balding men carried piles of paper and viewed him suspiciously. Finally he came to an obscure, unmarked door that led to a steep, creaking wooden staircase. This was lit only by a large unshaded bulb at the end of a long flex that disappeared into the gloom of the stairwell.

At the top of this flight was an imposing door with a large pane of frosted glass, through which he found two gate-keeping librarians sitting at a desk covered in papers. There was no-one else in the large room as far as he could see. He explained he had come to look up certain historical Health Service records. The two librarians, a man and woman with greying hair and rheumy blue eyes who might have been brother and sister, stared at him incredulously, then at each other. At first he thought he must have come to the wrong place. Their body language seemed to suggest there was nothing of the kind in their library, but after a muttered exchange he could not catch, the woman detached herself from her seat and, beckoning him to follow, led him to a glass case at the far end of the long room. A few minutes later he was sitting at one of the substantial desks with a pile of thick ledgers.

He wanted to check out Margaret's claim that there were an inordinate number of deaths at Needleham Hospital. It took him a long time to find what he was looking for. The information he needed was in various obscure places, and given titles that disguised the content he wanted, but at last he had it all in front of him. He checked it again, and there was no doubt about it. Mortality rates at

Needleham were consistently higher than in other comparable hospitals in the twenty years since 1980. Until that year Needleham had been unexceptional, but since then it had been in the top three for patient deaths every year, and the very top per capita in fourteen of the twenty years to 1999, the latest year for records. He was puzzled. Something must have changed in 1980, but what? Something slipped out from the shadows of his mind and was gone before he could direct his attention to it. It was a dark thing that did not want to come to light. There was a connection, a fact about 1980 he had read or heard recently, he was sure, but however he tried, he couldn't pull it back from whatever recess it had slipped away into.

SEVEN: July

In the decades between the wars, the population of Needleham Hospital reached its height. In 1933 the number of patients was around two thousand and five hundred, and so remained until the introduction of major tranquillisers in the 1950s. This development, and changes in economic circumstances in the 1960s which meant the old institutions were no longer financially viable, led to a decline in patient numbers. In the 1930s the hospital was in effect a small town in itself, and during the Summer would stage an open day to which people from the villages surrounding it were invited. Between the two world wars Needleham Open Day was a big event in the local calendar, and the Hospital Committee would invite patronage from wealthy citizens. Nursing staff would play cricket against a neighbouring team; produce grown by patients on the hospital allotments would be sold, and tours of the hospital would be arranged. The patients on such days were encouraged to wear fancy dress, which was considered to be good for their morale.

A History of Confinement in West Yorkshire,
Hubert Johnson

*

- We celebrate this day, the fourteenth of July, 2001, Bastille Day, for a particular reason!

The speaker's voice echoed flat and metallic through the public address system more accustomed to relaying bingo numbers. The bar room, noisy with a dozen conversations a moment before, quietened in anticipation.

- At the height of the French Revolution, in 1789, an angry crowd broke into the Bastille in Paris, the most notorious prison in the whole of France. They could no longer stand the oppression and poverty they were being subjected to. The prison seemed to be impregnable, but suddenly it was in their hands! They took the keys from the panicking guards. They ran through the whole place and let all the inmates free!

She lifted her hands upwards, and taking their cue, the desultory crowd in the upper bar of the Merry Prankster cheered and banged the abused tabletops with fists and glasses. The speaker seemed to swell and grow, as if the wave of emotion from her audience had flowed into her, filling her face with colour. She could hardly wait until the noise calmed enough for her to start again.

- But what was so amazing, so strange and unexpected, was that after they let out the political prisoners, locked up simply for disagreeing with the king and his sycophants, they found more cells, and when they got to the deepest and darkest cells, right at the bottom of the building, in the worst conditions of all, in cells running with rats and water - slimy, dark horrible cells, they found... people locked up for being mad!

The crowd booed and stamped their displeasure, cries of 'shame', and 'bastards'.

- People locked up not for politics, but simply because they were different! Because, according to the good citizens, they were making a nuisance of themselves on the streets of Paris! Their faces didn't fit! They were outcasts! For this reason, Bastille Day, July 14th, has become the international symbol for the mental health liberation movement, the day when we celebrate Mad Liberation!

Luke, who was sitting on the very front rank of the smoky room, in preparation for his own contribution to this event, had never seen Maria speak in public before. Where she had previously seemed pedantic and cold, now she seemed brave and fierce.

He turned to look at her audience, friends of the performers mainly, but many ex-patients from Needleham too, and some he recognised as current ones from acute wards, voluntary patients who had come out to the local pub to support the venture. The walls were decked with Max's abstract designs, and the work of other artists from the "Happy Daze" collective.

Already the crowd had seen great delights. The evening had begun with a rare performance from 'Bipolar Exploration', the band described in their publicity as: 'mad crypto-punk survivors' from Leeds, who had to be on early because their lead singer and song writer, legendary wild man Ginger Chris, liked to be in bed by ten o'clock. Ginge had come on stage in a pair of tartan slippers, and in between raucous songs demanding an end to bigotry and oppression, had poured and sipped strong tea from a Thermos flask.

There followed the poet Johnny Equinox, in his army surplus camouflage combat suit, with locks down to his knees, and his epic rant 'Quacks and Drugs and Shock and Dole' to the tune of an Ian Dury classic. Liron sang 'Fly Me to The Moon' unaccompanied and mangled the words to the great delight of the room. The creative writers from The Happy Days Centre made their unique contributions - Dol the Goth with her obscene rant against a junior doctor who had refused her weekend leave; James with an erudite love poem to the memory of Marlene Dietrich; Alex with a complex protest poem against those who had hacked into his computer and stolen his poems to sell on the poetry black market; Anthea with a reading from the Mabinogion which had left the bemused gathering staring into their pints.

The Countess had used her connections to good effect and had arranged for two young female musicians from the music college in Leeds to give a demonstration of Chinese classical music. The Countess was also responsible for the most surprising and glamorous moment of the evening, when the door at the back of the room opened, and a team of belly dancers from the local Adult Education Centre trooped in, shimmering and shaking in silk and sequins to a piped Egyptian love song.

Now Maria was winding up her talk.

- In October, when Needleham Hospital celebrates one hundred years of torture and oppression, we plan to picket their celebrations! We're proud to be different, to have flouted the fetid conventions of their so called normality! We have walked the lonesome valley of insanity, and proudly carry the light we found at the end of the tunnel! We are here to say to this medieval system, the world is not flat, we have sailed to the edge, fallen off, and returned to say 'there be no dragons, but those we make ourselves!'

The crowd roared its approval. James, who had been watching from beyond the raised platform that served as a stage in this little concert room, couldn't help feeling that Maria was rather over egging it. 'Don't gild the lily, darling!' he said to himself. 'Don't overdo it.' Some people, he thought, simply over reacted to the chance of a little limelight. As her speech ended, he clapped enthusiastically with the rest, and stepped forward in his billowing chiffon ball gown. The glow of its emerald sheen set off his bright red, curly wig, with its glittering tiara, and the dark, bold strokes of his mascara. He waited until the howls and wolf-whistles had died.

- ALL RIGHT, YOU ANIMALS!

He projected his basso profundo into the room with such gusto that Marjorie, who was sorting her change out at the bar and not paying any attention, jumped, and coins of the realm scattered across the bar.

- LADIES AND GENTLEMEN, MAD MEN AND MAD LADIES, FOR YOUR DELIGHT AND ENTERTAINMENT – A MUSICAL RE-ENACTMENT OF THE STORMING OF THE BASTILLE, AS PERFORMED BY EX-INMATES OF THE FORMER WEST RIDING PENNINE PAUPER LUNATIC ASYLUM!

The lights were dimmed, and the stage lighting turned on from the side. The crowd hushed in anticipation. Luke, the official prompt, had a pencil torch, which he now trained on the script on his lap, as Max strode onto the stage in his role of Carbamazanon, a man of the people.

Of course, it didn't turn out so smoothly. Walter as the guard had immense difficulties with reading his lines, even though he had James' script within three inches of his face, so there were long pauses. Marjorie as Mayfelda had to be fetched from the Ladies on her cue and Max's impersonation of Eric Morecombe was particularly bizarre, as he used a strong East European accent. It didn't matter. The crowd cheered and applauded everything as if it had been the Baftas.

James looked thunderous for a while until he realised that Max's improvisations involving catching imaginary objects in a paper bag were getting more laughs than his carefully crafted script. At that point he resigned himself to enjoying the travesty of his art as best he could, aided by bottles of expensive lager.

Maria proved a surprise success as Madame Bovinary, an aged crone, who sat stage left, knitting a voluminous scarf on which the words 'Moking', 'Tarpeau' and 'Drogham' were clearly visible. Anthea went down a storm as the revolutionary committee's advocate. But the biggest cheer was reserved for Alex's bumbling portrayal of Monsieur Tarpeau, the head jailer, whose every appearance was greeted with mighty boos and jeers.

The crowd cheered and roared as the intrepid revolutionaries gained entry to the prison by disguising themselves as the Prison's Day and Evening Community Support Team, come to start a drop-in. For Tarpeau they reserved the harshest punishment known to the revolutionary council - not Madame Guillotine, or garrotting, but compulsory attendance at the Happy Days Creative Writing Group. At the end the triumphant team raised a tricolor with the words

Liberty, Equality, Insanity!

Finally James, as the narrator, stepped to the microphone.

-   And so justice was done! And the moral is that anything is possible if we work together, if we … GET INVOLVED!

It was the cue for an extravagant arpeggio played by Max on a concealed piano. Then James, in his best Noel Coward voice, launched into The Involvement Song, for which everyone joined in the choruses, singing from the sheets that had been provided on their tables.

The Involvement Song

Let's get involved
- It's the greatest thing
Since human life evolved!
We'll be involved
- It's so wonderful!
Our problems will be solved!

(Solo) When Adam softly spoke to Eve
In that garden long ago
He said just tell me what you want
And I will make it so.
She thought for just a minute
turned to him and softly said,
the words that made his brain spin,
changed his mind, and turned his head.

(Altogether) Let's get involved
- It's so wonderful!
all differences resolved!
Let's be involved!
- The wall around this garden
will dissolve

(Solo) When Jesus climbed up to the Mount
And saw the people there
The sight just took his breath away
And he could only stare
Then Peter nudged him in the ribs
And whispered "go on man",
He gathered up his wits
And oh so gently he began...

(altogether) Let's get involved
Its the best thing
since this planet has revolved,
Just be involved
Your sins redeemed
And blighted souls absolved
(Repeat first altogether)
When we're involved!
Let's get involved!
We'll be involved!

As the disco kicked in, and strains of 'I Will Survive' burst through
the reluctant speakers, Luke found himself at the bar with Maria.

-    Nice speech! Never heard you talk like that before.

Maria coloured up, clearly pleased.

-    Did you go and see Margaret?

-    I did. She has... a lot of cats.

Maria snorted.

- She's batty. More so than any of the patients. She's completely cat crazy. When she worked here she kept giving me all these magazines and booklets from the Cat Protection Society.
- Did you read them?
- Well I took them because I didn't want to be rude. But I hate cats!
- Anyway it was good you put me on to her. She had some disturbing stuff to say about the Professor.
- She hates the Professor. She worked in the Unit for a few years. She thinks he's really incompetent.
- Worse than that. You don't happen to know anybody at the Pharmacy do you? I need to check back on some of the records of prescriptions.

Maria thought about it.

- Well there's Barbara, she's been working in Pharmacy for years. She's a Liberal Democrat, but she's all right really. She might help.

One of the belly dancers bumped against Luke. When he turned she was looking startled over his shoulder.

- Bloody hell!

He followed her gaze. Marjorie was in a crowd of women dancing unsteadily around a pile of handbags. On the choruses the dancers were shouting "I will survive" into each other's faces and waving their fists with real menace. James, who was in the middle of the group, tore the red curls from his sweating head and flung the wig, which made a bright arc through the air, and landed on a side table over a pint of cider. Walter continued to contemplate this with the same placid expression. The belly dancer laughed and took a pull on a large gin and tonic.

- I'm glad I'm not in charge of this lot.

- Me too!

Luke agreed. Maria frowned at them.

- Actually I don't think anyone is in charge. That's the whole point, isn't it?

There was a moment when Luke and the belly-dancer looked chastened, before the besequined woman caught Luke's eye and snorted, and the two of them erupted into uncontrollable laughter. After a few seconds Maria couldn't help but join in, and the three of them were still laughing with tears in their eyes when the music changed to Thriller, and space cleared round the Countess' extraordinary moonwalking zombie dance.

*

The following weekend, the heat of Summer settled on the house of Luke's father, and it sank into a sullen doze. The house had always seemed aloof from nearby terraces, detached as it was behind tall beech and privet hedges. As a child Luke envied his mates who peeled off into the terraced back streets of Myllroyd after school, while he had to walk home alone to the 'teacher's house'. Now on his father's death it seemed as if the house itself had gone into mourning. Luke wondered if he would ever be in a position to sell it. It was as if he too had fallen under a spell.

He lived in a corner of his childhood bedroom, long since become a store room, and full of teacher's lumber. He had cleared a space for a mattress and camped out there. The rest of the house was similarly packed, mostly with books and boxes of paper. He had a sensation the house was producing books while he slept. Rooms that he felt he had made progress clearing seemed next day fuller than ever. He spent a long time in the room where his father died. His father had been killed when a large bookcase of metaphysical poetry had come away from its attachment to the wall, and fallen onto him as he

181

worked at his desk, a hard wooden corner striking him a hard blow on the side of his head. His body was found by the woman who came in to clean for him, pinned down under the weight of shelves that had been overloaded for years.

There wasn't much of Luke in the house. He had really left when he was ten, after his mother's disappearance, to go away to the boarding school near York where the other boys were so well drilled in the eccentric ways of the old establishment. It had seemed only he floundered from one day to the next. He came home only during school holidays to the silent house and increasingly distant relationships with his earlier school-friends. Now he was back living here, the house overwhelmed him with its size and its silence.

One day he ventured into the attic that was given over to things that have no use but cannot be thrown away. He found his father's old papers, boxes of journals and books too obscure to take up space downstairs, too revered to dump. It seemed endless, but towards the back of the pile he found a box with his old mediocre school reports, along with his life-saving certificates (bronze and silver; he never made gold to the disappointment of his father), a couple of battered Corgi cars, an old school cap. There were childhood paintings of strange lop-sided animals, and scrawled words that might have been an insect's dream of language. Clearly these were things his mother had kept. They were too sentimental for his father. As he dug even deeper under the papers he found it at last and realised when he did that he had been expecting it.

A faded orange TV cat.

As if it had been waiting for him.

Bagpuss.

*

Needleham was relaxing in the warmth. An atmosphere of lassitude and indulgence fell over the dreaming hospital. For weeks the Flying Squad were rarely called, and its members organised football games

182

on the newly mowed lawns. Patients strolled the baking grounds or congregated on the bleached wooden benches by the disused fountain, where they conversed in meandering non-sequiturs. Sometimes they listened without words to the doves that had taken up residence in the higher towers. The toughest nurses thawed and allowed more concessions. On the locked wards patients who had been denied walking privileges all Spring now found themselves marched out twice or three times a day for longer and longer periods, as nurses smoked and chatted together in the benign brightness and heat.

One day Luke took a walk and explored deeper and deeper into the hinterland of the hospital, finding mossy courtyards with peeling doors bearing signs for 'Medical Supplies' or 'WC Staff/Visitors (Key On Jutland Ward)'. At one archway between wards he found a traffic light, still blinking red, orange, green, regulating an intersection of roads, and the ghosts of hospital trolleys and vans long since decommissioned. There were acres of untended squares now silent, home to colonies of wild grasses, doves and summer flowers. A white feral cat started at his approach and slipped into a broken ground floor window.

The hospital had taken on a new meaning for him since learning of his mother's death. He imagined her walking past these buildings when the hospital was thriving. Now there were cracks in many of the walls. The tarmac of the roads was pitted and in some places depressions had opened up a foot or more deep. One small storage building seemed to have fallen in completely, the stones crumpled in on themselves with the slate roof still more or less intact. This was on the edge of a square that was enclosed by the long two storey blocks of old wards.

There was a fenced-off area with the name 'Abetter Gas & Oil' stencilled on each section of opaque plastic sheeting. Rising from the centre was a thirty-foot-high, thin tower, like a telecommunications mast. Luke marvelled that he hadn't seen it from the road, or some other part of the hospital, but other buildings nearby were of similar height, and had shielded the tower. By its side there was a long metallic tube. He heard the rush of air or water emanating from behind the fencing like the noise of a subterranean ghost train, or a sudden underground flood. As he listened it seemed the sound changed to that of machinery, similar to the sound of a passing aircraft.

He looked round at the old blocks of disused wards, made of the discoloured stone of old mill-towns. The tarmac was covered with broken glass, bricks, odd bits of piping, and flawed here and there where tufts of grass had begun to break through. He could see no people, and despite the heat of the afternoon he shivered. The sound seemed to get louder, the buildings to tower over him, menacing him with history. There was another sound now, below the register of the underground railway. It was a seething sound of angry water, boiling unattended or forced through hose onto hard concrete. It was the kind of water that likes to overflow and drown; to race through streets and bring down mudslides; to carry off cars and homes. It was the violent sound of insects or lethal electricity. He began to walk quickly, then broke into a run to get away from this square, hurrying back to whatever small comfort the little cluster of wards that were still functioning at Needleham could offer.

*

The sign on the door of the church hall said 'Reiki Share' in the rounded hand-written curves a primary school teacher might use to demonstrate the art of writing. Anthea pushed the heavy door open with some difficulty and stepped into the hallway. There was a strong smell of sandalwood. The hall was badly in need of a paint job. The skirting boards were scuffed and scarred, and dark patches showed where people had brushed or leant against the walls. She moved instinctively to the door on her right. As she pushed, an intoxicating wave of perfumed air swept past her. In the room eight people were sitting in a circle, and beyond them a portable therapeutic bed had been folded out on its thin wooden legs. A tall man detached himself from the group and moved to intercept Anthea.

- Ah, Anthea! Nice to see you! Can I have a word?

His voice was honey and hymns, a gentle, peaceful drone. He smiled benignly from behind his trimmed grey beard, and his blue eyes beamed with good will. He blocked her way into the room, where over his shoulder she could see all faces had turned towards her. Anthea found herself ushered back into the corridor, and towards one of the other doors.

- What's wrong?
- Nothing's wrong, Anthea, nothing's wrong. We just need to have a little talk.

She found herself in a bleak little room with magnolia painted woodchip begging for a new coat. There were four plastic sit up chairs and a square wooden table with an artificial cheese plant, and little room for anything else. Outside was a yard with green wheelie bins and a tall wooden fence.

- I was wondering if you'd come back after...last time.
- O God yes, I'd forgotten about that! I suppose I was a bit out of order.
- Well you did upset Deidre.
- I know, Patrick, but she does get on my tits when she gets on her high horse like that.

Patrick looked pained.

- Anthea, I wish you wouldn't talk like that. It seems so......
- Truthful?

- Aggressive! It seems aggressive, Anthea, and that is a problem in a Healing Circle like ours. We try to create a space where healing can occur. The atmosphere is very important. People were very shocked when you raised your voice like that.

- Well, she was being very patronising.

- Even so.

- O, for goodness sake, Patrick. She just talks down to everyone, as if she was the only one who's ever opened a pack of Tarot cards. She was wrong, as simple as that. I don't think she's even read Deepak Chopra.

- Anthea, I have to be blunt. We know you've been in hospital relatively recently. Have you stopped taking your medication?

Anthea looked at him closely.

- Since when is that your business? Or anybody's business here. Aren't you the Healing Circle? You don't believe in drugs for God's sake! You're alternative healers.

- Complementary, Anthea, we do complementary medicine! We work alongside aleopathic medicine. We don't reject it outright. Anyway, the point is, Anthea, that the group have decided, for the time being at least, and this can be reconsidered at any time, but for now, as a temporary measure, we think its best if you take a break from it.

- You're banning me from the Healing Circle?

- That's a very negative way to look at it. It's not a ban. It's a kind of cooling off period, really. It's just until you...... get well.

- So let me get this right, I can't come to the Healing Circle to heal until I'm well?

- We think it best.

- So Deidre with her Diabetes, and Marcia with her thyroid problems, and Ruby with her haemorrhoids, they're all alright, but I'm not?
- We're not saying that you can never come back. Just that, for the moment, we think it's wisest if you don't come to the group.
- I can't believe you're saying this.
- Please don't cry, Anthea.
- You said crying was good. 'Crying discharge is a natural, healing emotional release', you said.
- I know I did, Anthea, but there's a time and a place.
- Patrick, you're a fucking, two faced, spineless hypocrite!
- Please Anthea! That's enough, I think you should leave.
- Don't worry, I'm going.

Anthea swept out into the street, crying into a cotton handkerchief. Patrick sighed and tried to compose himself sufficiently to concentrate on Elaine's explanation of the theory of healing runes.

*

The main office of the charity Luke worked for was on the little town's main street, a deliberate policy to put "mental health" at the heart of the community, and challenge stereotypes. The board outside read:

MINDFIELDS
Association for Mental Health
COMMUNITY CRISIS CENTRE
Making the field of Mental Health bloom

As Luke approached the doorway it shared with the Salvation Army charity shop, he saw a hunched figure approaching the door ahead of him, and hung back. It was Violet, a long stay patient at Needleham, recently discharged. She had never come to the advocate's office, always suspicious of anything official, but now it seemed she needed help. She shuffled to the door and pressed the intercom button, creating a fearsome electronic disturbance in the thick air, which made the people at the bus stop nearby turn and look with interest. Several long seconds passed with only the intermittent drone of passing traffic, before a distorted voice spoke, loudly and clearly over the sound of passing traffic.

- Needleham Mindfields Community Crisis Service, and how may I help you today?

Violet muttered something Luke could not catch. It seemed the several people at the bus stop were straining to hear too. The rasping voice from the metal box sounded again.

- Please speak a little louder into the mouthpiece please.

Violet's quavering voice rose above the traffic sound. Again the disembodied voice, even louder.

- Please speak up!

- I'M VERY DEPRESSED.

Great interest now from the bus queue, while a woman passing with a child in a buggy paused to see what was going on.

- It's Violet McKenzie. I've come to get some help.

- Can I have your date of birth, please.

Violet turned and gave a furtive look at the bus queue.

- You know my date of birth, I gave it you last week!

- Can I have your address please, then?

- Listen, Barbara, you know who I am. Now just open this door and let me in. I need some help.

When the voice came again it had dropped some of its previous formality and had an air of resignation about it.

- Violet, I've got to ask, it's me job. Now you're not due in today, are you? I don't know if there's anyone can see you.

- But I've got to see somebody. I'm desperate!

- Well what's been happening?

Violet again risked a quick look round. There was the young woman with a toddler in the fold up pushchair, a grey-haired older man and two middle-aged women with shopping bags. All five were watching with interest.

- Lucky, me cat's died and I'm very upset about it.

- Your cat?

- Yes, me cat.

- It's died?

- Yes.

- When?

- Last night.

- Well what have you done with it.

- I've done nothing with it. It's died. It's at home in its basket. I can't face it, I need some help.

- Well did you do something to it?

- I did nothing to it.

- Well was it old?

- It was old.

- Well there you go. It probably had its time. I mean cats do die love. It's not really a mental health crisis is it?

- Well it is for me.

-   Well what are we going to do? I mean we can't bring it back to life. The doctors are clever but they're not that clever, Violet.

-   Look just let me in.

There was a pause, while the soul at the gate was weighed, valued, and at last judged.

-   You can come in Violet, but you'll have to wait until someone's got time to see to you, alright?

The door at last buzzed open and Violet scuttled in grateful. Luke hesitated. One of the women at the bus stop turned to the other.

-   Poor soul, her cat died.

The other nodded ruefully.

-   It was old, but even so, it's still your cat.

-   She probably forgot to feed it.

-   I wouldn't wonder. Neglected probably.

-   Aye, like her.

The man turned to them and said seriously:

-   They're spoilt today. Just because your cat's died, doesn't mean you should get special treatment.

They nodded again. He dropped his voice to a whisper and mouthed.

-   She's from up there. Needleham.

One of the women nodded even more emphatically.

-   I know, they let them out and they don't know what they're doing half of them.

Luke walked past both the door and the bus stop and continued up the high street. At the library he took a left and went round the block before approaching the Centre from the same angle as before. A bus had obviously been and gone, and there was the start of a new queue looking at him with interest as he pushed the buzzer. Thankfully he was expected and allowed in without too much questioning.

Inside, the hall and stairs bore signs of neglect and a faint smell of urine. In the reception area upstairs there was no sign of Violet. The bespectacled woman who greeted him had long blond hair, blown back and fashioned around her ears like a Fleetwood Mac homage. She gave him a challenging look as if daring him to comment on it, but was otherwise polite to a fault, and gestured him through to the office of John Turbot, Luke's line manager, who greeted him warmly.

- Come in, Mark.

- It's Luke, actually.

- Sorry, Luke. It's been a long day! How goes it? I have to say I'm very pleased with the way you've been supporting that new campaigning group, er, what's the name of it?

- The Off-beats.

- Off-beats, yes, what a brilliant name. Brilliant. Such a hard slog trying to change these systems that have been in place for donkey's years. Sorry that case about ECT didn't work out by the way.

- Francesca.

- Yes, the Italian woman. Very sad, I understand they had to move her to intensive care at the general hospital. Anyway you gave it a good shot. I'm sure they'll be more careful in future, and that's a result. So, you asked for a special meeting?

- Yes, I've been collecting some information I think you should see.

He took out of his bag a red file and passed it over the desk. John Turbot looked at it suspiciously, opened it and began to read. His face betrayed a shock.

- You didn't think to mention this before?

- Well, I didn't really have any evidence before.

- This is extraordinary.

The manager began to read in earnest and for several minutes the only sound in the room was the sound of pages turning. Then he threw the file down on the desk and blew his breath out in a hiss.

- You're suggesting that the Professor of Psychiatry at Needleham Hospital has been...that's extraordinary.

- The evidence points to that.

- Good lord. If this is true...I think you'd better leave this with me.

- You think there's enough to go on?

- I certainly do.

- What do you think the next step is?

- Well, if this can be substantiated, and it looks as if you have concrete evidence, then I think this is really a matter for the police.

- You really think so?

- I think they'll have to be involved. There's no other way.

- So I'll leave it in your hands then?

- I'll talk to the chair of our board now, and let him know what the situation is, then I think the next call will be to our friends on the thin blue line.

- So I'll just wait to hear from you?

- Indeed, I shall keep you informed of all developments. By the way, do you have another copy of this file?

- No, I thought perhaps we could make another copy while I was here.

- I think in the circumstances we'd better keep the number of copies to a minimum.

- Are you sure?

- I think so. I wouldn't want this to be in the wrong hands, it could just muddy the waters. It's dynamite. Leave it to me, I'll get on to it right away. Thank you so much. I think you've finally given us the wherewithal to reform that rotten establishment once and for all.

Turbot shook Luke's hand heartily, and Luke walked out with a great feeling of relief taken from his shoulders.

*

That night Luke made a decision to be more decisive about dealing with his father's things. The clothes had already made their way to Myllroyd Cat Protection, and now he started to put poetry books into boxes, deliberately not scrutinising them to reduce any chance of sentiment. Once filled, he moved the boxes to near the front door so there would be no chance of them finding their way surreptitiously back onto the shelves. He worked resolutely and fast, and by the time Susan rang he had six boxes ready and taped up.

- Really you should try to sell them.

She had said such a thing before, but the effort of doing that seemed like another barrier in getting the books out of his way. He elected to change the subject.

- Anyway, how was your day?

- Don't change the subject! My day was fine. Have you made up your mind about coming to this wedding yet?

- I don't know, I'm not really very good at weddings.

- Look, you don't have to be "very good". It's not your wedding. You just have to turn up. You just have to be there, to put in an appearance! It's not really such a big deal.

Luke didn't really know why he had such a strong desire not to attend the wedding of Susan's brother.

- Luke, you have to decide! They want to know how many people are coming. It's next month.

- Ok, I'll tell you by next weekend. I've had a lot on my mind.

He hesitated, then went for it.

- I handed in the evidence to my boss today.

- Your evidence?

- Yes, you know, about the deaths at Needleham, and the prescribing records.

- O that. I'd forgotten all about it. Did you really go digging around? I can't believe you did that.

- Well it seemed important. I didn't tell you, but I found out that...hang on there's someone at my door.

There was indeed the loud sound of four hefty blows delivered on the wood of the front door as if the deliverer intended to knock it down. When he came back to the phone his voice sounded strange to himself.

- Susan I'm going to have to go. The police have come to see me.

- The police!

- Yes, they want to look for something.

- What on earth do the police want?

- I don't know. Look I'll call you later.

When he had placed the receiver in its cradle, he turned to face the suited officer. Uniformed men in the background were dismantling his computer. The man spoke in a censorial voice that it seemed he must have practised in a mirror beforehand.

- I'm afraid I must ask you to accompany me to the police station, sir.

- But what for?

- If you come with me sir, all your questions will be answered. We wish to take a statement from you regarding certain confidential items that have been removed from Needleham Hospital.

Luke thought about it.

- I made some copies of files relating to prescribing policy. Is that what this is all about?

- If you come with me sir, it will all be explained.

The man looked distastefully around at the piles of books still waiting to be sorted, and Luke had no option but to find his coat and follow the men to their waiting van, locking the old house behind him.

EIGHT: August

Is there a moment on the long and winding, slippery road to madness when you can make a decision to draw back? Could there be a time when you have a choice, a kind of mental equator that you step or sail across at your peril, and just before you do a warning message flashes on some inner screen?

'Alert! You are about to cross into insanity. If you do not intend to be mad you should stop now. From now on the water will go down the plug-hole in the opposite direction.'

Could you look at those uncharted waters, the dense undergrowth, perhaps the desert stretching away as far as the eye can see, and decide to turn back? And would your life be forever changed by the terrible knowledge of what you saw in that instant? Would you live under the shadow of fear for the country you dare not enter, but now will always wonder about? Or was it so much more complex than that? That no intelligible warnings are possible, and madness is a gentle slipping and sliding down an indiscernible slope, until the angle changes, and all you are aware of is the experience of falling.

Into what?

Experience so utterly transformed, language is hardly possible? Where only the scattered tangents of surrealism can serve any longer as speech? The loss of any fixed point in the human world? A detachment and isolation from the worlds of meaning and understanding?

What is the truth about mad?

In an ideal world you would stand at the crossroads, one big white sign pointing to SANITY, and the other to MADNESS, and in the broad light of day, with the sun on your back, you would make the only possible choice you could, and trot down the hill towards safety. Why make any other choice? The trouble is that when you personally get to that crossroads it's nearly always midnight, you haven't slept for a while, and some kids have been messing with the sign.

'The Metaphor of Mental Illness', Hubert Johnson

(unpublished manuscript)

*

Luke felt strangely light-headed. It had started coming on from the time he visited the Tannenberg Unit with Anthea. He felt that he had lost something important, and not just his parents or his old life in Wales. Whatever it was, it didn't feel like something that he needed, more like something that had been an impediment. Partly what he had lost was anxiety. Since his father's death he no longer felt someone looking over his shoulder, judging him. He felt released from the burden of being a son. He had nothing to live up to now. He was an orphan.

The police had released Luke after taking his statement, pending further enquiries. He was suspended from work of course, as was Maria, who was suspected of having helped him. He was not allowed to talk to any colleagues at the hospital, especially the woman from the Medical Records Department who had been so helpful. He could have taken his findings to the local newspaper. The only trouble was Turbot now had the file with the details of his discoveries. He had a sense of puzzlement.

His sleeping became erratic without the routine of work. He slept less, and one night didn't sleep at all. He went from room to room examining the house, looking with new eyes at what his father had left. He spent a long time in his old bedroom listening to the soft noises of the old house, and next morning rang Susan at work to tell her he would not be attending her brother's wedding. She took the news badly. She had been very upset that he had been suspended, and this was now a bridge too far. At first there was a long silence, then she said she was very disappointed, and the line went dead. He had an impulse to ring straight back. He hated disappointing people, but instead he put on his coat and walked out into the warm light. He didn't feel upset that Susan had hung up on him, he felt elated that he had come to decision, and had that strange sense again that something was missing, a filter or brake that would have stopped him deciding like that.

Myllroyd High Street was relatively quiet, as he passed Narcodale Country Supplies, with its racks of Gortex jackets and rows of hiking boots. Everything in the shop window looked clean and bright. It shone back at him as if newly created by some modern rustic god. A male manikin in a heavy purple fleece smiled benignly out into the day, with one arm outstretched, fingers open to passers-by like a blessing.

A car horn woke him from his reverie. The first part of its registration plate was BAD. Was someone trying to get a message to him by communication through registration plates? Was something even bigger than the Professor's misdeeds happening, a struggle between goodness and badness? Only a few white-haired couples were to be seen making their way to chemist and newsagent. Many cars were parked, but only one or two were carefully negotiating the narrow street. Everything around him seemed super real. He felt as if he was seeing it for the first time since... when? He could not remember colours so bright, or the intensity of sound around him from birds round the nearby concrete litter bin, the click of a walking stick on the irregular flags of the pavement. It was as if some filter that protected him from the immediacy of the world had been lifted.

Something was certainly missing.

He walked on down past the little Boots on the corner, the PDSA charity shop with its racks of Mills and Boon romances, wondering what it was that was different. He walked to the Merry Prankster, where he bought a fizzy apple drink and sat in a corner by the fruit machine. Half a dozen people were at the bar or sitting alone at tables trying not to look self-conscious. No-one was paying him any attention, in fact people were conspicuously trying not to pay each other attention, apart from one or two on the high stools at the bar who were trying to engage the bored barman.

Luke thought that if R. D. Laing was here right now he would surely have an angle on what was happening. He would help. He would reassure Luke that the strange thoughts he was having, this feeling of everything breaking down would lead to a breaking through, that there was a perfectly good explanation for the whole thing, that this psychotic interlude would pass and lead on to a new life of sparkling experiences.

-    I wouldn't be too sure about that, sunshine!

The soft Scottish accent seemed familiar and yet strange at the same time. The words were spoken so clearly and loudly that Luke started and turned half round to see where they had come from. But there was no-one within fifteen feet of him. Certainly no-one who could have spoken those words. It was finally happening to him, just like he'd seen it happen to Liron, and to Anthea, and to those countless others who'd walked into the advocacy office these last eight months. The voice had seemed so real.

-    Ah reality! Relax. All you can really say is that you're having an experience! You don't know what it is. Just watch it. Let it happen. Why try to categorise it?

The voice was reassuring, but lightly mocking too. A knowing voice. But if this feeling of fear that was coursing through Luke, making his hands shake so he could hardly raise his glass to his mouth, if hearing this voice was not a sign of madness, of the final descent into the oblivion of mental illness and all that entailed, then what the hell was it?

199

- Look, the only thing you're entitled to say is that you're having an experience. It's a phenomenon, that's all. You don't know what the hell it is! Why try to speculate? You're tying yourself up in knots and there's no need. Just look at it for what it is.

But it couldn't be right to have this voice inside his head, and especially not the voice of a dead maverick psychiatrist.

- Yeh, it's true I have been dead. But the trouble is that you never die with a certain kind of notoriety. People keep digging ye up, whatever ye do. Ye don't get rest.

But that was hardly honest, was it? Hadn't Laing courted controversy? Didn't he go out of his way to get the goat of the establishment of the time?

- Maybe when I was younger I was a bit of a show off. It was a wild time ye have to remember. Ye can't really imagine what it was like now, and I was older, even in the Sixties. People hated authorities, but they sought them out anyway. And it had to be said so ah said it - society is mad the way we do it. It drives ye fucking mad. Fucking capitalism!

So what you were really getting at was changing society? That if we lived in a different kind of world we wouldn't get 'mental illness'?

- Look, what we now call 'mental illness' is just the natural kind of experiences people will have if you put them into a world where everything is fucked, commodified, where they are alienated in their families, before going out to be alienated at their work. S'all I was saying.

Right, so there's not even any such thing as 'mental illness'. It's an illusion. Really you believed the same as that other guy, Thomas Szasz? Who said 'mental illness is a myth'?

Another voice entered the discussion, an older voice with a strong eastern European accent.

- I'm afraid I have to intervene at sis point. I simply have to say that capitalism is not se problem! Se problem is interference in people's lives! Capitalism, properly organised, is part of se solution! Capitalism! Real capitalism, by fich I mean se free market system – sat is se solution, not se problem! Doctors simply don't have se right to interfere in people's lives se way sey do! Sey should leave people alone!

The first voice joined the argument.

- Yeh, leave them alone! Of course! But under capitalism, leaving their families alone is to leave them to be fucked up by the system based around profiteering, and commodifying everything!

- Please my friend let us keep our language decent! Let us not descend into se gutter!

- To be fucked up I say, because that is the right word to use here. To be fucked up by their families, because that is how families behave in a capitalist system where everything is geared towards the production of objects for sale.

- I cannot agree, my friend. Capitalism delivers se goods! Literally! It creates se prosperity we all need. Look at the alternative! Se culture of Soviet Russia, or Mao's China, se society of control from se top where your ideas would not last fife minutes my friend. You would not even haf se opportunity to write them down!

Luke felt his head bursting with this increasingly loud exchange.

- LOOK CAN'T YOU BOTH SHUT UP! DON'T YOU SEE THAT YOU'RE ON THE SAME SIDE. FOR GOD'S SAKE YOU BOTH AGREE THAT FOR WHATEVER REASONS THE WAY WE THINK ABOUT MADNESS IS TOTALLY **MESSED**. SO THE DETAIL DOESN'T MATTER! IT'S ALL FUCKING POLITICS. SO JUST

FUCKING STOP IT, RIGHT! JUST FUCKING SHUT UP THE BOTH OF YOU!

He paused, and both the voices had gone. Actually all the noise in the rest of the room had gone too, except for the subdued murmur of a rolling TV news broadcast. The other drinkers were all ignoring the TV and staring at Luke. It was a curious stare, not threatening. Rather there was a certain puzzlement and even fear in it. He decided in any case it was time to leave. As he reached the door it occurred to him what it was he had lost.

It was his mind.

*

Rumours were flying around Needleham like an unruly bunch of starlings getting ready to leave for Winter. They accumulated in corners and lurked behind old clanking radiators, ambushing staff and patients alike, so that any time two people met there was speculation and intimation. Where they had come from was like much else at Needleham: a deep mystery. The whole hospital was about to be closed down according to the geriatric corridor. No, said the OT department, pornographic images had been found on the Professor's computer. The Acute wing was divided between financial indiscretions, and the discovery that the Professor was in fact a serial bigamist. Tarpow had called a meeting with Nurse Manager Moking, Ellis the consultant, and Blenkinsop, the Chair of the Trust Board, to discuss the file that John Turbot, Manager of Mindfields, Trustee of the Health Trust, and philanderer with skeletons in a cupboard that Tarpow had the keys to, had placed in his hands.

- It's an outrageous slur on a man of impeccable integrity who's devoted his life to the care of the weak and vulnerable!

Blenkinsop boomed at the initial meeting in Tarpow's room, and then added somewhat meekly,

- It's not true, is it?

202

Tarpow made a show of sighing, adjusting his tie, and then straightening the folder in front of him.

- It seems that the Professor may have been, shall we say, a little over zealous in his prescribing of certain anti-depressants and anti-psychotics.

There was a palpable silence in the gloomy room. Tarpow's office suddenly felt too big to them all, the sky outside too dark and overcast. Instinctively Moking glided across and flicked at a switch, which blared a sudden fanfare of fluorescence into the room. Now it seemed too stark, too bright.

- When you say 'over-zealous'...

Blenkinsop left his remark to dangle in the air, hovering over a chasm of horrific implications. Tarpow cleared his throat before continuing.

- I'm sure there was nothing intentional in the Professor's actions. I've looked over our Pharmaceutical Financing Strategy, which I think may have led to certain...problems.

Blenkinsop looked puzzled.

- Can you be more specific?
- Yes, but I think I'll hand over to Mr. Ellis at this point to explain, since these are essentially medical matters.

But Blenkinsop was still puzzled.

- I thought you said 'Financial Strategy'?

Tarpow laughed.

- Yes, well, Medicine, Finance, same thing really these days.

They all laughed at that. Ellis looked pleased to be called into the limelight. He adjusted his tie importantly.

- In the light of our independent status as a prototype flagship Foundation Trust, we entered upon certain... arrangements

203

with a commercial company, Toxico Pharmaceuticals. The more we prescribed their anti-psychotic drugs, the more they contributed to the Needleham Pharmaceutical Fund. This, as you may recall is an independent fund.

Blenkinsop, Chair of the Needleham Board, who had never heard of this Fund until now, still looked baffled.

- So a drug company paid money into an independent account, and what happened to the money then?

This time it was Tarpow's turn to look puzzled.

- Well it was paid into our main account of course.

- I thought you said the account was independent?

- It's quite independent. It's at a different bank from our main account and everything. Of course our admin team administers it, for convenience. It's accepted practice in industry. I forget the exact terminology for it.

- Laundering?

- Yes, that's it.

- Good lord!

Ellis continued.

- We were then approached by a second company, Venimo Pharmaceuticals, who market anti-depressant drugs, and entered upon a similar arrangement with them. The more we prescribed their drugs, the more the Trust benefitted. Unfortunately this led to patients being prescribed both sets of drugs.

Blenkinsop looked as if it was beginning to dawn.

- So you mean some patients were given both anti-psychotics and anti-depressants?

- Well, all the patients actually. It became hospital policy. The problem really came when we entered an arrangement with a firm that made minor tranquillisers, Abetter Pharmaceuticals. Some of the patients really had bad side effects from taking the three sets of drugs.

- Good lord, but isn't that terribly bad practice?

Blenkinsop seemed shocked, and Nurse Manager Moking felt she should stand up for the doctor.

- Major mental illness needs anti-psychotic medication, but of course this has the effect of flattening the patient...

- You mean flattening the mood of the patient?

- Flattening both the patient and the mood of the patient. It can, in effect, be very depressing, hence the need for an anti-depressant. And the whole thing, being ill and having to take all those drugs, can make people very anxious, hence the need for minor tranquillisers.

- But what effect does this have on patients?

- Well generally it's very helpful, with only a few serious contraindications.

- Serious contraindications?

- Yes. In common parlance... deaths.

For a while all that could be heard was electricity, charge becoming light, flowing innocently along its predestined path, humming to itself lightly as it did so, as though happy not to have to deal with the complexities of the human world.

*

The streets were deserted, and Luke walked on and on, taking any turn at random until he was irredeemably lost. He passed through a council estate that he had barely known existed. Big old brick houses with scrawny gardens rose on both sides of the street, flecked with litter, here and there the ruins of old toys and abandoned machinery. Paths disappeared into dark archways between some of the houses, and he could sometimes see the brighter rectangle of a TV screen, but no-one was walking on these streets. There wasn't even the company of an occasional car. He walked on and on, leaving everything behind, until he could no longer remember where he had come from, or what this place was. He crossed a major road and entered streets where the houses were bigger, and sheltered behind well-kept hedges of privet and beech. There were real trees here, not just the overgrown elders and privet of the council estate, and they stood silent and solid. Somewhere away to his right there was the sound of a vehicle, but it quickly passed.

He passed the last of the houses and came to an open field, with a disused building at one end. The place looked familiar. He climbed over the gate with some effort and realised how tired he had become. There were woods on the far side of the field, and the Pennine hills rolled out beyond and above them. He started to walk towards the little building, and noticed the top of a tower, visible through the trees. He understood suddenly where he was, and the voice of the Countess came into his head. "Like paupers. No headstones, no names." But this field had changed since he had been here in the Spring with the Countess. One whole corner of it was fenced off with the words ABETTER GAS AND OIL on each section of the fence. Rising behind this was one of the thin tower-like structures he had seen in the square in the old hospital grounds. There was the sound of machinery, a constant low grade droning, but he could see no people or sign of human activity. Everything was masked by the shielding fence.

He had walked in a long semi-circle from the pub to the edge of Needleham Hospital. He looked down at the tufted grass and trod more gingerly on the old graveyard. When he reached the building he saw it was a little stone chapel, in a state of disrepair. It had slim, arched windows, empty now of glass, and the old slate roof was mossed, with gaps where slates were missing and wooden beams showed. Old rose bushes gone wild trailed their barbs as if in protection. He stepped through them and pushed open the heavy door.

Inside it was dark and dry, smelling of earth. A dim light filtered through the doorway and windows. There were no traffic noises, but there was a kind of whispering in his ears, and nothing he could immediately see that would make such an unearthly yet strangely human noise. At first he thought the sound must be coming from the Abetter workings across the field. He placed his ear next to the stone floor of the chapel and the volume seemed to be turned up, like a kettle beginning to sing. Occasionally he could almost hear words, but never quite make them out. The very ground was seething with some enormous subterranean debate. When he sat up the sound became distant. When he put his head back to the stone there was the sound of human voices. He felt chilled to the stomach and reached inside his backpack for the familiar shape of Bagpuss. The pink stuffed cat remained inscrutable, but words formed in Luke's mind.

- What do you expect in a graveyard, particularly the graveyard of an old lunatic asylum? I don't think any harm is intended towards you. It's just, well, it seems the spirits are rather disturbed at the moment.

A light mist had formed in the room, and it intensified in front of the place where Luke was sitting up. The patch in front of him became slightly translucent and began to take on a human shape.

- Uh oh. What the fuck is that?

- I don't know.

- Bagpuss, you're supposed to know about these things.

- So sue me.

The figure in front of them reared up to its full height, which was actually not very tall for a human form. It was an old, rather raddled man. His body was shining with some kind of phosphorescence, but Luke could make out that he was wearing the old hospital uniform of a shapeless stripey dressing gown, belted loosely at the front.

- Luke, don't be afraid. You will come to no harm.

Luke struggled to find his voice.

- You look like Marley's ghost.

- Indeed. You are very astute. I do look like Marley's ghost, because that is the only form of my being which you can make any sense of. If I were to appear in a different guise it would be unfamiliar, or strange, and I could not communicate with you in the manner I wish to.

- So I created you? You are just a fig leaf of my imagination?

- No, I exist independently of you. But it is a sad fact about humans that they can mostly only experience what is already familiar to them. Once confronted with something totally unfamiliar they tend to blank it out completely. So if we want to communicate from our side we have to do it in such a way that it is recognisable in some way. And apparently this is what people like you expect to see in a graveyard. Personally I think it's rather, how do you express it? Naff.

- So I've simply created your form?

- Yes, but can we agree to drop the chains?

Luke noticed that the apparition was indeed weighted down with thick steel chains.

- Of course.

He said considerately, and the chains fell away.

- That's amazing. Obviously I am in the middle of a psychotic episode!

- Sadly, yes. However before that goes any further I have something to show you. Gather your things.

Luke turned to put Bagpuss back in his rucksack, but the timid creature had already apparently climbed back in. He scooped up the small rucksack just in time to feel his feet leaving the ground, and then he had the sensation he was whirling through the air. The stars seemed to blur, and the mixture of orange and blue light intensified, and became almost solid. A high-pitched hissing accompanied this change like bacon frying on a high gas inside Luke's head. As the white noise grew deafening, the scene in front of him faded, until his vision was like looking point blank at a TV set off station. When he became conscious again he was standing beside the old apparition, and both were looking down into the garden of a suburban house. It was newer than the ones he had seen earlier on the council estate, but smaller, with steel grilles over the small white windows.

- What is going on?

- Just watch.

As they looked down, a team of uniformed men ran into the garden, one carrying something Luke at first took to be a gun. On closer inspection he could see it was a blunt cylinder of solid steel around three inches in diameter, with a thick shoulder strap hanging. Across the shoulders of the navy blue overalls the men wore were golden letters, proclaiming:

HEALTHCARE
SOLUTIONS
Care that won't go away!

The men positioned themselves on either side of the door and the one with the steel tube stepped forward. Two blows at the lock and the door splintered and burst open. The other men disappeared inside, to re-emerge moments later frogmarching a dishevelled man who remonstrated with them angrily.

- Are these police officers?

- Dear me, no. These are community nurses. What we are looking at is one possible world. We are looking at the mental health system of the future, as it will be, unless something can be done in the present about it.

As they watched the man was bundled into a people carrier that carried on its side the motto:

Finally!
HEALTHCARE
SOLUTIONS

The car drove away at speed, and Luke turned puzzled to the apparition.

- So, let me get this straight. You are the ghost of the mental health system future.

The spirit looked uncomfortable.

- Well, had you studied quantum physics and been a little brighter I could have given you a more accurate explanation, but in terms that are acceptable to you given your cultural and educational expectations, yes, in fact I am the ghost of the mental health system future. Come, there is more.

The scene below them shifted to a brightly lit corridor.

- God, that looks like Needleham, but it can't be still open surely? What year is this?

- The concept of a 'year' doesn't really have a meaning in this realm. It is simply 'a possible future.'

It was Passchendaele Ward but slightly different to how Luke remembered it. The Staff Office had expanded and was now where the television room had been. The outer walls of the Office were of smoked one-way glass, so the effect was of a dark spacecraft that had landed on the ward and settled among the white walls. A door opened and a nurse came out. Luke saw that it looked like Nurse O'Price, but an older, more corpulent version. Behind him Luke could see a large room of desks and armchairs and several people, presumably nurses in relaxed mode, in front of a bank of TV screens. The nurse waddled down the corridor and the watchers could see that on each side were small cells with a glass panel. In each room a figure lay sleeping on a bed. The corridor seemed to be longer than he could remember, and at the end the nurse turned abruptly to the right and disappeared from their sight.

- God, it's so quiet. This must be the middle of the night.

- No, if it were the middle of the night there would be no nurses there at all. It is the afternoon, but the new drugs are such that they can predict to within five minutes how long patients will sleep, so they set them all to sleep for the whole afternoon. They aren't supposed to do that, but it makes for a quiet time for the nurses.

Through the door Luke could see that one of the nurses was reading War and Peace, and another was writing furiously.

- A dissertation for his Aromatherapy MA.

The ghost said, anticipating his thoughts.

As they watched, Nurse O'Price came back round the corner, this time followed by two of the uniformed community nurses, who carried between them the slumping figure they had earlier seen being taken from the house. O'Price opened the door to one of the cells and the nurses deposited him inside. As the cell door slammed behind them one produced a little electronic screen from the wide pocket on the breast of his navy jacket, and gave it to O'Price, who signed it with a flourish. Then the corridor was quiet again.

- So this is how it's all going to turn out.

- In one version of the future, yes. Not a very nice version, it has to be said. Particularly when the side effects kick in.

- The side-effects?

- Well, in this world there was a new wonder drug, which had such reliable effects it was only trialled on people for up to six months, before being introduced. Sadly it's lethal for anyone who takes it for more than that time, and unfortunately the effects lie dormant for a further year, before death occurs.

- Wait, go slower, I don't understand.

- Well, almost the whole psychiatric population is by this time on this drug, but the effects only start to show up after 18 months.

- And anyone who's taken them for six months has no chance of survival.

- That's right, so there was suddenly a huge wave of deaths in the late 2020s. Almost the entire population of mad people taken out. Of course some people thought it was intentional and a good thing all round, but I couldn't possibly comment on that.

- God, this is terrible.

- Hold on, it's not the whole story. There's more.

The scene below them changed again and they were looking into a crowded room. It looked like the interior of one of the crumbling houses in the part of Myllroyd where James lived. A woman was sobbing into a towel and two others were around her, trying to comfort her. A man with long hair sat on a worn couch, staring suspiciously around. Two other women were sitting by the window, one talking and laughing while the other listened. In a small kitchen a man was washing up dishes, while in the main room a man in a denim jacket was talking on the telephone. The watchers could hear his voice above the other noises in the room.

- We're going to have to make a move today. I think they're on to us. Is the other house ready?

There was a pause while he listened.

- Yes, I heard they got Joe and closed down Schoolbroke Avenue. You can't blame them for grassing. They give them extra leave and everything.

He put the phone down and sat staring at it for a moment with a worried expression before shuffling together papers and stepping into the kitchen to talk to the man there. Luke whispered to the ghost.

- What are we looking at?

- This is a 'safe' house. Since the introduction of Community Treatment Orders in 2007 a growing number of people became 'service avoiders', and a system of alternative treatments has grown up. There are houses like these in every town in the country, which the authorities obviously don't like. People try and look after each other as best they can, but they generally get found and mostly people are then locked up, and the people who set them up get prosecuted, if they can't prove they are mad.

- And is this how it has to be.

- No, the future can be changed. This is only how it will be if things continue as they are going now.

These last words were spoken against a growing background of white noise. Luke felt himself growing dizzy and had the sensation of his hands and face becoming huge. Then he was waking. The chapel walls were around him like a prison. He sat up. His body felt light and he heard someone laughing in a slightly hysterical way. He realised with a start it was himself. He had had a revelation! He had been granted a vision of the future and it was his duty to transmit this to other people! He wanted to tell James, Anthea and Maria. He wanted to see Susan. He felt at last he had the knowledge and arguments to convince them all, but especially her. He would go to the wedding after all. He would go to her and tell her what he'd seen, and she would understand what he'd been banging on about for these last eight months and try to help him. He stood, picked up his rucksack, and strode resolutely out of the chapel.

*

Although it was mid-afternoon, James had taken a long time to come to the door in his silk dressing-gown. After settling Maria and Anthea in the sparse elegance of his front room he disappeared into the kitchen and made coffee in a large caffetiere. Now he sat by the open window sipping and smoking, and showing no inclination to get business moving. The meeting was Anthea's idea. Luke was banned from contact with Maria, but Anthea had visited him at home and been taken aback by his unkempt appearance, and by the neglected messiness of the old house.

- What is this music?

James exhaled stale smoke through the sash window before answering. Anthea had insisted on this ridiculous arrangement if he wanted to smoke, which he did, since it was his flat after all. Gusts of yearning contrapuntal harmonies weaved around them.

- Ave, Dulcissima, Maria!

Maria looked at him suspiciously.

- Gesualdo. An Italian nobleman writing sacred music for Easter four hundred years ago. 'O all ye that pass by, behold and see if there be any sorrow like unto mine.'

She didn't look impressed and was happy to say so.

- Religious music is so pious.

James reflected sadly, not for the first time, that madness acquaints a man with strange bedfellows. Maria the didactical materialist for instance, suspicious of culture in all its forms. A trot with an imaginationectomy. Even now she was eyeing intensely the small green Victorian vase on his mantelpiece, a family heirloom from his mad granny, and probably disapproving of such an example of his bourgeois upbringing.

- Not so pious as all that. When he caught his wife in bed with a rival nobleman *in flagrante delicto* he murdered them both – brutally!

He smiled at her. In truth he felt a little sorry for Maria, thrown out by the other barmy revolutionaries for being just a little too mad. The loony left indeed. She had told him the sad story of that night during the miner's strike and her revolutionary fervour. She had once been a member of the Huddersfield Polytechnic branch of the Revolutionary Socialist Alliance. In the overheated atmosphere of 1985, as the Miner's strike dissolved, she became convinced that Britain was on the verge of revolutionary insurrection. Her comrades enjoyed arguing, but after several hours of it they really just wanted to have a pint, and when Maria was still going on at dawn they had no option, they felt, but to deliver her into the hands of the mental health system. She had never forgiven them. A sobering tale.

Anthea watched this interchange with a worried look on her face from the battered armchair positioned between the two large speakers, the only comfortable one in the room. It was James' music chair, and he would have claimed it but for the smoking stand-off.

- I think we should get on.

James leaned over and lifted the arm from the vinyl disc, carefully placing it back on its stand.

- I didn't mean to stop the music altogether.

James raised a forefinger.

- One must either listen to music, or not listen to it. There is no halfway. Gesualdo is not wallpaper!

He had a stern look on his face, which dissolved into a quick smile as he caught her eye and winked at her. That was the trouble with James, Anthea reflected. You never knew where you were with him. Half the time he made stuff up, the trouble is you never knew which half. It was horrible though, the way the gay scene had rejected him, once they knew he'd been in a mental hospital. It was the only time she'd seen that sophisticated exterior crack, the night he had cried on her sofa, telling her about being recognised by a nurse at the gay bar in Leeds, and from then being treated like a pariah on the scene.

Maria didn't really know what to say, but felt a start had to be made.

- Anthea and I are both worried about Luke.

James shifted himself in his seat and frowned.

- I share your concerns. He is acting strangely since the debacle of the Strategic Plan. I went to see him the other day and he seemed very paranoid.

- Exactly! He was like that when I went to see him. He insisted we went into the garden – he thought the house might be bugged. And today he doesn't seem to be there at all.

Anthea remembered Luke's haunted face. There was a pause as they all considered Luke and each other. In their own way they had all made a virtue of their altered states. They had learned to live with their diagnosis and to brazen it out in the 'normal' world. But it was a guerrilla war, a making the best of. The identity of being mad was not something they would wish on anyone. James sat back and blew out a big cloud of smoke that rushed towards the open window. His voice was suddenly enormous in the silence.

- He looks thin.

They looked at each other.

- Even thinner than usual.
- Strained.
- Like a man with a lot on his mind.
- Like a man on the verge of...
- James was the one to say it.
- Cracking up.

Maria couldn't help groaning, but whether from the thought of Luke's mental state or from James' use of such an inaccurate, populist term was uncertain, even to her.

- Do you think we've driven him...?
- Bonkers?

Maria screwed up her face.

- Look, I just hate this language! Can't we discuss this seriously!

James and Anthea exchanged a look. James gave a little snort of amusement, and Anthea looked as if she was trying to stifle a smile. This was the way they always were with her, Maria reflected – mocking, undermining, always ready to take the piss. How could they all work together if they didn't respect her? Now Anthea was making an effort to be serious.

- It is true, we should try and avoid using... inappropriate language.

She was looking at James with that irritating amused look on her face. Anthea was too soft with James, Maria thought. She was basically a hippy trying to avoid conflict, which after all is a necessary part of life. Thesis, antithesis, synthesis. Still, you couldn't help but feel sorry about the way the alternative types had rejected Anthea when she'd been in hospital, as if they weren't completely weird themselves with their potions and Tarot cards and angelic crystal healing runes. Not one went to see her. How could her peers just turn on her like that? Now James was clearing his throat to speak in that portentous way he had when he was going to say something ridiculous.

- Do we even know why he's been suspended?

Anthea responded.

- He told me he'd gathered evidence about the Professor. You know that rumour that goes around the wards? Luke said that he'd found proof, and that he could show that a lot of the deaths at Needleham were... not accidental.

Maria was incredulous.

- Why the hell did he have to do it all on his own? Why didn't he talk to us about it? Surely, he made copies of his evidence? He didn't just take the whole lot and hand it over to Turbot, did he?

- You know how naïve he is. It wouldn't occur to him that they all depend on each other for their jobs.

There was a silence in the room as they all contemplated the monolithic monster that was the mental health system - many headed, and with the ability to regenerate any head that was cut off, or turn opponents to stone with its neuroleptic potions. Anthea broke the silence.

- I still have my old key to the advocacy office. Luke says the police took everything from his home, but perhaps he left some evidence there? We could go in and have a look. They can't just cover everything up!

There was another silence while they all considered her last sentence. It was Maria who formulated the thought they all arrived individually.

- It seems they can do whatever the bloody hell they like.

*

The golf club was a mansion that stood close to the bank of the river. Luke reached it in the late afternoon after an eventful train journey during which he somehow lost the jacket containing his wallet with his money and debit card. Consequently he had to walk the three miles from Burton station along the road that followed the river, and at one point had taken a short cut across what seemed to be open meadow, but turned out to be treacherous swampland. He had sunk on occasion up to his knees in the soggy turf, and had to retrace his steps several times, but eventually he forded a stream. He found the golf club on the other side of the manicured fairways of the course, on a long curve of the river bank.

The building had the worn and aristocratic look that buildings get when they are listed and don't need to bother any more. It had timbered beams dividing the old stone of its walls, and part of the roof was thatched. Little brightly painted rowing boats and canoes were moored at an immaculate quayside, beyond which the river ran swiftly, swollen by a day of rain in the nearby Derbyshire hills. The first person he saw as he approached the house was a young woman with a gardenia in her hair, wearing a fairy frock, and sitting on a stone wall overlooking the river. She appeared to be muttering to herself, but as he got very close he realised she was singing in a very gentle voice. She had long brown hair tied behind her head, a burned down cigarette in one hand and a glass of red wine swaying precariously in the other. As he came near her she started.

- Wow, who are you? You look like a pirate!

There was an uncomfortable pause as they regarded each other and the sounds of a frantic fiddle band came out through the open window, across a stretch of lawn. Inside he could see people in lines joining and parting, swinging and parading.

- I am kind of looking for treasure, in a way.

- Where's your jacket.

- I left it on the train. I was having a bit of an argument at the time, with the ticket collector, and… anyway I got off in a bit of a hurry.

The young woman took a hefty swig at the wine and a long draw on the cigarette. She looked at him, or rather slightly to the left and a little in front of him.

- What were you arguing about?

- I didn't like his attitude.

She laughed in a surprisingly loud high raucous way, like an amplified woodpecker. When the sudden fit had passed she looked at him seriously.

- So who are you, pirate man?

- I'm Susan's…

Words suddenly failed him. What was he exactly? Anyway, apparently, he didn't need to add anything else, since the young woman nodded in an understanding way and squinted down into her glass.

- Ah Susan's. Sister Susie. Sweet Sis Sue.

She suddenly looked troubled.

- And you're her other brother?

- No, no, I'm not her brother.

Her face lightened as if she suddenly understood.

- You're her chap! She said you'd backed out. O, you're Susan's mysterious chap! Well that's amazing! I'm pleased to meet you. I'm June's best friend, you see! Your bird's brother is marrying my best pal! Bloody funny family if you ask me. A bit repressed, don't you think?

Luke looked in through the window of the building.

- Well I don't feel comfortable with that kind of jargon. It's not very accurate you know. It's….doctor speak.
- Doctor speak? Well this is a doctor's wedding – June and Harry are doctors, and so are most of the people at this wedding.

They both looked towards the building. Through a wall of French windows they could see a couple making their separate ways down two ragged lines of men and women, being swung round by each person they met to the frenzied repetition of a wild slip jig.

- What do you call a room full of doctors?

Luke considered this.

- I don't know. A doctrinairiat?

She laughed out of proportion to the humour of the comment, he felt. The band finished the number on a great flourish, and the dancers, no longer borne by the vibrant music seemed to have trouble standing. One man had passed out completely and was being attended to by a laughing group. Several others seemed to be struggling to walk.

- A bloody bore anyway. Actually there's a few social workers like Susan. Terrible isn't it? What they are like? I'm a doctor. That's how I know June. We trained together.
- You're a doctor?
- I am indeed. Fully qualified. Paediatrics.
- You just don't seem old enough.

221

- It's true I'm a doc. It's changed my life so much being a doctor. I used to get pissed out of my mind, but now I just get absolutely arseholed.

It was clearly a line she'd used before, and she laughed the charming, unbridled laugh of a young horse let loose in the paddock, the glass swaying in her hand, and wine slopping over the rim. She looked cross-eyed as if trying to look at something just beyond the end of her nose, and lapsed suddenly into a quiet contemplation of the end of her cigarette.

He left her there and went in through a solid wooden gate that opened onto a path of stone flags leading to the open door of the barroom. The caller was trying to muster enough people for another dance, and people were milling towards the centre of the floor, or hastily away from it, but he saw Susan near the crowded bar. She was leaning into a dinner jacket whose owner, he noticed, had his hand on her hip. Luke had been carrying an image of their meeting all day. Susan would be pleased to see him and they would embrace tenderly. In the event as he neared her she looked shocked and burst into tears. The dinner jacket had recoiled in response as Luke approached and now Luke saw that its owner was a tall, well-built, square jawed fellow with an immaculate brushed back hair-style who was glaring down at him.

- Susan, what's wrong?

Susan wept copiously. She took the pure white handkerchief from the hairy paw of the dinner jacket and wiped her eyes.

- Look at you...

Was all she managed to say.

- I had trouble getting here. I lost my jacket. I had an argument. I had to walk through a bit of a marsh. But I came!

This speech seemed to upset Susan even more.

- Where are your shoes?

222

He looked down and remembered how the one had been sucked into the marshy ground, and how the other one didn't seem much good after that.

- I suppose my feet are a bit muddy. I'll go and wash them in a minute. But the point is I wanted to tell you the most amazing thing.

The dinner jacket had been joined by a second one, an uglier, squatter version of the first, who had a deep, cultured and rather hostile voice.

- Look, I don't want to be rude, but this is a wedding reception, and well to be frank, you're a mess. I think you ought to go and get cleaned up.

- Yes, I will in a minute, but look Susan, do you remember once we were talking about your meditation class and I was being all sceptical and saying I thought Western people getting into Eastern stuff was avoidance because well, Christianity isn't sexy anymore? Anyway I was in the graveyard and had this amazing kind of vision.....why are you so upset?

Susan had continued to weep and at the word vision gave a small howl and sobbed even more violently. The two dinner jackets had been joined by a suit and he too was dark haired, big jawed, with the heavy shadow of one whose testosterone will not be denied.

- I think you're upsetting the lady.

He came over to stand close to and half in front of Luke, as if to block him should he make a sudden move towards Susan. The faces of the three men suddenly seemed to Luke like wolves, narrow eyed, focussed and still.

- Do you have an invitation?

- Well I did have, but I said I wasn't coming because well, I don't know June and Dave, and, well, I just didn't fancy it really, and anyway, who the hell are you, a bloody bouncer or something?

The squat dinner jacket stiffened and drew himself up.

- I'm Dave.

- O, ok, sorry, Dave. Ok, yes, well, you know I would have accepted the invitation, but it was....difficult, you know.....

The young doctor mentally summarised his knowledge of the situation, ordered it, analysed it according to his years of study... and produced an erroneous diagnosis.

- Are you a ... client?

The charged word crackled out into the room and there was a sudden stillness. A shock wave travelled out from the small group, so that even at the far end of the room where most of the earlier dancers had gone to sit down and rest, there was a discernible pause. Luke heard the last word repeated in different registers and tones, as if by a flock of chuntering game birds. The Dance Caller who had been remonstrating with the crowd to get back on the dance floor heard the word and faltered, turning toward the group uncertainly. He was tall, with long red hair and a full beard, and with his long arms reminded Luke of an orangutan. The band who had been preparing to play again looked on with interest. The pause lasted the briefest of seconds before the closest of the suits gripped Luke's arm. It was a grip that had spent a lot of hours preparing itself in the gym for just such a moment. Luke tried to laugh but the light-hearted effect he aimed for aged considerably on the way from his brain, creaking out drily into the gaping desert of the room.

- I'm not a client! Susan, please! I'm not a client, I'm......

But Susan was still crying, and he didn't quite know what he was. It was the fairy girl who had followed him in who spoke first.

- He's a pirate!

And she lifted her face with its elongated muzzle and laughed a long, howling laugh. Her teeth showed long and yellow. The pack of suits and the dinner jacket moved in as one and Luke felt himself pulled down and overpowered.

*

Maria was anxious, in a city where some terrible impending disaster had emptied the streets and cast a threatening shadow into every alley and shopping precinct. It was like Leeds in November, but a Leeds gone feral, even more dissipated and tawdry than usual. She was walking past shop windows with improbable goods – old bicycles and grandfather clocks, piles of polystyrene packaging and picture frames. She didn't know which direction the danger was going to come from, but it was imminent and would be lethal. She approached one window, which had a huge stuffed owl in the centre, and as she got close enough to look into its enraged eye, the air erupted with the sound of an alarm.

It was too early for the phone to ring. She took a moment to register and place the sound. It took a further few seconds to drop her feet onto the bright red rug and locate the phone on the floor under a pile of discarded clothing. Anthea's voice didn't give her the chance to speak. She listened for several minutes before she managed to get a word in edgeways.

- Hang on, hang on, ok, don't panic. So Margaret says that Luke was taken into Passchendaele during the night. What else did she say?

- He came in last night, in the middle of the night. She rang me on the patient's phone. She heard people shouting and she saw it was Luke. He was really drugged up. We've got to do something.

Maria listened to Anthea's repetitive version of the phone call. There wasn't much meat on the bone of it. Margaret was sure it was Luke, drugged enough so that he could still just about walk and protest a little, but once they had him there several nurses disappeared into a side-room with him and he was quiet after that.

A deep calmness came over Maria. Her moment had come as she knew it would. Her breath slowed and deepened. Her mind stepped off the train of exile, waved to the gathered crowds, who cheered, and welcomed the return of the charismatic leader.

- What time is it? 6 o'clock. Ok, look they won't let us in until ten. Tell James to meet us at nine at the Town Hall bus stop.

When she'd put the receiver down Maria sat for a moment at the edge of the bed. A strange feeling of elation filled her. Not that she didn't feel for Luke or sympathise with his situation. It was just that the forces of evil were so good at public relations these days it was hard to lay a glove on them, but every so often they played a false move and you had your chance.

*

Jonathan O'Price could not stop Anthea and James from visiting Luke, but Maria was a different matter.

- I'm sorry, love, but you know the score. You're suspended from work, so you shouldn't even be on the premises.

The nurse's office was his lair, the natural habitat where he was top predator. It was the one place in the world where his word felt like law. He adjusted a paper clip on the desk and brushed a piece of cotton from his jeans. Anthea tried to intervene on her friend's behalf.

- Come on, we're his friends. We just want to see him for a few minutes. What's the problem?

- No problem for you Anthea, and no problem for you chief (indicating James), but Maria is suspended, not supposed to be here at all. End of.

Maria went through the motions of pleading and O'Price of giving her plea full consideration but they all knew he had the upper hand and had never been known to yield it.

Two young nurses led Maria back to the ward door. Anthea and James went the other way towards the side room. O'Price, alone again, turned back to his familiar office with the satisfaction of a job well done. He had Luke's bag on his desk and out of curiosity he opened the flap and found inside what looked like a soft toy. It couldn't be! He pulled it out. It was. Bloody Bagpuss. What the hell was the advocate doing with Bagpuss in his bag? He gazed at it for a moment. He hadn't seen or thought of Bagpuss for twenty years.

"Even Bagpuss himself, once he was asleep, was just an old, saggy cloth cat, baggy, and a bit loose at the seams, but Emily loved him."

And Jonathan O'Price had loved Emily. However horrible it was, there was always Emily, so kind to all the broken toys; Emily, with her magic world where violins could play themselves.

He remembered the relentless teasing once his older brothers had figured out his Bagpuss fascination. He shook himself sternly, grabbed the forlorn figure of Bagpuss from the bag, and threw it with considerable force onto a shelf above the desk. (How fucking childish can you get?) He sat down in front of his word processor to finish his coffee and get on with some paper work, slightly jangled by the sudden appearance of his favourite childhood TV character.

The pink woollen figure hit the wall at the back of the shelf and bounced. It teetered on the edge of the shelf to which it had been thrown for the briefest of seconds, and then as if making a decision, fell, hitting the hot cup of coffee, which tipped over the desk and into the lap of the nurse who leapt, scalded and screaming.

*

227

Luke was sleeping heavily. He was lying on his back with a troubled expression on his face when Anthea and James walked in.

- What was that scream?

James shrugged.

- You get used to that on Passchendaele.

- It sounded like O'Price.

- Just wishful thinking my dear.

Their attention was fixed on the unconscious form on the bed.

- He doesn't look very peaceful, does he?

Anthea pulled a plastic chair closer to the bed and the figure there roused and stared at her. Luke tried to raise himself, but the effort was too much, and his head fell back against the pillow.

- Anthea.

A dry whisper, as if a leaf from last year had blown in and was crossing the plastic tiles of the floor in a draught. After a pause Luke's lips began to move again. The draught started up, the leaf began to move. Anthea tried to decipher the sounds but they meant nothing. She could only make out the word "see". He opened his eyes and with difficulty trained them on Anthea.

- What did you see, Luke?

He looked as if he were thinking hard.

- Saw the ghost!

Anthea stared at him and suppressed a shudder. Memories from the previous Winter came back to her, of her sense of the ailing hospital, a figure she had sometimes seen or sensed, and the words he had seemed to whisper to her. Memories she had had to put aside to rejoin the world of normality. She had stopped talking about them. People either became irritated with her or humoured her. Luke continued.

-   You said the hospital had spoken to you?

Anthea considered this.

-   Needleham?
-   And the future!
-   The future?
-   How things will be. The calamity. It's going to be awful. So
    much dying.

His eyes filled up with tears and he tried to raise himself, but the effort was too much and he collapsed back. James stepped to the bedside and spoke.

-   Luke, did you make copies of your research? Do you have
    the evidence about the Professor?

Luke turned towards the new voice, but his eyes were already going distant with concentration, before the eyelids fluttered, and he lapsed back towards sleep. His two friends looked at each other. James broke the silence, drily.

-   It will be a while before we get any sense out of him. God, it
    annoys me when they drug people up like this. What's the
    point?

Anthea considered this.

-   Well, it sure shuts them up.

James sighed his agreement. He looked round the clinical room.

-   O, that's not good.

Anthea turned to see where he was looking and saw the sign on the end of the bed that showed Luke to be a patient of Professor Drogham.

*

Maria didn't leave Needleham Hospital immediately. Instead, at the end of the drive, she slipped into the dense undergrowth that marked the hospital's boundary and followed a line of trees round to the old playing field, which she crossed with a self-consciously confident gait. She found a passage between old disused wards and went through the square where the Abetter Gas & Oil machinery was in full grinding song behind the high fence that blocked out any view of its activities, entering the hospital through a side door without attracting attention. Jutland corridor was deserted as always, and she quickly used Anthea's old key to gain access to the advocacy office. Once the door was closed and locked no-one was likely to bother her while she worked out what to do next.

The first thing she noticed was that the word processor that had stood on the desk had gone. She sat down in the uncomfortable plastic chair in front of Luke's old desk. The office had a forlorn, dusty look. The drawers of the desk were empty but for leaflets about the advocacy service, a stapler, some scrap paper. The drawers of the filing cabinet were open, even the one marked confidential, normally containing patients' records. This was meant to be kept locked, and she looked more closely. The drawer had been forced. Inside was a row of sliding green pockets, each one with a person's name in a little plastic name tag at the top, containing details, she assumed, of frustrating phone calls, tedious copies of nurses', social worker's and doctors' reports, but nothing that suggested anything so uncomfortable for the hospital that they would suspend its advocate.

She sat back in the chair and looked around for clues. She noticed a jagged crack had appeared on the wall behind the desk. It was very fresh. Dust from the plaster had formed piles on the desk and covered it with a gritty film. The crack was an inch wide in places, running diagonally down like a representation of a lightning strike. It was as if one half of the wall had simply slipped to one side. At one place she could put her fingers into it. She had an urge to pick up the phone and report it to the maintenance people, but she wasn't supposed to be there. She reflected that Needleham was hard on its advocates. Perhaps gravity was being equally hard on Needleham?

The crack disappeared below the desk, and Maria moved the desk forward and looked under it to see if the crack continued right to the floor. The action of moving the desk released a file that had fallen, or been placed between the desk and the wall. With routine inquisitiveness, she got on her hands and knees in the desk well, and picked it up. It appeared to be rough notes in Luke's handwriting, and as she read her breath came quicker.

NINE: September

Chlorpromazine was the original 'breakthrough' drug, which paved the way for the 'revolution' in treatment in the 1950s. If psychiatric drugs are a chemical cosh, then chlorpromazine is the original knuckleduster. As the one might tear the delicate human skin of a face, so the other hollows out deep voids in the consciousness of that most complex creation in the universe, the human brain.

'*A Meditation on Medication*', Hubert Johnson

(Unpublished manuscript)

*

A silver terrier pauses on the edge of a flat, square plain. It sniffs the air as if to take its bearings. It is a dog on a mission, a silver dog beloved in the annals of stories of dog and man. It will bring great gifts and riches to its owner. It will gallop at a given word, and where it lands, money will pour out of the very pavement, and its Master will be pleased. So it waits in silent reverie, transfixed and staring at the silver infinity of the future, down a world of squares.

A pair of plastic cubes raps and turumbulakatacks onto a hard surface, coming to rest on a board that shows obscure writing, numerals, instructions in an arcane language.

A designated priest interprets the signs with a triumphant 'yes, my son'. He is a hirsute, biblical man with a plastic badge and hard blue eyes.

A silver top hat held by a giant's pink and hairy-fingered paw hops past the terrier, coming to rest on a red edged square. The priest rubs his hands. 'Come on, pay up.'

Oblongs of thin paper are sifted from massed piles of blue, green and pink sheaves, formed into a new pile and handed over reluctantly.

The dog waits, barely able to contain himself.

On Passchendaele Ward, the room is washed in light from a soft, grey sky that looks as if the colour has been rinsed out of it. A small group of pilgrim souls huddles in a corner of the room, gathered round one of the flimsy dinner tables, on which various artefacts of ritual are scattered. Luke has flickered awake from a long period of otherness like a switched-on TV and wonders where he is. He examines his hands and does not recognise them.

- Come on Walker, it's your go.

Luke knows from the man's expression that the words refer to him but does not recognise the name, or know what is expected of him. The other man raises his eyes to the emulsioned ceiling.

- Give me strength!

He leans over and places the plastic cubes in Luke's hand.

- Shake them!

Luke stares at the square objects with strange markings in his hand. The other man sighs again, grips Luke's hand and tips the cubes onto the table. They fall with a clatter.

- There, you've got a five. Two and a three, see, five. Go on then!

Luke stares at the board.

- Move the bloody dog!

Luke looks down and there is indeed a silver dog, waiting to go. He picks it up tentatively between index and thumb. For several seconds he continues to stare at it, while the other people at the table, two in rainbow dressing gowns, and one in tee shirt and jeans stare at him. At last the angry looking one who has done all the talking so far takes his hand, complete with dog and taps it on the table five times, pulling the little silver dog out of Luke's fingers and placing it on the board with a sigh.

Such is therapeutic activity on Passchendaele Ward.

Luke had no memory of how he'd come there, or even that he had been there before. He wandered through the rooms of the hospital ward as if they and he were new created. The psychiatric medication had done its job so successfully that he didn't remember what a knife and fork were. Only the visits of his friends, reminding him who he had been, gradually prompted memories that after some days began to create a picture of a person who could conceivably be him. Yet the daily heavy ration of drugs weighed down his mind, or splintered it into uncomfortable fragments, so that thinking at all was an immense effort. The world intensified around unpredictable details.

One day while watching the news he had the realisation that it was mirroring his own state of mind, and that he was possibly even responsible for the terrible things he was seeing. The loss of his own father and mother, those twin towers of his existence, was being re-enacted in front of him. The graphic image repeated over and over on the screen from New York was the result of his own preoccupations. He cried over the implication of his responsibility for so many deaths, and the nurses responded by increasing the dose of Haloperidol.

So Luke's world shrank to a shuffle from the six-bedded dormitory to the day room with its oversized armchairs and dying potted plants, and the featureless corridor that linked them.

The other patients were a cross-section of exaggerated humanity. Some were equally disoriented as he was. Others were not noticeably different from the average inmate of Needleham town. Some were clearly in their own world, not wishing contact, smoking and occasionally talking to themselves or looking out with suspicious glances. Others were cheerfully gregarious and voluble, though not always in ways that made sense. One afternoon an old man with matted locks down to his shoulders and wild blue eyes peering from a face that was full-bearded and therefore mostly hidden sidled up to Luke's armchair in the day room and greeted him.

- You're the advocate aren't you?

Luke stared back and considered. The word had no immediate meaning for him. It was a foreign sounding series of syllables suggesting exotic foodstuff. The man's eyes darted round the room, and his hands were never still, playing with each other, reaching out to touch the formica surface of the coffee table, reaching into his pockets.

- I created this place.

Luke stared back at him. He looked back wildly.

- I know, it's incredible. It's all my doing, everything you see. My invention. I dreamed it up. I wrote it. Wish I'd never bothered. I wouldn't have done it if I knew what trouble it was going to cause me.

- What do you mean?

- I'm a writer you see, a historian actually. I thought I'd try my hand at writing a novel, but it all got out of hand. The characters got out of control. You, James, Maria and the rest. It was all going to be so simple, and now it's a complete mess, and now I don't know how to end it, or where it goes from here.

Luke stared at him.

- So if you made this place, what are you doing being a patient in it?

- Research.

- What are you researching?

The man looked around furtively.

- A book. *The History of Incarceration in West Yorkshire in the 21st century.*

Somewhere in the dark recesses of Luke's mind, off a small corridor, just the other side of the old Industrial Therapy Unit, a small bell clanged once.

- Hubert Johnson?

- That's me.

- I read your first book.

- This is a sequel.

- And is it different in the 21st century? Surely incarceration is better than it was?

Johnson gave a nasty laugh.

- You'd think so wouldn't you! No, it's just the same. The PR is better, that's all.

He tapped his nose.

- Keep it to yourself. I'm working undercover.

- I read your first book when I came to work at Needleham. Is it all true?

- I made the bit up about grouse beating. But apart from that - more or less.

Luke considered, which took a lot more effort than it should have done.

- What about the Off-Beats?

- Hubert Johnson gave a snort.

-   I've abandoned it. "The Pharma Bums", my great unfinished novel. Can't be doing with fiction. There's enough with what's actually happening without making stuff up.

-   But the group? James and Anthea and Maria decided to call the group The Off-Beats. What about them?

The older man looked at him pityingly.

-   You're on your own kiddo.

The door of the dayroom opened and a frowning young man in a new suit stepped into room. He saw Luke and moved towards him.

-   Mr. Walker? I'd like to ask you a few questions. Can you come with me?

A look of alarm crossed Hubert Johnson's face and he leapt up and moved towards the door, pushing past the newcomer at high speed.

*

Needleham Mental Health NHS Foundation Trust Your Mental Health Is Our Business				
Schizophrenia Diagnostic Tool				
	Yes	**No**	**Unclear**	**Comments**
Delusions (e.g thinks is Jesus or other historical figure)				
Hallucinations (Aural, visual, etc)				
Hearing Voices				
Disordered thoughts				
Feelings of persecution/ paranoia				
Scoring: (4/5 = Definite, 3 = Probable, 2 = Borderline, 1 = keep an eye on)				
Other comments:				

The young houseman was on his first placement and hid his terror under a calm front that he had learned from observation of his seniors. He fixed Luke with a smile that had a distant benign vacancy about it. He held a clipboard in front of him.

- Do you believe that you are Jesus Christ?

Luke felt exhausted. For a week now, each time he had woken up from the drugs he had been given, it was to be given another dose, so that deciphering the words in the question was an act that would require far more energy than he had. Outside, the sun was shining, and he wanted the man to put down his flipchart and for them to wander out together beyond the steel grid of the window panels, and find somewhere to fall asleep. When he spoke his words slurred together as if they'd been stirred and were dissolving.

- Insofar as he said "I am you and you are me and we are he and we are all together", then yes, I think I am!

The doctor looked him warily. He had trouble making out what Luke was saying. Luke added

- And you are too.

The doctor looked down at his checklist, honed on 120 years of academic study and in-depth research and analysis.

- That sounds like a 'yes' then. How about hallucinations? Have you heard or seen anything you would consider.....strange?

Luke thought about this for a moment.

- Everything is strange here.

He leaned forward and nipped the end of the plastic board, which announced 'Krapzil – Keep Them Safe!" on its underside. The doctor jumped, and pulled the board automatically towards himself, recovering to adjust his glasses.

- Yes, but I mean, do you see unusual things? Things that would be unusual…. to the rest of us?

Luke took his time to process this.

- We are stardust.

- Stardust?

- Golden

- Golden?

The doctor looked uncertain.

- We've got to get ourselves back to the garden.

The doctor's pen poised over the clipboard. Luke had a sudden thought.

- I did see a ghost!

- A ghost?

- The ghost of Needleham! What it will be like if we don't...

His voice trailed off in reverie. Lewis placed a tick against the 'yes' column for hallucinations.

- How about voices? Have you heard any voices that seem to emanate from outside yourself?

Something was stirring in Luke. The doctor wanted to understand, and he wanted to tell him! He had a sudden burst of energy.

- Yes! The ghost! Of Needleham future! It's true, I heard it, and saw him! And Bagpuss!

- Bagpuss?

- My guide! I heard the voice of my guide! There are voices everywhere! Your voice! I hear it loud and clear! Especially the things you don't say! Your need for stability and to be somebody and have a proper career and that. Maybe there's been a lot of pressure somewhere along the line to do that and get your act together, to study and give up the best years of your youth to fulfil some ambition, not your own but foisted upon you by ambitious parents and...

- Yes, alright.

The doctor sounded testy.

- But what about your voices?

- Well there are voices everywhere in this culture, noise, radios TVs, it's a constant babble. Then all the internal voices.

- Ah! Internal voices, tell me about them.

- Teachers and parents, every time you reach out to touch something, saying 'DON'T', or every time you want to move in any way beyond your boundaries, a voice says 'How dare you', and suchlike voices that we internalise, and come out when we least expect them.

- And you hear these voices in your head as it were?

- Where else?

- And many of them?

Luke considered.

- Call me legion?

The doctor wrote this comment carefully in the space reserved for 'other comments'.

- You don't hear any voices telling you to harm yourself or others?

- Drink this! Smoke that! Put some sugar into your body to stop you thinking about it all? Watch TV? Eat? Almost all the acceptable things in this consumerist culture you can legitimately do to yourself are harmful in some way.

The doctor put an uncertain tick in the 'Voices' column.

- If I ask you what it means to say 'A stitch in time saves nine', what would you think I meant by that?

- That you're displaying what the existentialists call 'bad faith', hiding behind the façade of "doctor" in order to escape from the terrible anxiety of being real and actually here right now with me, the only moment there will ever be. Would you like to dance?

The doctor placed an emphatic tick in the 'yes' column for 'disordered thoughts'.

- Thank you but not now.

- I think you're trying to work out if I'm a danger to myself, which is a bit rich coming from someone who works for Needleham Trust, who after all have been responsible for an unusually high number of deaths in the last twenty years, actually the highest in the country taken overall and mostly coming from the wards under the professorial unit. Don't you think that's strange?

The young doctor stared at Luke and then emphatically placed a tick in the 'feelings of persecution/paranoia' column.

- But don't take my word for it you can just see the evidence in my...

Luke's voice trailed off. There was something somewhere that was very wrong. But what was it? Whatever it was he had good evidence for it. But where was the evidence?

*

Later that afternoon Professor Drogham and his houseman discussed Luke.

- So you have him on level one, on constant supervision?

- We've had a nurse with him all the time today, even when he goes to the loo. And we've taken blood tests.

- And any further observations?

- Well, according to the nurse's report, he made various comments to the effect that he felt he was being watched, and that he resented it.

- He felt he was being watched? Ah! Paranoia!

- Yes, the nurse noted various references to 1984.

- Ah, regression!
- And to hidden electrical equipment in the walls.
- How fascinating!
- Yes, he kept talking about surveillance equipment. We actually captured some of his comments on film through the two-way mirror in the Quiet Room if you are interested to see.
- Typical schizophrenic paranoia! Deluded, a classical case! That's the clincher, clear as a bell!
- He did seem rather thought disordered, with a tendency to ramble off at a tangent.
- That's very common too. Knights Move Thinking!
- Nice move?
- No! Not 'nice', 'Knight'! K-N-I-G-H-T! As in chessboard knight.
- Sorry I'm not quite with you?
- The knight in chess. It moves in a different way to all the other pieces! The point is that the schizophrenic will suddenly veer off in a totally unpredictable direction, making it impossible to understand what they are talking about. Did they have any jackets left by the way?
- I beg your pardon?
- Jacket potatoes? In the canteen? I'm getting rather peckish.

*

James, Anthea and Maria convened at the Chi Café. It was in a sullen, Autumnal mood today. James distinctly heard the skittering of dry leaves blown in from the street caught in a draught behind him, but when he turned there was only an old man stirring a pint of tea with a metal spoon and such vigour that it produced the effect of a squall in a beech copse. He was sitting very erect and had a military look. The café was half full, and other people looked weary or vacant. James looked back at Anthea and Maria, both serious and intent on the matter at hand. The women's intensity gave him the sudden feeling he was in a Second World War spy film, and he immediately tried to stifle the thought. He knew the Chi Cafe's ability to amplify mood. Anthea was saying something.

- We can get Luke to appeal for a Mental Health Review Tribunal, and for a Manager's Hearing.

Maria snorted at this. Anthea glared at her.

- It's better than nothing. And we should keep going to see him every day. We know they're far less likely to take liberties when there are people around to witness.

James felt a chill. The two women had been talking in low voices, almost whispering. He looked at the other people in the cafe, a middle-aged couple, the elderly man pretending to read last night's evening paper, a man in a leather coat and his blonde Aryan female friend. They could all be spies. A sudden thought occurred to him.

- Did we ever hear back from London?

Maria had left telephone messages at the National Association for Users and Survivors, a campaigning organisation which they had hoped might give them some advice. After a phone call with a rather disbelieving worker, she had written to them explaining their concerns about what was going on. They had been hopeful that this national body, set up to encourage user involvement and protect the rights of patients, might take up their case.

- Nothing yet. I suppose they're pretty busy.

James snorted.

- Either that or in the pay of the big charities.

-   Don't be cynical. (James thought that was a bit rich coming from Maria.) Anyway they'll be coming to speak at that conference at Needleham in October, so we can try and talk to them then in person.

James was unconvinced.

-   I won't hold my breath. They won't want to rock the boat.

Anthea spoke.

-   I wish we had more idea what Luke gave to Turbot. The file you found of his rough notes show figures, which are pretty appalling, but they're hand-written, and we don't have the originals they were taken from. And they don't really give any evidence as to why the death rate in Needleham is so much higher than anywhere else.

Maria nodded her agreement.

-   And his writing is so hard to read. I wish Luke was a bit more coherent and could tell us about it. They've got him so scrambled on those drugs that he can't think straight. He's rambling all over the place. I wish he could explain some of his notes. That German stuff for example. I don't understand the significance of that.

-   German stuff? What German stuff?

James stared at them. He had taken their word that Luke's notes were complicated and inconclusive, and hadn't looked at them himself.

-   The notes Luke made in the file Maria found in the office, have some scribbled notes that seem to be in German. I suppose you speak German?

-   Gnadige Fraulein, naturlich spreche ich Deutsch! Je mehr sie es jagte, desto geschwinder wurde es! Let me see.

James took the file and read:

- This part that says "Drog papers"...
- I thought that said "Drug papers".
- Well, it could be, but it looks to me like it might be "Drog", as in "Drogham". Our beloved Professor.

He read on.

- A Miscarriage of Justice? Published by D. in... "The Freedom Journal" 1987. God Luke's writing is terrible. It looks like "Lebensunwerten Lebens: under pseudonym. Ref: Binding K, Hoche A."

He looked thoughtful. Maria was impatient.

- What does it mean?

James said nothing for a few more seconds.

- Die Freigabe der Vernichtung lebensunswerten Lebens.

Maria looked disgusted.

- This is no time to be quoting opera!

James turned to look at her.

- It's not opera. It's the title of Hoche and Binding's 1920 research paper. Basically calling for the destruction of what they called "life unworthy of life".
- What does that mean?
- I'm afraid, Anthea darling, it means us. It's rather a famous work. Or notorious I should say. Alfred Hoche was a German professor of psychiatry, and Karl Binding was a law professor. In 1920, long before Adolf Hitler showed up on the scene, they came up with a theory that one way to deal with the economic problems Germany was having was to get rid of surplus people. The useless ones. The ones who were not productive, the disabled and the mad especially. They began to quietly eliminate people in institutions where there

was no-one around to meddle. It paved the way for all that the Nazis did later to the Jews.

He was still, but intensely so, like a computer given too many commands.

- It seems our Professor Drogham has an interest in eugenics.

*

Blenkinsop was a drowning man flailing around in Tarpow's office, ready to push anybody else under to survive – or more likely take them down with him, thought Tarpow. He had already jumped off his seat twice and marched to the end of the room and back as Tarpow explained the situation to him. He would have to go at the earliest opportunity. But who would replace him? John Turbot was a good man, he could do it.

- I don't understand. There must be some terrible mistake.

Blenkinsop's voice was to Tarpow a whine utterly incongruent for the Chairman of a major Northern Health Trust. So Tarpow deliberately made his voice as calm and considered as possible.

- There does seem to be some very unusual behaviour on the Professor's prescribing behaviour. It seems that the advocate had, illegally I might say, obtained copies of pharmacy records concerning the use of certain drugs around the time of the deaths of Professor Drogham's patients.

Tarpow waved the dun coloured file, which he had removed from the Pharmacy Department. Better such sensitive information were in his personal possession.

- Drugs? But we know about the drugs – the major and minor tranquilisers, the antidepressants.
- These are different drugs. Additional drugs. Pain-killing drugs. In particular diamorphine and tramadol, but also

247

insulin. Just before many of the deaths, there was a surge in the Professor's prescribing of those drugs.

- A surge?
- Well, a significant increase.
- How significant?
- A trebling.

There was a pause while Blenkinsop took in this information. Then his face seemed to crumble.

- O my God!
- Yes, it looks bad, on top of the drugs we know he was already over-prescribing.
- But why on earth did none of this ever come to light before.

Tarpow almost lost control of his temper at this ridiculous statement, but he managed to hold onto himself and respond in a measured voice.

- The Professor is our senior psychiatrist. There is no one empowered to question his judgement. He is the authority on all things to do with medicine and prescribing at Needleham.
- But he's not above the law!

Blenkinsop's naivete irritated Tarpow.

- Of course he's not above the law. But what is the law, and who does it come to when it needs a judgement about all matters to do with mental health? As far as mental health matters go, the Professor, in effect, is the law!

It was true, he reflected. The law huffed and puffed and blew a few houses down, but when it crossed the demarcation line and entered the territory of the mental health system, built as it was out of the stone of tradition, it behaved like any other uncertain, intimidated patient. Blenkinsop looked as if he'd reached a sudden conclusion.

- We must tell the police everything we know.

Tarpow considered this.

- We don't actually know anything yet. We merely have what
you might call circumstantial evidence. The Professor is due
to retire in a year's time. It's possible he might be persuaded
to move to a more managerial position and concern himself
with policy.

There was a pause while they both considered the Professor's
ignorance and obtuseness about policy matters. Tarpow continued.

- It could be managed. It would hardly be the first time we've
promoted someone to stop them doing more damage. I need
hardly tell you what a scandal of this nature might to do all of
our careers. Especially coming so hot on the heels of the last
one.

- But it has nothing to do with us!

- We have been running the hospital. It will not reflect well on
either of us. No, I think discretion is the better part of value
in this case.

- You mean "valour"?

- No, I mean "value".

- But what about that advocate chap who started it all off?

- Yes, our whistleblowing advocate, the one who sparked all
this. And ironically is now a patient on one of our wards.

Blenkinsop considered this and a light dawned in his desperate face
as he saw a straw to clutch.

- Do you think he imagined the whole thing because of his
illness? Or at least that it could be made to look like that?

- I think it could.

- You don't think the truth will out?

- There is the small matter of evidence. But truth is a relative concept, particularly in the world of mental health. It's a mess certainly, but it does potentially help our cause if our advocate friend can be shown to be …unstable.

- Obviously he must be treated with respect.

- It goes without saying. He must be treated with absolute respect.

Tarpow thought of Passchendaele Ward and its senior nurse. A small smile came to his lips for the first time in a while. He relished the sound of his own words in this, the sanctuary of his office, so much so that he said them again.

- Absolute respect.

He repeated.

*

In the Professor's room Luke was trying to stay awake.

- So you are feeling no better?

It was a statement disguised as a question. Luke's head was swirling. On pain of being given an involuntary injection, he had that morning taken several different tablets and a small glass of thick brown sludge that tasted bitter and sharp as disinfectant, with no satisfactory explanation as to what any of them were for.

- I don't think I will while you're making me take these drugs.

Drogham consulted the file in front of him.

- Apparently you took your medication willingly.

- They told me they would force me to have them if I didn't take them voluntarily. Which they have done on several occasions. So hardly voluntary.

- Mr. Walker, you must trust our judgement. The nurses and doctors at Needleham have studied these issues for many years. You seem to have the attitude that we don't have your best interests at heart. I assure you we do.

Something itched at the back of Luke's mind. What the patient who had escaped on the first day Luke came to Needleham had said.

- You are not trying to kill the patients then?

The Professor looked suddenly startled.

- Kill?

- Some patients think you are. You gave a talk, I understand. About a paper by two German psychiatrists.

Drogham looked at him sharply and considered his answer carefully.

- Mr. Walker. Our duty is to prevent suffering. I think what you people who complain so much don't understand is the depth of torment people with mental illness suffer. You yourself are having a small taste of what some people have to face. Not just the odd bad day, or week, but year on year of absolute mental and spiritual agony. Unbearable suffering. Mental disability so crushing that life is an intolerable torment. And we are able through the medication we administer to give some relief.

Luke was struggling to marshal his thoughts. He felt as if he was walking through a bog in a mist, and the clouds were swirling in thicker every moment. But there was somewhere he had to get to.

- You gave a paper on two German psychiatrists. Ho….Ho….not Ho Chi Minh…

- Hoche. I think the name you are looking for is Hoche. I did write a paper. I have actually written many papers.

The Professor's voice had become thin and thoughtful. It was almost as if he was talking to himself.

251

- I think the times have vindicated Herrn Hoche and Binding. The epidemic of mental illness rampant in the world today is evidence that our current ideas about the causes and treatment of mental illness have been lacking. The number of sufferers is rising exponentially. With our increasingly complex world we are encountering new forms of mental breakdown every year. Gambling addictions, social phobias, disorders of the personality that are terrifying both to the people who have them, and to the people they may come into contact with. We are running out of options, Mr. Walker, and we have a duty to prevent such suffering. There is clearly a genetic disposition to mental illness. Ten years ago the Human Genome Project began to analyse DNA. One day, we will be able to detect and eradicate mental illness at source, before birth.

- By aborting all foetuses that don't meet your standards?

- Please, don't be melodramatic. By then we will be in a position to make adjustments to the genetic code. But sadly we are not in that position yet. Until then we must help people as best we can.

- And that help might include… putting people out of their misery?

- Mr. Walker. You have a severe paranoid psychosis, which makes you think these strange thoughts. I'm so sorry for you. It must be a terrible thing. This kind of aberration will not yield easily to treatment. In cases of this kind, which will not respond to medication, sometimes only electric convulsive therapy can create the kind of decisive effect we need.

There must have been some switch under the desk, because the door behind him opened with a click, and he found the arms of two nurses securing him in his chair, and then the sharp invasion of a steel needle into his thigh. The colours of the room swirled in front of his eyes, as his balance shifted and spiralled upwards and leftwards, and then he was pitching forward, falling towards the dark pile of the carpet.

TEN: October

Minding the World's Mental Health: October 10ᵗʰ, World Mental Health Day 2001.

A day conference to celebrate 100 years of mental health care at Needleham Hospital, with guest speakers from the National Association of Users and Survivors, plus a photographic exhibition of photographs of the hospital through the years.

*

On October the 10th, the early sun rose to shine equally on the insane and the normal. The day conference had been hastily moved from the old ballroom to a large seminar room, following the unaccountable collapse of a stone fireplace. This was given by Nurse Manager Moking as one reason why James, Maria and Anthea could not attend, when they presented themselves at the hospital.

- There is not room. We are having to be very strict about seating. And even if we had seating, there are fire regulations and in any case you do not have tickets.

Maria considered this.

- Since when have there been tickets for this event? It's a public event. There are no tickets.

Moking looked shifty.

- There were...invitations. There is a guest list and... virtual tickets.

- Virtual tickets?

- Indeed. We have a list of people who will be attending.

She had sudden thought, which seemed to clarify everything for her and broke into a canter.

- The event is fully subscribed. If we let you in then we'll have to refuse entry to others who have booked places. And that's not really fair, is it?

It was a masterstroke to appeal to justice and fairness with the hospital user involvement worker and her clique, and Moking knew it.

The three retreated to reconsider. They sat on a wooden bench near the main doors inscribed with the words: TO THE MEMORY OF WILLIAM PEMBLETON, OUR DAD, "STILL CRAZY AFTER ALL THOSE YEARS", on a little steel plaque. There had been no contact from the national organisation in the intervening weeks, but Maria was still hopeful.

- We can try and see the National Association people afterwards. They must be staying somewhere in Needleham village.

James was doubtful.

- They'll probably be going off to some posh place to have tea if I know Tarpow. He'll be spending the involvement budget on buttering them up. They won't get back til late, and we don't even know they'll be staying in Needleham.

He had an idea.

- There is a back way in. It's an emergency door into the conference room. If we can get in, they won't risk the bad publicity at a public event by throwing us out in front of everybody, and we can try and talk to the National Association people at the break.

They both looked at him as if they didn't believe he could think of something so practical, so ingeniously simple.

- That's a great idea!

- We could sneak in after it's started. It's a plan!

James found himself distracted by something in the corner of his vision.

- Have you seen that!

They looked around to see what had caught his attention. The stone wall of the clock tower building, which housed the offices of Tarpow and the administrative block, had a distinctive line running up in steps from the ground to a second-floor window some twenty feet above. It looked as if someone with a thick marker pen had drawn a staircase in the stonework, marching up the wall one step at a time.

- It's like the building's sagged.

- It's bigger than the crack in the advocacy office.

They stepped across a forlorn flowerbed and looked at the fissure closely. It was tiny at the base, but grew wider until at the level of the window frame it was at least two inches wide. The whole wall of a section of the wall had slipped.

- Is this place safe?

- It must be. They check it regularly because it's so near the old mine workings.

- This is the same 'they' who think that electric shock therapy is safe?

The others turned to James with a sudden startled look.

*

There were exhibition stands obscuring the fire door at the back of the conference room, so they were able to enter without being seen. About two hundred people sat in twenty rows of red backed plastic chairs before a speaker's plinth, making the room look half-full and rather sparse. It was, Anthea noted, a soulless room, part of a block that had been new in 1984, a modernist box with plain, off-white walls and too close a view of older and grimmer blocks through the double-glazing. Tarpow sat on the raised plinth, with the Chair of the Board, and a man and a woman who were presumably the guest speakers from the National Association of Users and Survivors. Moking was with the small crowd near the door, overseeing the pinning of badges and handing out of papers. She was distracted, and the three interlopers sneaked out from behind the screen declaring the merits of Spectforalcapone to join Liron sitting by himself in one of the back rows, nicely obscured by a row of well-built nurses.

Liron greeted them as if he'd been expecting them all along. He didn't stop humming "Red Sails In The Sunset" as he waited for proceedings to begin. Anthea gritted her teeth. She was too tense to appreciate the Hugh Williams 1935 classic. She looked impatiently at her watch, and surveyed the speakers on the plinth, who represented their hope of getting the air of publicity into Needleham.

Anthea did not share Maria's faith that the National Association of Users and Survivors would help them to expose the wrongdoing at Needleham. They were survivors of psychiatry like she was. They had been through the same system, and now had funding and a national brief to make changes that would mean the patients voice would be heard at the highest level of planning. Why was she not convinced? The two speakers on the platform looked benign enough. They had been shuffling their notes, rearranging their glasses of water and adjusting their microphones for some minutes, while the audience of staff and local personages sat expectantly. Now two younger managers, also a man and a woman, joined the speakers on the plinth to explain something about the microphones. As they sat with the hospital managers she looked from manager to survivor, and from survivor to manager, but already it was impossible to say which was which.

Liron stopped humming for long enough to turn to Anthea and pass on a piece of information.

- Bad news about Luke.

- What bad news?

- About the shock. Prof got him down to get buzzed this morning. Not good.

Anthea took a moment to take in this news.

- What do you mean? Why would they give Luke shock? He's not depressed.

Liron shrugged elaborately, as if the ways of this world were beyond him. Anthea was agitated by the news, but her attention was now taken by something that was happening in the room. It had been relatively sparsely occupied just moments before, but now it began to fill up with people, who seemed to be appearing through the same door where Anthea, James and Maria had come in.

They filled the space behind the rows of chairs and began to occupy the vacant seats around them. Who were these people, and where did they come from? They were not workers, yet did not seem either to be local residents, service users, or carers, or at least none that she had ever met. Some seemed to be in contemporary dress, others in the dress and fashion of previous decades. Others wore old-fashioned, outmoded styles of the 1940s and earlier, and some had the dark clothes and formal style of people from sepia coloured Victorian photographs. This strange army filled the available chairs further and further forward, then began to congregate at the sides of the room, and at the front in the space in front of the plinth. Anthea thought that perhaps they had opened some kind of portal by coming

258

in through the fire door, but dismissed it quickly. It was a thought worthy of her "breakdown" the previous winter. She experienced a tightening in her chest, and a feeling of panic. James and Maria, from their expressions, seemed to be seeing the same thing, and even Liron had stopped humming and was staring with his mouth slightly open.

As she watched, people seemed to materialise through the walls of the room, and one elderly man in a sepia, ill-fitting suit rose through the floor in front of the speaker's plinth with a pained expression on his face, as if he were struggling to free himself. Slowly his whole body became visible and he moved away awkwardly to join a group by the side of the stage. Some of the people were sharply defined, hardly distinguishable from the nurses and managers among whom they sat. Others were indistinct, almost blurred at the edges, like people drawn in ink on porous paper. Anthea saw a disembodied arm move across the room, with suggestions of a shoulder and neck, but no person appeared at all.

The hospital workers in the audience seemed unaware of the presence of these uninvited guests and continued to ignore them. Nurse Moking had taken up a seat on the front row, and beside her sat a woman with wide lapels and a victory curl who turned to look at the Nurse Manager with curiosity, slowly from head to foot, as if it were Moking, and not her who had suddenly appeared from nowhere.

The room filled to capacity and more people kept coming until they were overlapping. Bodies shared the same space, like figures superimposed in a film. As she looked, Anthea had an insight that the room was not a real room at all, but a light source in an infinite void to which souls were being drawn out of the darkness from all points of the compass. There was an immensity beyond this space, filled with nameless people, the wretched and the starved, the damaged and the hopeless, all making their way towards the brightness, across an enormous plain stretching away in all directions.

The people on the plain seemed numberless; wave on wave drawn out the void towards the light. The further from the room they were the more featureless they were, congealing into a mass of dark-clothed bodies, each with the lighter patch of a face above. As they neared the room, she saw that the ones coming now were skeletal, scarecrow people, their eyes dark hollows, their heads bald. The walls of the room were gateways through which people from all times were streaming. She closed her eyes but could still see the holes in time, and feel the vastness of space from which they came. She started to shake with fear. It was such experiences that had led her to be a patient at Needleham at the beginning of the year. She felt a hand on her shoulder, and looked up to see Liron peering into her face with a worried expression.

-   Ok?

She could not answer. She tried to nod or shake her head, but he could not understand which, the movement of her head could have been interpreted as either. There was a painful squeal of electronic feedback, and the attention of everyone in the room was drawn to the podium, where Tarpow's voice boomed suddenly, then became human as he found the right distance from the microphone. He was clearly unaware of the visitors thronging the hall, and spoke as though already rather bored with proceedings.

-   Good morning, and welcome. Today we celebrate World
    Mental Health Day, a day to reflect on the advances we have
    made in the past year, and look forward to the future.
    Before beginning proceedings, I'd like to first of all give
    congratulations to Julie Graytfell, our Senior Social Worker,
    who we have just learned will be leaving us to take up an
    appointment as Senior Social Work Advisor at Richmond
    House, the headquarters of the Department of Health. Julie
    has been a dedicated and untiring member of staff at
    Needleham for almost eighteen months. I haven't actually

had the pleasure of meeting her myself, and unfortunately she is unable to join us today, since she is giving evidence to the Select Committee on Health at Westminster...

The door to Tarpow's left had opened, and a frisson passed through the crowd, both invited guests, who whispered to each other, and the nameless strangers, who emitted a high sound that sounded to Anthea like insects. Four unknown men had come into the room and stood just inside the door. Two were in police uniforms, and two in nondescript dark suits, who might have been local government or hospital managers. They consulted the greeters at the door, and then the older man, who seemed to be the leader, walked over to where the Professor was sitting in the front row. After a whispered conversation the Professor followed them out. The room broke into a frenzied murmuring.

Augustus Tarpow took the microphone and intoned in his most magisterial voice.

-   There will be a short delay before the start of the conference.

He whispered to Moking, then hurriedly disappeared in the wake of the policemen and the bemused Professor. The room grew noisy, as people discussed this turn of events. Anthea turned to James.

-   What's going on?
-   I don't know. It looks like the Professor's been rumbled. Do you know who these people are?
-   I think they are the ghosts of Needleham's past.
-   James looked her sharply
-   I think they seem too well dressed for that.

They both looked again at the thronging crowd around them, Anthea at the ragged scarecrow figures, the formless skeletal faces and the blurred and missing limbs, and realised with a shudder that even she and James were seeing different things.

The microphone at the table on the plinth crackled and boomed and called the room to order. It was Moking who had taken the initiative, under orders from the Chair of the Board, who had suddenly disappeared in the wake of Tarpow and the policemen. She introduced the speakers in a laboured fashion, and they began their PowerPoint presentations.

Anthea slipped past James and Maria, and went out through the fire exit at the back.

*

In his office the Professor stared at the policemen in bewilderment. Then he sighed deeply and nodded three times. His face drooped until he was staring at the floor, and a knobbly hand came up to rub at his head as if he were massaging a hurt, or trying to wake himself up. Everyone else in the room watched, and a silence fell. The Professor stopped rubbing his forehead and was utterly still for a few seconds. When he raised his head again the face that greeted the policemen and Tarpow was like a different person. It was as if the Professor had aged a decade in a few seconds. His face seemed deeply lined, his expression one of misery. He began to speak in an uncertain voice that was barely recognisable as his own.

- You don't understand, you see. You don't understand how it is.

The plainclothes police officer seemed almost embarrassed.

- You don't have to say anything now.

But the Professor carried on anyway.

- The pain of these people. You don't understand what they go through. It is unbearable, literally unbearable. It's inhuman to let them suffer like that. It's like if an animal is in pain, you can't allow that to go on. It's just the same. What else could I do? What else could I do?

His question hung on the air, and as if on cue the detective stepped forward, and placed a gentle hand on the Professor's elbow.

- We just want you to come to the station to answer a few questions at the moment.

The Professor stared up at him suddenly, as if noticing him for the first time, and nodded again.

- It's all over, isn't it? Well, thank goodness is all I can say.

And with that he strode out of the office, with the two inspectors having to start suddenly to keep up with him, and the uniformed men in their wake. Tarpow was left alone. General Cardew's gaze suddenly looked rather accusing. Tarpow was puzzled. Something had just happened, but what was it? One minute life was continuing along its appointed track, and the next a point had been switched. Masked men leapt aboard. The gold bullion disappeared into vans that drove away. He picked up the phone on his desk.

There was a time when nothing happened at Needleham that Tarpow didn't know about. 'Get them by the balls and their hearts and minds will follow'. He knew them all, and how they ticked, who to push and who to pander. But now, god, he almost said 'The world is going crazy'. For the first time in thirty years he didn't know who to call. He put the phone back in its cradle, just as the fire alarm went off.

*

When the alarm began to blare, Anthea was walking down the deserted main corridor, making her way towards the ECT Suite where Luke was. The sound was unbearably loud, ricocheting off emulsioned walls and the glass of window and display case. She put her hands over her ears and began to run. People appeared from side corridors and doors that opened onto the corridor and moved past her in the opposite direction. She could not tell who was real and who was not. Some seemed substantial enough, and one woman grabbed her by the arm and tried to turn her round.

- Come on love, you have to go to the nearest exit.

But Anthea wriggled out of her grasp and continued to head towards the ECT Suite. There were more and more people running the other way. Some seemed almost transparent, like a pattern of steam on the air, streaming past with open mouths, emitting high notes of anguish and panic. They grew thicker, until she felt she was running against a great crowd like masses of commuters at Leeds station in the rush hour. The ground seemed to be moving under her feet, like a funfair trick in a haunted house.

She found the steps down into the ECT suite, and the crowds and noise of the main corridor fell away behind her. As she clomped down the ill-lit staircase, a window higher up broke, and glass fell around her, bouncing on the stone steps, so she had to tread carefully to avoid fragments on the lower steps. The reception area was deserted, and she started to open the doors of side rooms. She found Luke in the third room and shook him violently but he did not wake up. She went out and found a sink in a toilet and returned with a glass of cold water, which she threw in his face. He stirred then and opened his eyes. The wailing of the fire alarm was still blaring.

- We've got to get out of here.

She pulled him to a sitting position, and he gingerly put his feet on the floor. The room seemed to jolt and there was a crash from a nearby room.

- Come on, we've got to go.

He got to his feet with difficulty and she supported him to move out of the room and to the door of the unit. In the corridor outside, the building was heaving and groaning around them, pieces of plaster falling in front and behind as they hobbled together. Somewhere there was the sound of more glass cracking and shattering onto a hard surface. They reached the stone staircase and laboured up it, Anthea kicking broken glass out of their way.

At the top a drugs trolley stood abandoned. As he went past Luke pulled on it to give himself leverage for the last step and it moved towards him with surprising ease, and sidled past him as he fell out of its way. He turned just in time to see it dip as the front wheels went over the first step, then the back wheels followed and it was clattering down the staircase. Each time a pair of rubber wheels bounced onto the next step a great crashing of steel and plastic exploded like a drummer hitting a cymbal irregularly in some avant garde performance. The doors of the mobile cabinet fell open and plastic containers cascaded out, some without tops, so the little blue or pink tablets, and two-tone red or green and white tubular capsules leapt and bounced on to the step and off into space through the iron railing, down into the corridor below. At first the trolley seemed to be hesitating, juddering and grating like a steel bucking horse. Step by step it descended, the slender hope of science itself going down through the years. Then it began to pick up speed and the metallic crashing became a constant harsh waterfall. At the bottom, the front of the trolley hit the floor and the whole thing flipped up and over, coming to rest on its top. Its doors were open and tablets were scattered all around it like hailstones and globules of blood. Luke felt Anthea gripping his arm.

-    Come on, we don't have time.

They went on, past the long radiators in the main corridor, into the admin block, with its mosaic floor of blue swans, into the carpeted area where Tarpow had his office. Then the big front doors were in front of them and they were out into the grey air of the day. She pulled and pushed Luke away to the left of the car park, and a group of conifer trees that offered some kind of shelter. When she turned round, she saw a mass of people watching from the gathering point on the car park a hundred yards away. She picked out James and Maria, Tarpow and uniformed policemen among the crowd. Then her attention was drawn back to the stricken building.

The end seemed to come in slow motion. It was like watching old TV footage of a demolition, the only difference being the sound. Seconds before anything shifted, the rumbling began. Instead of the tinny sound of a TV repeat, this was a noise that started as vibration through the soles of her feet, emanating upwards like the birth pangs of some mountain's child. The building in front of them seemed to shiver. It was as if the main part, from the Admin offices on the ground floor to Tarpow's office running across the whole of the second, sank inwards from the sides. The noise grew in volume and violence, now a screaming protest of stone jammed against concrete with unimaginable force. The heart of the building fell away, disappearing from view, leaving the clock tower suspended for a fraction of a second. Then it began to fall as if crumbling from the bottom. A cloud of angry smoke and dust pummelled the surrounding air, and the tower fell down into it like a failed missile subsiding into its launch pad. There was a deafening noise of metal grinding on stone that sounded to Anthea's ears for a moment like the exultant scream of a freed prisoner. The cloud expanded, thinning, and began to settle as thick dust on the tarmac around them.

Aftermath: March 2002

The air in the taxi seemed intolerably hot to Ellis, but in the back there was no control he could see to wind down the window. The driver's bull neck was separated from them by a thick partition of plastic and glass, and communicating with him seemed as if it would require an enormous effort. He wiped his brow. Perhaps he was getting a fever? How could it be so hot? He turned to the corpulent shape sitting beside him.

- This whole episode has been appalling. It's a shambles. There'll be an enquiry into how this place has been run, and I hope everything comes to light.

Tarpow turned slowly towards him, as if from some deep thoughts of his own.

- Of course, there'll be an enquiry. There will be recommendations. Some of them will be fulfilled, some not, and life will carry on.

The sodden gardens and wintry trees of well-to-do West Yorkshire were passing as they travelled towards the new temporary offices of the Needleham NHS Mental Health Trust in Myllroyd. The stone houses looked like good investments, and Ellis felt himself suddenly insubstantial, a passer-by whose achievements would soon be forgotten here, in this world of solid facts. These bulky objects were on paths he would never understand. Yet Needleham Hospital itself,

267

with its enormous size and shadow in both space and time, had been so suddenly destroyed – at least the main administrative block. It all seemed incomprehensible. He felt the need to speak out against the complacent, solid nature of things.

- Tarpow. It's all over. This time things are going to change. I know you can't see it, you and the old guard. You think you can just go on the way you've always gone on, but it's over, it's finished, can't you see that? There's a new way of doing things. What Needleham stood for has gone. We just don't do things like that anymore. There's no place for you and your kind now, you'll be swept away, the way you should have been decades ago.

There was a pause, as if Tarpow was letting the words sink in. It lasted so long that Ellis wondered if his remarks had really hit their mark. Then Tarpow's frame began to shake. It was a strange thing to see, and to feel, and at first Ellis thought that Tarpow had broken down with the strain of it all and was crying. He almost felt sorry for his harsh words. But he quickly realised that Tarpow was laughing, laughing so hard that no air could get into his lungs to express the mirth through the blessed release of sound. He rocked backwards, and little by little the noise began to come out. It was a wild, unrestrained noise when it came, resounding in the little cab like a wild animal throwing itself against the bars of a cage. The hefty driver glanced into the rear-view mirror as the laughter surged in loud waves of unrestrained delight. Tears did start to roll down Tarpow's cheeks, and at last with monumental effort he pulled himself together and pulled a white handkerchief from his top pocket to mop his face.

- You are right, Ellis, quite right. Things will change, things will change. But, plus ca change...

His accent was appalling, and again he gave himself over to great howls of laughter, whooping and barking like a huge sea animal come to shore to seek a mate and fight off all comers. When he subsided again, he managed to say, between deep breaths.

-   Look Ellis, there are two things that will always be with us. And I'm not talking about the poor. Fuck the poor. I'm talking about the two great terrors of the human race. There is of course death, the thing we will all come to, and mankind's greatest dread. But the second, and by no means the weaker - death's younger brother, is…. madness! The only thing men fear as much as death! Because madness is indeed death in life! To lose your reason! To be in the world but lost to the world! Is there anything more terrible?

Ellis could not speak or look at Tarpow. He stared at the passing countryside with a kind of horror.

-   There will always be fear, Ellis. Look at the twin towers, and this 'war on terror'. What is terror but the fear of those two brothers, Death and Madness? We are frightened of death, the commonplace end to all our dreams that creeps along and takes us by surprise in the night. Yes, that's frightening. But a death that knows no reason? A death that is not accidental, and not because of some unforeseen but natural cause? Or for greed or gain, or some other motive we understand? That is the truly terrible thing. Where there is terror you will always find the fear of madness. And that's where we come in. A frightened world will always have a need for a system to contain the madness it cannot live with. We are the dream catchers for society's nightmares. No Ellis, I think that this is not an ending! I think that we will be in business for some time to come!

The heat in the car was insufferable. Ellis felt the strength of Tarpow's attention on him, and was at last forced to turn and look into those terrible eyes. Tarpow's pupils were huge in his triumphant face. Ellis turned away shuddering and the overheated atmosphere in the car lapsed into silence. The car sped on towards the next meeting, the next strategic development, the next agenda and set of decisions, leaving behind the mistakes of the past like the dark tarmac of the road.

*

The Yorkshire sky was threatening rain again as Luke approached the administrative block of Needleham's new psychiatric unit. The door of the new building was reinforced glass and aluminium. Luke had to gain entry through an intercom.

-   I have an appointment with Maria Paraskeva, Senior Patient Involvement Coordinator.

There was no reply, but the door opened cautiously. At the low reception desk, a young bespectacled man (not the son of Henry, surely?) made a phone call and gave him a visitor's badge "TO BE WORN AT ALL TIMES". The young man pointed him towards a lift with mirrored walls of dull steel. On the third floor he turned into a corridor that still smelled of fresh carpet and the blond wood of new fire doors. He found Maria's office on the right. Maria seemed pleased and a little embarrassed to see him. She had a mock pine desk and a view of the tree fringed car park.

-   You've gone up in the world!

She looked uncomfortable.

-   I think technically I've been shifted sideways. I seem to spend all my time in meetings these days. I thought Anthea was coming with you?

-   She's gone to visit Alex on the ward.

Maria frowned.

-   Poor Alex. I went to see him the other day. He was very traumatised by the collapse. He seems to think he put the idea of blowing up the place into the head of Arman, that Armenian bloke who absconded.

Luke remembered Arman very well from his first day of working at Needleham, and particularly the sight of him running down the drive to freedom.

- I remember him from my first day at Needleham.

- He claimed his family had links to Chechen rebels.

- I don't think it was Chechen rebels. I think it was all that tunnelling by that Abetter lot, wasn't it?

- You might think that, but I'm not in a position to say.

She picked up a letter from her desk and waved it in the air.

- "All employees of the Trust should avoid any speculation of the causes of the collapse of the building until the enquiry into it is completed."

- And when will that be?

She shrugged.

- This year or the next, or the one after that. Sometime when management judges it's been sufficiently forgotten.

Luke sighed.

- What I want to know is who set off the alarm?

- That is a mystery. None of the actual alarms had been triggered. The central system just went off for no apparent reason. It gave everybody the chance to leave the building anyway. You were lucky Anthea came to get you.

- Yes, they said they were having a change over and somehow in the panic thought I'd been sent back to the ward. For some reason they were short staffed that day anyway.

Maria nodded.

- Well you know why that was? Two of the nurses from that unit had been taken for questioning about links to Yorkshire Uber Alles, and their ties with Professor Drogham. O'Price went too, sacked. They found a load of anti-Semitic literature under his bed, claiming that Yorkshire is under the control of a Jewish cabal, operating through the fish and chip shops.

Luke paused to think about that, but couldn't think of a suitable reply. Instead his mind went to another imponderable.

- The only thing I still don't understand is who took the file from Tarpow's office and delivered it to the police? Without that none of this would have come to light.

- Apparently it was an old guy. It must have been a long-term patient, but I can't think who it might have been. No-one fits that description. An old man with long flowing grey hair and beard. Surely we'd have seen him around? And he had chains around him or something. What was all that about? He just disappeared as soon as he'd handed over the file and was never seen again.

Luke immediately thought about his afternoon in the Needleham graveyard. He considered telling Maria about this, but it seemed too complicated. She was watching him as he clearly struggled for words. In the end he remembered something James had said more than once, when he wanted to cover himself.

- "Whereof one cannot speak, thereof must one be silent".

Maria looked dubious. She was about to argue with that, but a sudden flurry of rain or hail struck the window, and she moved across to shut it.

- That sounds like Broussine. I do miss him, even though he is an anarchist. Do you ever hear from him?

- He's got a boyfriend. They met at an exhibition of electronic music and visual art in an old mill in Huddersfield. James

272

started insulting one of the exhibits in that cantankerous voice he has. Anyway it turned out the artist was standing next to him. They had a massive row that ended in the pub and they've been together ever since. What about Walter and Margaret? Do you see them?

- They've got a tiny flat in Needleham village with a massive TV and hundreds of DVDs and they just seem to eat popcorn and chocolate all day, watching films. They're particularly fond of The Shawshank Redemption at the moment. It's like they've reinvented the life they had at the hospital but without nurses and with a bigger TV.

- We were going to go and visit them next. What about Max and the Countess?

- Max got a job in Iceland.

- Well it's a start.

- No, I mean he actually went to Reykjavik. He made contact with a survivor organisation there and they found a grant to run a radical art project in a day centre. He's very happy. The Countess has joined the Needleham Board of Governors and is not letting them get away with anything from what I hear. How about you and Anthea? I was pleased when you got together. You seem suited in a weird kind of way. How are you getting on together in the big city?

Luke was used to Maria's heavy-handed compliments and took no offence. He smiled at her.

- Thank you, we get on well. And Leeds is great. Everybody's a bit mad there so ex-mental patients don't stand out so much.

Maria smiled.

- That's true.

- We found a housing co-operative in Meanwood and everyone seems really friendly so far. I don't know where Anthea is. She said she'd be here by now.

He looked at his watch and experienced the mild anxiety he felt when Anthea behaved unpredictably, which was most of the time. It wasn't a completely unpleasant feeling, more a benign cousin of the dark panic of the old days. He hoped she was not getting into trouble. This was, when all was said and done, a psychiatric unit.

*

In the new Unit all the wards were named after the manager and players of England's 1966 World Cup winning team. After seeing Alex in the day room of Ramsey Ward, Anthea had slipped into the TV lounge. There were as yet few patients and the room was deserted. She lay down on the floor and felt the rough grain of the thin cord carpet under her head and her back, and on the down-turned palms of her outstretched hands. She breathed deeply, taking in the carpet's sharp smell of newness, and for a long time was motionless, eyes closed, listening to the small noises of a building settling; the rush of water in a pipe; the dull sound of a door banging in a corridor high and to her left; faint intermittent traffic sounds and voices beyond the window in the distance, fading to nothing. She felt as though if she stayed there long enough she would begin to hear conversations in the terraced houses of Myllroyd that surrounded the new hospital, and beyond these the sound of the winds that troubled the gorse and heather of the moorland that stretched away towards Lancashire on one side, and on the other down into the valleys that led to the big old woolen towns of West Yorkshire.

- Lead me not into conformity, but deliver me from medication. Let me never forget the joyous unpredictability of being. Thine be the Madness and the Glory. Forever and ever, so be it.

She lay still for a long time listening, but whether to her own voice or that of another was impossible to say.

I intended death, having grown tired of all done in my name, and of the terrible gap between intention and gruesome actuality. I planned my own downfall, even though you and others were a comfort in my old age. I could communicate with so few by then. I went willingly, gladly. But then, amazement! I woke here in this new place, afresh. I am reborn! It will go on. I will go on. I am ready to go on. But whether to better things or worse it is impossible to say. It will be different. Perhaps that is all one can say for certain.

Is that good enough?

It is the best I can do. Men will recreate me in their own image. Men will seek to use me for their own power and ambitions, for their own profit. So few understand.

Sanctuary?

Thank you. Yes, that is exactly right. A place at the end of the world when there is nothing else...

Mercy.

There was nothing then for a long time. Outside the sun had gone, and soft rain was falling from a slate blue sky, drenching everything. It fell across the hills, into the deep clefts of valleys, onto the backs of Pennine sheep, billowing through woods and scattering fat drops on each individual leaf, saturating the thick banks of grass by the roadside. It fell on the heads and backs of people who hurried along in the little towns and villages of the moors, drenching the mad and the sane equally, until it was impossible to tell the two apart.

For a moment, the sound of rain striking a sheet of tautly stretched polythene sounded almost like laughter.

THE END

Acknowledgements

Thanks to my partner Gail Bolland for constant enthusiasm and encouragement; to the other members of Chapel Allerton Writers group Debbie McPhee and Alison Ravetz; to Char March and the wonderful novel group she set up, including Mandy Sutter, Bridgid Rose and Katie Jukes; to Rommi Smith and her fabulous poetry workshop; to Ruth Steinberg, a co conspirator; to Jack and Vincent Simpson for making me laugh; to Pete Coleman for the same reason and for his conversation and friendship.

To the 'survivors movement' for kindness, support, ideas and inspiration, including Derek Hutchinson, Peter Campbell, Graham Estop, Justine Morrison, Patrick Wood, Andrew and Roberta Wetherell and many more; to Leeds Survivor Poets including Steve Bindman, Ushawant Kaur, Jacquie Bingham, Owen Turner and Margaret Boyes; to the Orphans of Beulah theatre company – Johnny Solstice, Tom Leader, Andrea Chell, Daphne Hubery, Chris Minns and Chesh; to the 3 muskateers Jenny Martin, Heather Parker and Renuka Bhakta.

To good friends and colleagues who've passed on – Barry Fox, Chris Ginger, Jan Wallcraft, Edna Conlan, Janet Foner, Migs Noddings, Colin Gell, Arike and many more; and especially to the ones who chose to leave early – Jenny D, Pete S, John T, Julian O – who wouldn't let me give up once I started.

Other novels, novellas and short story collections available from Stairwell Books

The Keepers	Pauline Kirk
A Business of Ferrets	Alwyn Bathan
Shadow Cat Summer	Rebecca Smith
Shadows of Fathers	Simon Culleton
Blackbird's Song	Katy Turton
Eboracvm the Fortess	Graham Clews
The Warder	Susie Williamson
The Great Billy Butlin Race	Robin Richards
Mistress	Lorraine White
Life Lessons by Libby	Libby and Laura Engel-Sahr
Waters of Time	Pauline Kirk
The Tao of Revolution	Chris Taylor
The Water Bailiff's Daughter	Yvonne Hendrie
O Man of Clay	Eliza Mood
Eboracvm: the Village	Graham Clews
Sammy Blue Eyes	Frank Beill
Margaret Clitherow	John and Wendy Rayne-Davis
Serpent Child	Pat Riley
Rocket Boy	John Wheatcroft
Virginia	Alan Smith
Looking for Githa	Patricia Riley
On Suicide Bridge	Tom Dixon
Something I Need to Tell You	William Thirsk-Gaskill
Poetic Justice	P J Quinn
Return of the Mantra	Susie Williamson
The Martyrdoms at Clifford's Tower 1190 and 1537	John Rayne-Davis
The Go-To Guy	Neal Hardin
Abernathy	Claire Patel-Campbell
Tyrants Rex	Clint Wastling
A Shadow in My Life	Rita Jerram
Rapeseed	Alwyn Marriage
Thinking of You Always	Lewis Hill
Know Thyself	Lance Clarke
How to be a Man	Alan Smith
Here in the Cull Valley	John Wheatcroft
Tales from a Prairie Journal	Rita Jerram
Border 7	Pauline Kirk
Homelands	Shaunna Harper
49	Paul Lingaard
When the Crow Cries	Maxine Ridge

For further information please contact rose@stairwellbooks.com

www.stairwellbooks.co.uk
@stairwellbooks